Greg M̶i̶ ... y imagination.
The Stra ... ers down dark
paths, e ... derstanding of
the spiritual conflict that confronts us all. I hope this is Mitchell's
next step in a long career.

—ERIC WILSON
NEW YORK TIMES BEST-SELLING AUTHOR OF *FIREPROOF*
AND *FIELD OF BLOOD*

Greg Mitchell's debut novel, The Strange Man, is everything a
supernatural suspense should be: thrilling, mysterious, creepy,
and thought-provoking. My kind of story. An all-around solid
performance. Can't wait for the next book!

—MIKE DELLOSSO
AUTHOR OF *SCREAM* AND *DARLINGTON WOODS*

In The Strange Man, Greg Mitchell takes the reader on roller-
coaster ride through the shadows of evil and shows the power it
can have on a town and a family when good people do nothing.
He also shows that one man can make an eternity of difference.

—ALTON GANSKY
CHRISTY AWARD FINALIST, ANGEL AWARD WINNER,
AND AUTHOR OF *ANGEL* AND *ENOCH*

Mitchell's The Strange Man is as mesmerizingly written as its story
is chilling. A macabre treat of the highest order!

—CONLAN BROWN
AUTHOR OF *THE FIRSTBORN* AND *THE OVERSEER*

Greg Mitchell did such a masterful job of immersing me into his
surreal world of monsters and impending calamity that it was only
after the imaginative fog cleared that I realized the monsters and
his hero's ultimate decision were made of the stuff that transcends
a mere story.

—TIM GEORGE
NAddict.com

THE STRANGE MAN

THE COMING EVIL TRILOGY | BOOK ONE

GREG MITCHELL

REALMS
A STRANG COMPANY

Most STRANG COMMUNICATIONS BOOK GROUP products are available at special quantity discounts for bulk purchase for sales promotions, premiums, fund-raising, and educational needs. For details, write Strang Communications Book Group, 600 Rinehart Road, Lake Mary, Florida 32746, or telephone (407) 333-0600.

THE STRANGE MAN by Greg Mitchell
Published by Realms
A Strang Company
600 Rinehart Road
Lake Mary, Florida 32746
www.strangbookgroup.com

Unless otherwise noted, all Scripture quotations are from the Holy Bible, New International Version of the Bible. Copyright © 1973, 1978, 1984, International Bible Society. Used by permission.

Scripture quotations marked NAS are from the New American Standard Bible. Copyright © 1960, 1962, 1963, 1968, 1971, 1972, 1973, 1975, 1977 by the Lockman Foundation. Used by permission. (www.Lockman.org)

The characters portrayed in this book are fictitious unless they are historical figures explicitly named. Otherwise, any resemblance to actual people, whether living or dead, is coincidental.

Cover design by Gearbox Studio
Design Director: Bill Johnson

Visit the author's website at http://www.thecomingevil.blogspot
.com/.

Library of Congress Cataloging-in-Publication Data

Mitchell, Greg, 1979-
  The strange man / by Greg Mitchell. -- 1st ed.
     p. cm. -- (The coming evil ; bk. 1)
  ISBN 978-1-61638-194-3
  I. Title.
  PS3613.I8546S77 2011
  813'.6--dc22

                                    2010041706

E-book ISBN: 978-1-61638-414-2

First Edition

11 12 13 14 15 — 9 8 7 6 5 4 3 2 1
Printed in the United States of America

PROLOGUE

Be of sober spirit, be on the alert. Your adversary, the devil,
prowls around like a roaring lion, seeking someone to devour.
—1 Peter 5:8

STORM'S COMING."

When he was ten, Eldon Granger broke his arm, and the bone was never set right. Even now, at age sixty-five, he felt it ache whenever a storm approached. Today, although the skies over the small town of Greensboro were bright blue and thickly populated with dramatic cumulous clouds, Eldon felt the approaching storm in his bones.

He sat in his tattered clothes atop one of the charred stone foundations that lay scattered in the tall grass of the North Woods, which bordered Greensboro, using an old buck knife to scoop beans out of a can. At his feet sat a semicircle of children, boys and girls, ages ranging from nine to thirteen, ashen-faced and speechless as Eldon continued spinning his tale.

"Mighty big one's coming, I reckon. You know, a storm came through these parts over a hundred years ago. A *bad* storm, if you know what I'm saying."

The children blinked back at him, spellbound.

"Some storms, see, they just make a racket with all the thunder before they blow on through. Harmless, you'd say. But other storms..."

Eldon lifted a row of beans to his scraggly face and slurped them down. Gulping, he leaned toward the kids, lowering his voice to a whisper.

"...other storms, you see, they have a way of staying. Sometimes they leave something behind."

He sat up and dug in his can for the last scraps of his meal.

"That's what happened back then. Something got left behind. Not from this earth, neither. No sir, came from the world beyond."

One of the kids looked to the sky, squinting against the sun as if hoping to see a flying saucer pass overhead on cue.

"No, no," Eldon grumbled. "Not up there, boy!" With a jerk of his wrist, he stuck his knife hilt deep into the soft earth, eliciting a gasp from the girl sitting directly across from him. "Down *there*."

He could almost hear the thumping hearts of the frightened listeners. Reaching down, he plucked the blade from the dirt, wiping it off on his stained jeans then using it to scrape the last remnants of beans from the can.

A couple of the girls made "eww" faces at each other as Eldon finished his canned supper.

"They come up from time to time," Eldon began again. "Devils, they are. Walking the earth. Looking for little boys and girls who don't mind their elders."

He leveled an appraising glare at each of the children, his eyeballs bulging to almost grotesque proportions.

"I sure hope that ain't none of you. I don't wanna be seein' your pictures on the news, how no one can't find ya. Too many kids have already gone missing 'round these woods ever since that first storm. *Creatures* out here, haven't you heard?"

Eldon took a deep breath, his mind wandering.

"Maybe that's why you come. You out lookin' for the monsters of the North Woods, that it? Thinking you might spot something out there? A bogle, perhaps? Or maybe the king himself, the *bogeyman*?"

He gestured at the yawning forest beyond, dark and imposing despite the brightness of the afternoon.

Some of the kids turned to face the woods, imagining they saw strange shapes and heard otherworldly noises.

"Well, God be with ya, if that's yer intent," Eldon said. "Believe you me, you don't want to see those monsters. Because once you do...you don't see nuthin' else, if you catch my meaning."

One of the older boys interrupted him. "Ah, come on. Everyone knows those are just stupid stories."

Eldon's eyes grew wide, as though he'd been slapped across the face. "You don't believe in the bogeyman?" he asked.

The kid stood and turned to his friends. "Come on. My dad was right. This guy's just a crazy old man."

The old-timer rose, towering over the children. "You callin' me a *liar*?"

Deflating just a bit, the boy said, "How are we supposed to believe you?"

Eldon's eyes darkened. "That's the scariest story of them all." He sat down again. "Y'see, I had a friend back when I was a runt. Name was Joe Hallerin. Not much younger than some of you. He ran afoul of the thing out in these woods...Terrible, terrible."

"Tell us." The boy sat.

Whether the boy was eager to hear something gross—as most boys are—or he wanted to ridicule the vagabond further, Eldon didn't care. He was fearful and excited, all at the same time, at the prospect of telling his best story.

"All right," he began, scanning the small group, "but don't say I didn't warn you. What I'm about to tell you is not fer young ears. Yet seeing as how your parents ain't doin' a good job a teachin' you the fundamentals, I guess it's left to me."

Once he was certain he had their attention, he dove into the tale, splaying his hands in front of them as though warming himself on the fire of their anticipation. His eyes lit up with mystery.

"Folks in the hills speak of a nasty bogle-king, one that even Sally-Bally, Gowerow, and Old Raw Head are afraid of. No one knows from where he comes. They say he comes for all bad children who pay no mind to their mamas.

"Folks don't speak much about Wolf Hollow anymore, but it used to be that every autumn old-timers and youngins alike would go to the apple orchards there and pick the sweetest apples you ever did taste. And it was up there in Wolf Hollow that there used to live an ornery cuss of a boy named Joe Hallerin.

"When Joe was just a baby, his father took ill and passed on, leaving his mother to raise the boy on her own. She worked day and night, that poor woman, but that ornery son of hers never gave her no respect for it. He would practice his moans and groans so he could lay out from school on Monday. And when his mama went to work, Joe Hallerin would sneak off to the fishing hole and catch frogs all day. And even iff'n his mama managed to drag him to church, he would plug his ears when the preacher started talking about hellfire and damnation. Some said Joe Hallerin stole chickens from his neighbors, though they never could catch him in the act.

"One day, after catching a whole sack full of frogs at the fishing hole, when it was getting late and the sun was hiding behind the trees, Joe Hallerin made his way home. As he was passing by the old woods of Wolf Hollow, he heard the most peculiar thing. Something from the bushes said:

O Joe Hallerin, where are you off to?
O Joe Hallerin, where have you been?
When our master comes to get you,
Open the window and let us in.

"When ol' Joe heard that, he went white as a sheet and lit a shuck outta there. When he got home and his mama asked him why he was late, Joe wouldn't tell her. Fact is, he wouldn't tell no one but me.

"A couple days later, Joe was on his way to town. He always liked to go off to town and hide in the bushes and throw mud at all the ladies in their fancy new dresses. On his way there, though, he happened by them same old woods. The peculiar sounds came again, and this time Joe stopped to take himself a look. What he saw in the bushes is indescribable in human words. The closest thing he could make out was that it was a whole bunch of critters with smoky, hollow, black eyes and mouths full of needles. They had long knives for fingers, and they all huddled close together, like a swarm of angry bees.

"'Who goes there?' he asked.

"Again, the critters spoke:

O Joe Hallerin, where are you off to?
Going to do no good, I'd say.
At the stroke of twelve, we'll come for you.
Open your door and come out to play.

"Again, Joe became all stricken with a fright and lit outta there, all the way home. And when his mama asked why he was in such a hurry, he never did say, 'cept to me.

"Now it happened that evening that Joe Hallerin was off to bed. He was all tucked in for the night, the covers pulled to his little chin, when he heard the most awful clatter outside his bedroom window.

"'What...Who goes there?' he stuttered from under his covers. And a voice that sounded great for storytellin' called back to him from t'other side of the window:

O Joe Hallerin, where are you off to?
Gone to the land of dreams?
I am the master, and I've come to you.
Open your window; it'll be such a scream.

"Joe pulled the covers up a little bit tighter, afraid to go out into the dark, y'see. He remembered the times the preacher told him to stay away from evil, but evil seemed to be so much fun. He thought of his mama, but even though he would miss her so, Joe wanted to go and see what the matter was with the stranger at the door.

"So, throwing the covers aside, he got out of bed and loosened the latch on the window. There was such a gust of wind come in that it blew out the fire in the woodstove. The house grew cold, and Joe saw his own breath.

"Then a crooked man with a crooked smile came a-hoverin' in that old cabin, looking like a hanged man at the gallows. The man had a snow-white face and lips black as a thick pool of blood, and he grinned wide to show his yellowed old teeth and said:

O Joe Hallerin, where you off to?
Never did listen to what the preacher would say.
Now you've got a lot of paying to do,
Your name will be sadly remembered today.

"And just like that, Joe Hallerin was whisked away on the wind, never to be heard from again. His mama woke up the next morning, her son gone from his bed, and she let out such a cry, knowing that Joe's dirty deeds had finally caught up to him.

"That's why ever after in ol' Wolf Hollow, this sad, strange tale is told to all the little boys and girls to keep them mindin' their mamas and their preacher-folk and to remind them to stay far away from Old Scratch and his kin."

Eldon hunkered down, suddenly quiet.

"And if the Strange Man ever come knockin' at your door"— he stood tall and roared—"don't you ever, *ever* let him in!"

Story time was over. With Eldon's tale complete, the breezy pre-storm cool called to the youths, appealing to their greater sense of adventure. Gathering their bikes from their resting places in the tall grass, the children rode off to live out the rest of their Saturday afternoon, talking excitedly about crazy old Eldon and his ghost stories.

Meanwhile, Eldon resumed his regular duties, using a pike and black garbage bag to collect discarded beer cans and other trash around the Old Greenesboro ruins. "People just don't have no appreciation for heritage," he grumbled, marveling at the refuse left behind in such a historic location.

These days it seemed the ruins served only as a giant receptacle for the town's garbage. Teenagers would sneak here at night to hold wild parties, far from their parents' watchful eyes. In the morning, all that remained of their revelry was smashed cans, broken bottles, and cigarette butts. Eldon did his best to keep the place clean—as much as the weed-entangled remains of a forgotten settlement *could* be kept clean. Nature had reclaimed the ruins, true, but there was no reason why the place had to be treated with disrespect.

Still, the teenagers' disrespect was Eldon's gain, as he was sure to earn a small fortune after handing in the cans and bottles for recycling at Don's Barber Shop in downtown Greensboro.

Eldon had dropped out of school after the sixth grade and wasn't fit for much but factory work. He eked out a decent living over the years without a family to support. His was a simple life of work, drinking with the fellas, and watching bad TV. But hard times hit Greensboro a year ago when the highway moved. Factories closed. Men lost their jobs. Families lost their homes. Eldon was an unfortunate casualty of the economic downturn. The bank foreclosed on his house, his car, his life. The North Woods became his sanctuary. This far out in the country there were some rotten old cabins abandoned by Greensboro's early settlers, and the bank didn't seem to have claim on any of them. Eldon moved in with the raccoons and cobwebs with nothing but the clothes on his back, a crate of Jim Beam, and the last of his earnings. Now living at a level slightly above homelessness, Eldon spent most of his days like today, scouring the town and surrounding woods for salable junk.

Every once in a great while he'd come across something spectacular, like an old pocket watch half-buried in the dirt that might fetch ten bucks at one of the pawn shops in town. But this Saturday he seemed destined for another catch of beer cans and bottles. If he were *really* lucky, the bottles would still be in one piece.

Like Ahab battling Moby Dick, Eldon raised his pike high and brought it down, piercing an aluminum can. His quarry impaled on the end of the stick, Eldon stuffed it in the bag with his other felled prey and continued the hunt.

Life in the North Woods wasn't that bad, for the most part. His daily sojourns in the country gave him ample time to think about things and enjoy his golden years. After spending so much of his life slaving away in the factory, it was refreshing to be among the trees with the warm sun on his face and open air as his companion.

Only at night did Eldon second-guess his decision to live in the woods.

In the beginning nothing seemed out of the ordinary, but these days the nighttime made him feel thin and frail. Lately he'd been having bizarre nightmares, at first sporadically, but now they were increasing in frequency and intensity. Sometimes at night he had fevered visions of strange, man-shaped dark figures, their slippery arms raised to the starless night sky, dancing and uttering horrible, gut-twisting wails of pleasure and pain. On those nights, when he woke up, soaked in sweat, he'd swear the shadows surrounding his bed were looking at him.

Watching him.

He never told anyone about the things he saw in his nightmares, not even the kids who came to listen to his stories. Truth be told, Eldon Granger never knew a boy named Joe Hallerin and was pretty sure there was no Wolf Hollow in Maribel County. It was all just a story his mother told him when he was little to keep him in line, and he supposed she heard it from her mother in a time when every mother in Greensboro told her children that story or one like it. But time had moved on, life had changed, and Eldon didn't hear the old stories anymore. The world no longer believed in such things. Eldon himself didn't believe in monsters or bogles or bogeymen or any of the colorful creatures he sprinkled into the receptive minds of children.

But the dreams…they were almost enough to change his mind.

As the blue day turned a smoky orange Eldon's dilapidated

shack beckoned to him, despite the words KEEP OUT he had spray-painted in black on the windows. The setting sun, now a big ball of red in the late afternoon sky, continued its descent as charcoal-colored clouds formed in the distance, promising a night of wind and rain. Eldon was glad to be home and sighed in sweet liberation as he hefted the black bag off his shoulder and dropped it onto the rickety porch. He'd tarried in the forest longer than he meant to and was glad to have made it back to the cabin before dark. Tomorrow he'd make a trip into town to exchange his garbage for greenbacks. After that, a trip to the store for groceries. He thought he might make a day of it.

Entering the dark house, he fumbled for the box of matches he kept by the door and lit the gas lamp. He intensified the flame, moving into the sparsely furnished living room. Here, arranged in front of the cold fireplace and dusty mantel, a moth-eaten couch he'd collected from the curb, three milk crates, and a scratched-up coffee table awaited him. He set the lamp on the table and called out, "Honey, I'm home."

An old sandy-colored basset hound named Cougar sauntered into the room. Its jowls hung loose, giving the dog a perpetually sad expression. Eldon smiled and bent down to scratch the dog's neck and back.

"Hey, ol' Cougar. Ya miss me? Huh?"

The dog obviously did not reply, but that didn't stop Eldon from snuggling up to its loose skin.

"Hey there. Been a long day, hasn't it? Sorry I've been out so late, boy. Found some good stuff today. Tomorrow it's the best stuff for you, don't you worry. The *canned* stuff."

Grinning to himself, happy to be home, Eldon stood and chuckled as Cougar hobbled toward the front door, his interest piqued by the sound of some critter outside.

"What did you make me for supper?" Eldon inquired of the hound's retreating backside. "Ah, I guess it's up to me. *Again*."

Bent low, Cougar sniffed at the crack beneath the door. Suddenly, the dog jerked back with a whimper, then growled. Eldon looked over his shoulder, mildly curious.

"What is it, boy? Huh?"

Cougar stepped away from the door and took a defensive stance, growling once more. Eldon's smile faded, replaced by a frown. He moved toward the door and knelt at his faithful friend's side.

"What is it, Cougar? What's spookin' ya?"

Cougar let loose a thunderous bark, and Eldon bolted to a standing position, startled. The dog gnashed and scratched at the floor, clawing at the wood, then began jumping against the door.

Eldon shouted, "That's enough, now! Enough! What's wrong with ya? You smell that storm coming or what?"

But the dog could not be sated. It barked and growled and scratched and clawed, determined to get outside. Eldon pushed the dog aside and threw open the door, looking out into the ginger light of dusk. Dark clouds hovered on the horizon.

"What is it, boy? There's nothing out here!"

Nevertheless, Cougar tore through the open doorway toward the sooty, overcast sky, barking all the way before disappearing into a dark thicket.

Eldon yelled after him, "Hey, now! Git back here, boy!"

He stepped onto the rickety porch, listening to the yapping of his hound in the woods. Sounds of struggle replaced the barking, and Eldon's aggravation with the dog's erratic behavior melted away. A somber hush blanketed the woods, time drawing out like an eternity.

Finally, a lone yelp split Eldon's heart.

"Cougar?" he called urgently. "You all right out there? What'dya find?"

His questions were answered with silence.

"Cougar?"

A rumble of whispering snickers undulated between the thin trees as a subtle green fog roiled the fallen leaves, turning them crispy and colorless. The mist unfurled like emerald tendrils, a fitting prelude for the tempest that hovered patiently overhead, biding its time. Cold unlike anything Eldon had ever felt before crept into his bones, freezing his soul.

A second yelp was followed by another round of impish laughter.

His heart beating fast, Eldon grabbed a rifle from just inside the doorway and headed into the North Woods, the darkness surrounding and terrifying him.

"Don't worry, Cougar! I'm comin' for ya!"

As the old man stomped through the forest, the chilly green mist moved between his feet, veiling his path. Overhead, low-hanging branches grew together, shutting out the few remaining rays of sunlight.

From somewhere deep within the murky woods, Eldon heard Cougar yelp again. He picked up speed, determined to save his last remaining friend on Earth.

"Hold on, boy! I'm right here!"

The gloom enveloped Eldon, mocking him, but he did not relent. Drumbeats pounded inside his mind, and he felt as though he'd stepped out of the waking world and into the landscape of his nightmares, a place where the shadowed man-shapes of his dreams slithered and danced beneath star-less skies. His eyes widened, and he prayed that he might find Cougar and return home before the storm claimed them both.

"Cougar! Where ya at?"

Eldon paused, his eyes scanning the dim forest, fighting to see through the strange green mist. Then, as if the North Woods themselves conceded, the fog parted like curtains to reveal a stage. The stage was the Old Greenesboro ruins, and sitting atop one of the stone foundations, as if prepared to tell a story of his own, was none other than Cougar.

The dog just sat there on his haunches, sadly facing his master.

"Cougar?" Eldon asked, a curious smile forcing its way onto his lips. "What is it, boy?"

Whispers, soft cackles, and voices rippled in the shadows of the tall trees. Old Cougar whined, bent low, and covered his head with his paws.

"What is—?"

Eldon gasped and watched in dumbstruck horror as the shadows surrounding his mutt suddenly came alive. Numerous shapes—impossible to count—flew past Cougar, leaving the dog unharmed as they initiated a frenzied pursuit of his master.

Screaming, Eldon dropped his rifle and tore back through the North Woods, the sounds of wild beasts bearing down on him while Cougar, the bait of this tragic charade, continued to whimper and hide his face in his paws.

The fog lifted and the branches split, allowing Eldon to glimpse the dusk's welcoming light. His humble shack before him, he tore free of the woods' entanglement and the storm's baleful glare on his back. He raced for the front door, nearly tripping up the steps of the porch before crashing into his home. Landing hard on the floor, Eldon picked himself up and hurled his full weight against the door, desperately holding it shut as the things outside pounded on it and cackled.

"No…No…Go away…Go away!"

To Eldon's dismay, the green mist seeped beneath the crack

in his door. He began stomping at it furiously, hoping against hope to send it away.

"No...Please, no!"

Eldon never believed the stories about Joe Hallerin and the bogeyman. But now he thought of Joe Hallerin—if such a boy had ever existed—and wondered what shadowed lands the bogeyman had taken Joe to on that fateful night. As he fought against the mist, Eldon worried he'd discover that hellish place soon enough.

Suddenly, a powerful force caved in the door, throwing Eldon across the room. He staggered to a standing position as shapes invaded his sanctuary. Futilely, he shielded his face, crying out in shock and agony, but the living shadows overwhelmed him, and soon his cries were forever silenced.

Meanwhile, dark clouds continued looming in the east.

CHAPTER ONE

J EFF WELDON STOOD in the kitchen of his parents' white two-story Victorian house on one of Greensboro's most picturesque streets looking out the small window over the sink. He sipped a cup of coffee and watched the storm clouds circling Greensboro's eastern border.

"If it's going to rain, I just wish it'd hurry up already," he muttered into his cup, the worry lines on his face belying his twenty-seven years.

His wife, Isabella, nudged him as she passed by with mischief in her ebony eyes and a full plate of fried chicken, steaming mashed potatoes, and green beans in her hands.

"You going to eat or what?" she asked.

Jeff heard his parents talking and laughing in the other room. He gave the upcoming storm a final glance.

"Yeah, I'm coming," he said.

His mother, Louise Weldon, blonde but graying, straightened the napkin on her lap as Jeff and Isabella took their seats. As usual, Louise maintained a pleasant smile. Her face patient and trusting, she beamed with pride at having her family together in one place.

Well, except for—

"Where's Dras?" Louise asked Jeff.

The phrase "Am I my brother's keeper?" flashed in Jeff's mind, but he stifled it, knowing what his mother would say in response.

"Probably with Rosalyn," he said.

Louise turned to her husband, Jack, seated at the head of the table. Jeff and Isabella also turned to the aging man in overalls. His shoulders slumped with an invisible weight, his cobalt blue eyes wise, yet sad and fading.

"Should we wait for them?" Louise asked, her brow furrowing a bit.

"Boy's always late," Jack said without anger.

It's no excuse, Jeff grumbled to himself. *Dras knows how much these family dinners mean to our parents. Especially now.* Aloud, he said, "Let's just eat. It'll be cold by time he gets here."

Louise frowned but agreed. "Jack, do you want to say the blessing?"

The elder Weldon closed his eyes and bowed his head. His wife took his hand. Having been a pastor most of his life, the man was well practiced at praying. But today, the words weren't coming.

After a moment of silence, Jeff peeked and saw his dad wincing. Pain registered on his aged face. Jeff's heart hurt for the man. Before this sickness he'd never known his father to be weak. Growing up Jeff swore his father was ten feet tall and bulletproof. The man had every answer and could fix any problem. Now he struggled to say grace over a simple meal.

"I got it, Dad," Jeff said softly.

His father kept his eyes shut but nodded.

Jeff prayed, not really listening to his own words, just saying the usual, "Thanks for food and family." His words did not reflect his heart. There he prayed, *Why God? Why does my father have to be in so much pain? You could heal him if You wanted. I know You can. He served You his whole life. Doesn't he deserve that? Please, God, don't take my dad.*

"Amen," he finished.

A solemn chorus of amens echoed around the table.

Louise, ever the light-bringer in the room, initiated dinner conversation with one hand in her lap while the other scooped a spoonful of potatoes.

"So, how are you kids?" she asked.

Caught in mid-chew, Isabella nodded. Swallowing, she said, "Good."

"How are things at the church?" Louise asked routinely.

"Fine," Jeff responded quickly, not wanting his father to think for a second that he didn't have everything under control.

You left her in good hands, Dad. I'm doing a good job. I'll make you proud.

A smile broke through as his father bit off a chunk of dinner roll. "Deacons aren't giving you a hard time, are they?" he said.

Isabella snickered and looked to her husband, the question triggering a private joke between them. Jeff just shook his head. "Nah. They're all right."

"Good," his father nodded. "Don't let them get the best of you. If I'd done everything they wanted, the church would have folded by now."

"Oh, Jeff," his mother said wistfully. "I wish we could hear you preach more often. It's just, with your dad—"

"I know, Mom," Jeff said. "It's OK. You're not missing much." He smiled. "I'm not near the preacher Dad is anyway."

"Bah," his father grumbled, taking a bite of chicken, the drumstick trembling in his painfully swollen hands. "You're God's man for the job. That's what matters."

Thanks, Dad.

Jeff beamed at his father's approval. He was proud that his dad could still think so highly of God's will despite his current circumstances.

"Jeff's doing great," Isabella said proudly, patting her husband's knee under the table. "You'd be really proud of him."

"Well," Louise chirped, "with everything going so well, have you two given any more consideration to...adding to the family?"

Isabella nearly choked on a mouthful of green beans. Jeff reddened.

"Subtle, Mom," he said.

"I'm just saying," Louise defended herself, "I know you wanted to wait until things were stable financially, but you've been married seven years now. Don't you think it's time to start a family?"

"They'll start when they're ready, Louise," Dad said from his end of the table. "Call off the hounds."

Isabella retained her smile, though Jeff knew the question had stung. They wanted to have kids. That wasn't the issue. They weren't able. Maybe they never would be.

The doctors had already broken the news to the couple. Jeff just didn't know how to break it to his family. His mother had never ardently pushed for Jeff and Isabella to deliver to her a batch of grandbabies, but they knew that with Jeff's father edging closer every day to eternity, the elder Weldons wanted more than ever to share the birth of their first grandchild.

Mercifully, the doorbell rang. Jeff jumped up, nearly toppling over the table in the process. "I'll get that," he said.

Sighing with relief, Jeff opened the door. On the front porch stood Rosalyn Myers. Though he had known the twenty-two-year-old auburn-haired beauty all her life, he was still happy to see her.

"Hey, stranger," Rosalyn greeted him, her smile widening. She leaned up to give Jeff a warm hug and kiss on the cheek.

He returned the gesture, a flood of childhood adventures cascading through his mind.

"Hey, Roz."

"How long's it been?" she asked. "A month or two?"

"Well," he cracked a lopsided grin, "if you're missing me that much, there's a surefire way to see me more often. Once a week, even. Sunday, perhaps?"

"Smooth, Weldon," she said, playfully raising an eyebrow. "Is that how you charm all your converts?"

Jeff laughed and stepped aside, inviting Rosalyn into the house. His good humor faded when he saw she was alone.

"Where's Dras?" he asked, frustration rising in his voice.

Rosalyn regarded him with genuine surprise. "He's not here? I went by his apartment to pick him up, but he wasn't there. Bike was gone too."

Jeff fumed, the tips of his ears glowing crimson.

Where is he?

With sandy-blond hair that never retained a coherent shape and a face young and untouched by the rigors of the world, twenty-two-year-old Dras Weldon possessed a little brother quality that women found attractive on a platonic level. Dras owed his name to a mythical knight his five-year-old brother read about in a children's storybook. Dras seemed destined for quirkiness. His odd moniker was hard to pronounce, and he spent most of his introductory conversations explaining that it was pronounced *Droz* and not *Drass*. Apart from his unusual name, Dras had been reared in a "traditional middle-class American home," most would say, surrounded by the love and support of a doting mother and the strong Christian principles of a hardworking father.

Despite his upbringing, or maybe because of it, Dras Weldon was a man of addictions—dark, unseemly addictions that kept him bound in a vice-like grip, drawing him deeper and deeper into a web of insatiable hunger, feeding a lust that could never be quenched.

And so it was, while his family enjoyed a pleasant meal in the sun's dying light and the gray storm drew its plans against Greensboro in the distant eastern sky, Dras found himself down in the gravel pits near a small trailer park just outside of town serving one of his many obsessions.

"We had a deal!" Dras shouted, his heart racing and his brow covered in a sheen of cold sweat. Though he knew it would be of no use, he pleaded with the unscrupulous dealer. Sean Patrick was exceptionally ruthless.

Especially for an eight-year-old.

Angrily, Dras picked up the small plastic bag that contained the Snake Eyes G.I. Joe action figure in question. "You said you had one with Snake Eyes in the original package!"

Sean shrugged. "I sold it to Bobby."

Dumpy, freckled Bobby stood next to his bike behind Sean, his arms crossed, a stern look on his face. He gave a quick jerk of his head as if to say, "Wanna make something of it?"

Dras steamed. "You said you'd hold it 'til next Saturday!"

"He paid me sixty for it."

"Sixty!" Dras came unglued, throwing his hands about wildly, poor Snake Eyes jiggling in the wake. "I paid you *seventy* for it!"

Sean shrugged again.

"Look at this!" Dras pressed the toy into Sean's face. "It doesn't even have accessories! What about weapons? How is he supposed to defend himself against deadly Cobra assassins?"

"That's your problem," the precocious youngster said, folding his arms, mirroring his chunky back-up.

"You could have at least thrown in Timber! Snake Eyes has to have his dog, man!"

Sean leveled a cool gaze at the grown man throwing a fit over an action figure. "That's an extra twenty."

Dras's face flushed. He pursed his lips, ready to tear into the pint-sized menaces. Bobby took a step forward, standing shoulder to shoulder with his partner, and Dras backed down.

"Forget it," he said, pointing an accusing finger at the two cutthroats. "This is highway robbery."

Bobby broke his stoic silence. "It's business."

Dras glowered at the two of them. Then, with his overpriced Snake Eyes toy, he moved toward his own bicycle.

"This isn't over," Dras threatened, swinging a leg over the side of the bike.

Bobby raised his arms in a "bring it on" gesture.

Dras pedaled in retreat, but not before calling out, "I'm telling your mothers!"

Jeff chewed his food, his thoughts on his tardy brother. Isabella felt the tension emanating from him and nudged him in the ribs, while Louise and Rosalyn chatted over the dinner table. Jeff glanced at his wife out of the corner of his eye.

OK? her expression asked.

He exhaled and gazed at the empty chair where Dras should be sitting. Isabella shook her head at him almost imperceptibly and reached for her sweetened tea.

"I guess I should tell you guys," Rosalyn said, raising her voice a bit. "I mean, you're the closest thing I've got to family, so you should be the first to know."

Louise set down her fork, her eyes sparkling with curiosity. Even Jack seemed to overcome his usual distance, leaning forward to engage in the conversation.

"What is it?" Isabella asked.

Rosalyn looked at Jeff, then Louise, then pulled a folded envelope from her back pocket. She waved it proudly and declared, "I've been accepted to Vermont!"

Louise clapped and leaned over to hug the girl. "Oh, that's great!"

Jeff frowned. "I didn't even know you had applied. I mean, you had talked about it, but..."

Rosalyn smiled with a mixture of accomplishment and guilt. "Well, yeah, I thought I should give it a shot."

"Education's important," the elder Weldon said. "You'll do great there."

Rosalyn said, "Thanks, Jack. That means a lot."

Her eyes brimming with tears, Louise brushed the girl's hair with her fingers. "Your dad would have been so proud, Rosalyn."

A tinge of sadness passed over Rosalyn's face but quickly vanished. She turned to Jeff. "You're not mad, are you?"

Now it was Jeff's turn to blush. "*No*. No, of course not."

Isabella grinned. "He's just going to miss you. Expect an exorbitant phone bill."

"I will," Rosalyn said.

Jeff rose and moved toward Rosalyn. She met him halfway. The two embraced. "Congratulations, Roz," Jeff said. "I'm really proud of you."

"Thanks, big brother."

When they parted, Louise was dabbing her eyes with the corner of a napkin and Jack was rolling his. She laughed in surrender and swatted her husband with the makeshift handkerchief.

Isabella was proud of her husband for being strong, knowing how much he'd worry over Rosalyn being so far away. But she knew Rosalyn would be OK. She could take care of herself.

Still, one question hung in her mind.

As Jeff and Rosalyn stepped back uncomfortably, Rosalyn punching Jeff in the arm in an attempt to tell him she appreciated his concern, Isabella probed, "Uh...I hate to bring this up, but...what did Dras say when you told him?"

Rosalyn froze as all eyes at the dinner table focused on her. "Um...Yeah, see, that's kind of the thing. I haven't told him yet."

"Oh, he'll be crushed," Louise said.

"He'll be fine," her husband assured her.

Jeff scratched the back of his head and sat down. "This isn't going to be pretty."

Rosalyn said, "I know. That's why I was sort of hoping you guys wouldn't say anything. I'll tell him. I just have to pick my moment."

"Tell me what?"

Dras entered the dining room, his hand buried elbow-deep in a bag of Cheetos.

Rosalyn swallowed hard and eased back into her seat. "Nothing."

Jeff scolded his brother, partly to cover Rosalyn's fumble and partly to voice his own disapproval. "You're late."

Dras looked at his family gathered around the table, realization dawning on his goofy face. "Oh. Were we eating dinner tonight?"

"We saved you a seat, son," his father said, sad resignation in his voice.

Dras, still clutching his bag of snacks, plopped down next to Rosalyn and took note of the empty plate. He surveyed the table. "Man, this looks good too."

"It's cold," Jeff said. "Where were you?"

"Busy," Dras snapped. Then, to Rosalyn: "You OK, Roz? You look like someone just ran over your cat."

Jeff scraped the remains of his supper into the trash can, peeking into the dining room, where Rosalyn and Dras joked and laughed with his parents. He scowled. Isabella noticed his expression as she entered, following his lead in dumping the leftover scraps into the trash.

"He knows how much these family things mean to Mom," Jeff griped. "He should have put forth a little effort."

"He's here now. That's what's important."

Jeff slumped. "I guess so."

"Thanks for leaving me alone earlier, by the way," Isabella quipped.

"Yeah, I sort of left you to the lions, didn't I? Sorry. Mom's really on a baby kick, I guess."

Isabella patted his arm to show that there were no hard feelings. "I can't say that I blame her. Especially with your dad."

Jeff tensed, and Isabella was afraid she had reopened the wound. Jeff's father meant everything to him. Losing him would be the hardest thing her husband ever had to deal with.

She tried to soften the sting, nuzzling his side. "Though I wouldn't mind someone taking up that spare room in the house, you know?"

"Iz," he said. "The doctors…"

"What do they know?" she said, fiery conviction in her eyes. "*My* God created the world. Can't He create a little baby for us to love?"

Jeff stared in awe at her. Lovingly, he hooked his arm around her waist and pressed her familiar body to his. "Yeah. I guess all we can do is pray and, well…"

She smiled flirtatiously. "Yeah. We can still do *that*."

The sound of Dras's laughter filtered in from the dining room. Jeff's passion cooled. "Until then," he said, "we've got *Dras*."

Jack had long since retired to his recliner, loaded down with painkillers and ready to sleep the evening away, by the time the kids were leaving. Dras and Rosalyn stood on the front porch of the Weldons' home, while Jeff and Isabella exchanged hugs with Louise in the doorway.

"So, did you get it?" Rosalyn whispered to Dras.

Dras's eyes widened in panic. He checked to make sure his brother wasn't paying attention. Once he was satisfied the coast was clear, he retrieved the plastic bag from his pocket, revealing Snake Eyes.

Rosalyn examined its contents. "Where's the rest of it?"

Dras grumbled, still wounded from the encounter. "Stupid Sean Patrick gypped me."

Rosalyn stifled a chuckle. "I told you."

"I know," he groaned. "Hope springs eternal."

"And so does your parents' bank account, right?"

Dras paled. "Don't tell them, OK?"

"That money was supposed to be for rent, remember?"

"What are you, Jeff now?"

Dras quit talking as the big brother in question moved within hearing range.

"I'll call you tomorrow, Mom," Jeff said. He purposefully bumped Dras's shoulder.

"Hey!" Dras protested. He received a glower from his older brother in return.

"Bye, Dras," Isabella said amiably. "Bye, Rosalyn."

"Bye, Isabella." Rosalyn waved. Dras was too busy rubbing his sore arm to wave.

As Jeff eased behind the wheel of the car, he leveled a through-the-brow look at his brother. "Stay out of trouble."

Dras snarled and would have returned his brother's gesture with a choice one of his own were it not for his mother standing nearby.

Louise and Rosalyn hugged once more while Dras awkwardly kept his distance, unsure what to do with himself and feeling rather guilty for wasting his parents' money. When it was his turn to hug, Dras held up a hand and meekly peeped, "See ya, Mom. Thanks for supper," and jogged down the porch steps.

Rosalyn offered an amused shrug on his behalf and joined him in the yard while Louise went inside to tend to her husband. Rosalyn gave Dras a quick kick in the seat of the pants.

"*What*?"

"Don't be such a goof. Can't you hug your mother?"

"Ha. You're one to talk."

"If I had *your* mother, I'd be hugging her all the time."

Dras pulled his bicycle from its crashed position on the ground. "So, what are we gonna do tonight?"

Rosalyn dug in her jeans pocket for her car keys. She refused to carry a purse. "Same thing we do every night, Pinky."

"Pick me up in an hour?"

"Sure," she said, climbing into the car. "Wear something nice, will ya? I've got a rep to protect."

"Hardy har," Dras scoffed.

"Later."

"Hey, Roz?" His tone became serious. "You sure nothing's wrong? Something you want to tell me?"

Rosalyn faltered a moment, then said, "Nothing you'd want to hear. I'll see you later."

Dras nodded as Rosalyn drove away, heading in the direction of the imposing storm clouds.

CHAPTER TWO

RUNNING. BREATHING HEAVILY. *Leaves crunching beneath his feet. Moonlit branches slapping his face, fighting to keep him back. To keep him from seeing.*

Still he runs. The woods are familiar but out of place. He thinks he knows where he's going, but he's lost out here in the darkness and the soupy green fog.

He hears drumbeats. Already he can make out the sounds of alien howling, inhuman chants in constant rhythm. His stomach tightens, for he fears what he'll find.

Yet he pushes on. Unable to stop.

"It's coming."

Lightning flashed, and instantly the thunder rumbled.

Jeff Weldon sprang up in bed, covered in an icy sweat. A staccato of white-blue light flickered through the partially closed blinds. Pushing the strange dream to the back of his mind, he rose and moved to the bedroom window.

"Guess it finally decided to rain," he said sourly over his shoulder as he peeked through the blinds. Outside a violent wind leaned on the trees. When he received no reply, he looked toward the bed and saw his wife facedown in the covers, snoring lightly. Even like this, she was beautiful. Her dark, wavy locks were cast this way and that over the pillow, hiding her face. A soft mocha-colored arm had found its way outside the covers.

A quilt covered the rest of her body, forming a lump, though a nicely shaped one.

Isabella said she got her looks from her mother. *She certainly didn't get those fiery Latin eyes from her father,* Jeff reflected. He never knew Isabella's mother. She abandoned her husband and five children when Isabella was an infant. *Probably why Isabella learned to be so tough.* Good thing too. On occasion he needed her to protect him from things like big, scary storms.

"Iz?" He tried to stir her, to make sure she was asleep and not just ignoring him.

No answer. Isabella slept soundly, just like she did when she was nine and a tornado tore through her daddy's farm. Despite the intensity of the storm outside, Isabella remained peaceful.

Not Jeff.

The lightning and thunder combined forces, rocking the house to its foundation. Jeff jumped a foot. Isabella didn't so much as flinch. *How can she sleep through this?*

Digging around on the floor in the dark, Jeff searched for his robe. Once he felt its worn fuzziness, he slipped it on and left the bedroom.

No sleep for me tonight.

Jeff didn't like being caught unprepared. While there was no indication that this storm was the Big One, he knew it would only take one bad storm to sweep their rickety country house off the map. If that was to be the case tonight, Jeff wanted to face the situation head-on. His was a life carefully cushioned to safeguard against trouble, and that was just how he liked it.

Safe and predictable.

His instincts led him downstairs into the kitchen to sit out the storm. He flicked on the light to give him some guidance and prevent a toe stubbing and sat at the kitchen table, where his Bible and notes were still sprawled out from his study earlier that evening.

Taking his insomnia as a blessing in disguise, Jeff began to sort through the papers, trying to make some sense of them. Tomorrow was Sunday, and the congregation of the Good Church of the Faithful would expect him to fulfill his duties as pastor and deliver a powerful sermon. True to character, he was prepared, planning a rousing message featuring the prophet Ezekiel preaching to the dry bones in Ezekiel 37. He thought he'd reread the passage once more, just to make sure he was ready for the morning.

The pauses between the lightning and thunder were growing shorter, and Jeff knew it would only be a matter of time before the winds and rains would be assaulting his old house with full force. The anticipation caused his mind to wander. Storms had always frightened him. In his youth he had never been able to sleep when the rain poured and the thunder boomed. He feared each storm would herald the coming of some greater evil.

The bogeyman. Just like in the stories.

The thought of a creature scratching on his bedroom window wracked him with anxiety until he was well past the age of believing in ghost stories and urban legends. Even now he unconsciously checked the closets and peeked through the blinds before going to bed, much to his wife's chagrin.

Again the lightning and thunder double-teamed the house. Jeff glanced out the kitchen window. *That was really close.*

He thumbed through his Bible, trying to gather his thoughts. However, his mind returned to stormy days when he was a frightened child. His mother told him that when it thundered, God was bowling. The image always brought a smile to his face and temporarily eased his fears, though the feeling of dread in the pit of his stomach never entirely went away.

As he grew older, Jeff sought to conquer his fears by learning to prepare for storms—and any other threatening circumstance he could imagine. He reasoned that he wouldn't be afraid as long as he kept control of the situation, as long as he stayed alert.

Just in case.

The Bible stared up at him from the kitchen table. Jeff stared back, indifferently at first, but then something caught his eye. Suddenly, his familiar Bible appeared *odd* to him. He had studied the book profusely, reading its pages countless times, but tonight it seemed different. He couldn't describe it. It just seemed…alive.

Like it's breathing.

For a moment, he had to convince himself that it was, indeed, a book and not one of the random critters that Isabella brought home from the banks of the pond out back. It was *that* real to him.

At once, Jeff felt as though he were on fire. He started to sweat beneath his robe, and his face flushed, even though Isabella kept the house cool. Recognition dawned. He'd felt this way once before. This same burning intensity filled him when he felt called to follow the Lord. Maybe God was calling him to something else, preparing him for a special task.

Excitement and nervousness collided in the pit of his stomach. He stared at the words on the page of the Bible as if trying to fall into the text.

The Bible remained unchanged. It was as though he was a new parent trying to decipher the cry of an infant.

I want to understand.

"What is it, God?" he asked. "What am I looking for?"

Maybe he needed to change his sermon. Maybe there was

something else God wanted the people of Greensboro to hear tomorrow morning.

Something else...

Turning the pages, Jeff searched the Scriptures, praying to find something that would jump out at him and give him direction. But nothing spoke to him. *What am I looking for?*

Suddenly a powerful gust of wind blew open the worn back door in the kitchen, whistling some wild nightmare melody and spitting a flurry of leaves inside. Jeff started, his muscles tensing in fright. He hurried to the door to bar out the storm.

Then he saw it.

Over the troubled waters of Grover's Pond, the storm galloped toward him like a mighty god awakened from its slumber, ready to conquer and subjugate the world. With violet spikes the thing pulled itself along the midnight sky, its open throat straining to devour the entire town. Within its cumulus body, lightning flickered, illuminating the frightening beast.

It was unlike anything he had ever seen.

The clouds, brilliantly dark and blue, rolled over his home like a hungry predator. And they were moving *fast*. From the mouth of the storm came a roar of thunder that shook the heavens, the earth, and the core of Jeff's soul.

The sight so moved him—so disturbed him—he thought to wake Isabella, to let her bear witness to it too. Maybe she could convince him there was nothing to worry about, that it was just another storm. Yet he stood frozen in place, paralyzed by the same fear that haunted him as a child. And as he stared at the encroaching darkness laying siege to his little town of Greensboro, one truth reverberated in Jeff's mind: This was *not* just another storm. Not by a long shot.

"Mommy?"

The little voice was intent. Rebecca Walker gazed down at her daughter, Millie, as she tucked her into bed.

"What, honey?"

"The man on the TV said a storm was coming."

Rebecca stifled a laugh. Millie was only five, but sometimes she sounded so much older. She raised an amused eyebrow. "When did you start watching weather reports?"

Millie didn't have an answer. Rebecca didn't really expect one. She pulled the covers up and kissed her daughter on the forehead.

"It's way past your bedtime, Millie. You need to go to sleep now."

"I'm scared."

"Millie, it's just a storm. You know I've got to work tomorrow, and I need to get some sleep. You do too."

"But—"

Rebecca placed a gentle yet firm finger to her daughter's lips. "If you go to sleep, the storm will be gone in the morning, and everything will be OK. OK?"

Rebecca switched off the light. Before she could make it out the door, Millie called her back.

"Mommy?"

"Yes, honey?" she said, growing exasperated.

"Is the bogeyman real?"

The question took Rebecca by surprise. She had never heard Millie say anything about a bogeyman before. She didn't even know her daughter knew what a bogeyman was.

"Why do you ask?"

"TJ said the bogeyman is real. He said he comes for little boys and girls who are bad."

Rebecca frowned. She would talk to TJ later. "Is that why you don't want to go to sleep?"

Millie nodded.

"Your brother's just trying to scare you, honey."

"So there's no such thing as the bogeyman?"

Rebecca smiled. "No."

Millie smiled back, revealing a missing tooth. It was obvious the matter had been bothering her a great deal, and now that her all-knowing mother had clarified the safety of the situation, she felt secure going to sleep. "Good night, Mommy."

"'Night."

Rebecca waved, closing the door behind her.

Alone in the dark, Millie turned toward the bay window. Mommy had forgotten to pull the curtains closed. She stared out the window. On clear nights the stars and the moon would lull her to sleep with their twinkling. Tonight, there were no twinkling lights. She frowned.

A blast of lightning cut the darkness, splitting the black sky in two.

Millie jumped. Three heartbeats later, thunder followed. A chill ran down her petite frame. After the thunder subsided, she heard something.

Scratching.

It didn't register at first. She thought it was lingering thunder. But soon she realized the thunder was gone, yet the scratching remained. She strained her ears, trying to determine where it was coming from. She didn't dare get up.

Scratching.

It was louder now. Closer. Millie pulled the covers to her chin.

All was silent. Seconds passed. Millie began to feel silly for being afraid.

Scratching.

Chubby fingers ventured from beneath the covers, reaching under the mattress.

Found it!

Her pony flashlight.

She powered the flashlight to life. She shined it around the room but saw nothing out of the ordinary. Her fright began to subside, only to be replaced by an insatiable curiosity.

The scratching sounded again.

Millie aimed the light in the direction of the sound.

It came from the window.

Armed with her pony flashlight, little Millie Walker climbed out of bed and headed for the large window, the beam of the flashlight leading the way. She stopped, listening for the scratching, but the sound didn't return. She smiled, feeling more comfortable.

Laying her flashlight on the windowsill, she put her tiny hands on the glass, watching them meet their reflection. She looked up and noticed a large branch from a twisted tree blowing in the wind, the source of the scratching.

She giggled. "Silly old tree."

The breeze picked up outside. The storm was coming, just like the man with the toupee on television said it would.

Millie felt the glass grow colder and colder. She shivered, imagining how frosty the wind must be out there. Even the warmth of her skin did little to thaw the windowpane.

Suddenly, lightning flashed, illuminating the sky and her bedroom.

She looked at the reflection of her hands in the glass. They weren't her hands! They were the hands of a man!

The room plunged into darkness. Millie screamed. She jumped back, aiming her pony flashlight at the window. The strange hands were gone.

Thunder rolled. Without warning, the batteries in the flashlight died. Millie screamed again and ran to her bed. Abandoning the pony flashlight, she leaped into bed and pulled the covers over her head, her screams echoing in the room.

After what seemed an eternity, her mother burst through the door, brandishing a candle. Millie was so scared she couldn't speak; all she could do was tremble and wail.

Her mother embraced her with one arm. Setting the candle on the nightstand, she wrapped both arms around her daughter and rocked her, combing her fingers through the little girl's hair.

"It's OK, honey. It's just the storm. The electricity went out, that's all."

Millie found her voice. "It was the bogeyman! I saw him! It was the bogeyman!"

Thanks a lot, TJ. Rebecca sighed, trying to think of the best way to handle the situation. She said, "We talked about this, Millie. There's no such thing as the bogeyman. TJ's just being mean. Don't listen to him, OK?"

That didn't help. Millie clung to her mother, wiping tears on her shirt. Rebecca's mind raced. *She really could use a dad right now. Thanks a lot, Steve. I hope you're having a super time with your midlife crisis wife.* A nurse at the ER in addition to being a single parent, Rebecca had been forced to take on extra shifts just to make ends meet.

Feeling helpless and frustrated, Rebecca hugged her daughter and wracked her brain for something to say. She had to work in the morning and couldn't risk a sleepless night just because TJ decided to traumatize his little sister. She had to think of something that would dispel this bogeyman business.

Then she noticed the light of the candle.

Gently nudging Millie, she whispered, "Look. Look, honey."

Millie's cries died down to a dull sob. Rebecca pointed at the candle. "You know what?"

"What?"

"See this candle? It's protection. The bogeyman is scared of light."

"He is?"

"You didn't know that?"

"No."

"I can't believe you haven't heard that! Everybody knows that light keeps the bogeyman away."

Millie was buying it.

Rebecca continued, "As long as this candle is here, the bogeyman will stay away."

"Really?" Millie's eyes filled with hope.

Rebecca nodded. "Really. Now, go to sleep."

"OK."

Millie lay back and tucked herself in, keeping one eye on her mother. Rebecca smiled, and Millie decided everything must be all right.

"Good night," Rebecca said.

As Rebecca walked out the door, she muttered under her breath, "TJ Walker, we're going to have a *long* talk."

Turning from Millie's bedroom window, the bogle-king strolled down the abandoned streets of Greensboro in the form of a man, unrelenting rain pelting him as he savored his newfound freedom.

Having prepared for this moment for so long, to his dismay he discovered the townspeople huddling in their homes, fearful of the dreadful storm that signaled a new era. To make a grand arrival without benefit of a proper audience was disappointing. But he was free at last, loosed upon the earth once more. The independence was exhilarating.

Prowling alone down the back roads and side streets, he took in the Greensboro sights. So much had changed since he was last here. The town was considerably larger than he remembered but somehow smaller too. Few stores were open, and the buildings that did house businesses were falling apart. A cloud of apathy hung over every roof. The town was dying, and for a moment he thought his efforts would be wasted. The people of Greensboro were going to hell without his help. Still, he reminded himself, he had plans involving so much more than simple eternal torment. The town's state of disrepair would make the people weak and unsuspecting, and he would have free rein to wreak as much havoc as he desired before he ended all their earthly woes.

A steely calm washed over the Strange Man's handsome face as his large, black eyes surveyed the horizon, searching for his first destination. Something in the air caught his attention. He knew he was close. Through the downpour he heard laughter. A party. His mouth watered at the prospect of the lost souls he might find here in downtown Greensboro, a town defenseless and unwatched.

Like unsuspecting cattle bound for the slaughterhouse, a troupe of young people lined up outside the doors of a brightly lit dance club. Clustering beneath umbrellas and pulling hoods over their carefully styled hair, they joked and roughhoused with one another, wild and carefree despite the devastating storm that ransacked their town.

And despite the monster the storm brought with it.

The Strange Man halted across the street from the club, watching with the patience of power as he imagined how effortlessly he could snatch them all away from the living world with one fell swoop. The papers would be filled with the news, and, oh, what grief their parents would feel! Such a tragedy might cripple the community for good and leave the surviving families ripe for picking.

But why rush things? He stood in a dying town that begged him to lead it to its final demise. The highway had moved; the days of prosperity were gone. No one knew this town existed anymore. The outside world would do nothing to save Greensboro and its families.

He might as well have a little fun.

CHAPTER THREE

Y MIDNIGHT, HEAVY rains assaulted the small town of Greensboro in relentless waves as lightning and thunder raged overhead, and most of the sleepy town's denizens were tucked safely away in their homes.

Not everyone, however, was in bed. Some had found their way to The Rave Scene, the hottest club in town. In truth, it was the *only* club in town. The place was an abandoned shoe factory converted into a sanctuary for twentysomethings and teens with fake IDs. Remodeled when the highway relocated a little over a year ago, The Rave Scene was the failing community's last-ditch effort to dissuade the college crowd from moving to the City and taking their parents' hard-earned money with them. The town's leaders claimed the establishment benefited the economy and kept the youth out of trouble, but people knew the truth, no matter how vehemently they denied it to each other. The club was old, run-down, and had a peculiar smell of oil, which mattered little to its patrons. Alcohol flowed freely, and the music was always loud. Here, where there were never any parents watching them and frowning upon the choices they made, the embittered youth of Greensboro could remain children forever.

Dras Weldon *loved* it.

He stood in the same position as many of his peers, delicately poised on the precipice of adulthood, faced with an uncertain future and tempted to remain in the comfort of adolescence. Driven by an insatiable call to fun, Dras reported almost nightly to The Rave Scene, avoiding responsibility whenever it reared its ugly head.

Tonight, as on most nights, he danced with the most beautiful girl in the club, his best friend, Rosalyn Myers. Despite Dras's usual Saturday night drunkenness and the fact that he had the grace of a one-legged elephant, the couple moved wonderfully together. Already beyond tipsy, he tried not to pass out in drunken laughter as he leaned against his partner.

"I think I'm going to ralph," he said with a goofy grin.

Rosalyn laughed. "Yeah?"

"Yeah." He smiled, all his woes forgotten. "I think I need another drink. You want one?"

She smiled back at him as if he were a toddler too cute for his own good. "Maybe later. Save me a seat."

With a drunken salute, Dras made his way toward the holy grail of The Rave Scene—the bar. Pulling himself onto a stool, he flopped down and signaled to the bartender.

"Give me another one."

He could barely make the request without slurring his words. The bartender raised an eyebrow. Dras had seen that expression before. That same look of disappointment seemed to be permanently fixed on his brother's face.

Dras whined, "Come on, Sam. Don't be such a wisenheimer. I'm young. My brain cells regenerate more...rapider."

"Kid," the bartender scoffed, "I don't think I can give you any more with a clear conscience."

"It's OK, Sam. I'm of sound mind. I *order* you to pour me another." He slapped the counter as if he'd just declared law while trying not to hiccup.

The bartender hesitated, then gave in. He reached for a glass. "God help me if your brother catches me."

Dras waved him off and turned back to the dance floor, where

Rosalyn was swaying her curvaceous, though toned, figure in the midst of several hunks of man-meat, each one vying for her affections. She tossed her auburn locks and flashed her dark doe eyes, soaking up the attention. Dras knew what the guys would say about her come Monday morning: "Trysdale Trash." "Lives on the wrong side of town."

And she knows that's what they think, Dras groaned inwardly. *I don't know why she puts up with those sorry...*

The bartender slid a drink at Dras. His righteous indignation fell away. As soon as the liquid reached the rim, he downed it, then slammed the glass on the counter for more.

The bartender pointed at Rosalyn. "Your girl's looking good tonight."

It took Dras a moment to register what was said, his focus having shifted back to becoming as drunk as possible on what little money he had in his worn Velcro wallet, still wallowing in the humiliation at the hands of that no-good Sean Patrick. Sluggishly he searched the crowd, struggling to understand what the bartender had said to him. He spotted Rosalyn. With a silly smile, he said, "Rosalyn? She's not mine. We're just friends."

"Friends?" the bartender said. "*Right.* I see the way you two are together."

"No, really. We've been friends since the womb. She's like a sister to me, man."

The bartender laughed. "If I had a sister like *that*, I'd have to join the priesthood."

"My brother's a priest," Dras said. Then after thinking about it, "Or a pastor." He threw up his hands. "I can't seem to remember at the moment."

Rosalyn approached the bar, out of breath but glowing with an energetic smile. She took a seat next to her best bud. Dras decided a formal introduction was in order.

"This is Sister Rosalyn," he said to the bartender. To Rosalyn, "And this is Sam. He's a priest."

Well, almost a formal introduction.

The bartender smiled at Rosalyn and extended a hand. Rosalyn returned the gesture. They shook.

Rosalyn, fluent in drunken Dras, smiled and said, "Hi, Larry."

"Hey, Rosalyn." Then whispering, "That's how I know your friend's had enough. No matter how many times you guys come in here, when he's had his limit, he calls me Sam."

They laughed.

Larry said, "You want a drink?"

"Nah. Better not." Gauging Dras's condition, she said, "Looks like I'm sober gal tonight."

"Again," Larry said.

"Thanks, though."

The bartender left to attend to his other patrons, many of them trying to keep pace with Dras.

Watching him leave, Dras groaned, "Come back, Sam! I'm not finished!" In his effort to appeal to the nice man with the booze, Dras slipped off his stool. Rosalyn caught him and helped him back up.

"I think you're overdoing it tonight, Dras."

She worried about him when he got drunk. It hit her a little too close to home, reminding her of her mother. She'd told him so several times. But Dras couldn't stop. *Why does she put up with me?* Dras shooed his problems away. "What are you talking about? Aren't we having fun?"

"Same as always," Rosalyn said halfheartedly. "But it's only fun until someone loses an eye."

As if to test Rosalyn's point, Dras began poking his face, pretending to poke his eye out. Rosalyn brushed it off with a smile—until Dras actually poked a finger into his right eye. He yelped with surprise and pain and laid his head on the counter.

Rosalyn patted him on the head with humorous pity. With Dras momentarily blinded and distracted, she took the opportunity to survey the room.

"Oh well," she said, rubbing it in. "I'm sure there are enough good-looking men here with both eyes in their sockets."

Dras raised his head, holding a hand over his right eye and pouting. "It's not funny. I think I'm blind."

Giggling, Rosalyn continued surveying the crowd. All the faces were familiar, a side effect of growing up in a small town, she supposed. Dras loved Greensboro—its familiarity, its quaint charm—but for Rosalyn, the town had lost its shine when she was twelve.

When her father killed himself.

Greensboro no longer felt like home. It was a scrap heap littered with the remains of her childhood dreams. Besides, there was nowhere to hide. Everyone here knew her. Everyone whispered about her suicidal father and her drunken mother, and she could do nothing to escape her family's legacy or the label "Trysdale Trash." Seeing nothing in Greensboro but the past, Rosalyn longed for a future far away from this little town and its haunting memories.

Suddenly she remembered Vermont.

I've got to tell Dras.

She knew she had to tell him, but she dreaded it. Heaving a wistful sigh, she said, "What are we doing here?"

Dras glanced up, still nursing his poked eye. "I dunno about you, but I'm getting plastered."

Rosalyn ruffled his blond mop top. "Well, that much is

obvious." She knew better than to get serious when Dras was drunk, but at the same time it beat trying to have a serious conversation with him when he was sober. Despite their closeness, there were some things they didn't discuss.

Leaving Greensboro was, most assuredly, one of them. But since he was pretty far gone tonight anyway and unlikely to remember anything in the morning...

"Don't you ever get tired of this place?" she asked.

In typical Dras fashion, he replied, "No."

Rosalyn turned to the counter, rethinking her decision not to drink. "Dras, I...I've been accepted to a school in Vermont for next semester."

"Vermont?" Dras sputtered. "Why Vermont?"

"'Cause it's far away from Greensboro. Besides, I think I'd like it there."

Dras considered her announcement as gravely as was possible given his condition. "But...what about me?"

"I was thinking maybe you could come with me."

"But...but...all my friends are here."

Rosalyn laughed. "Goof, I'm your *only* friend."

Stiffening in defense, Dras protested, "That's not true. That guy...that guy at the video store...that...what's his name?"

"Dave?"

Dras snapped his fingers. "Yeah! *That* guy! Me and him, we're like this." Dras attempted unsuccessfully to cross his fingers.

"Well, then you and Dave will be happy together while I'm in Vermont."

All the humor drained out of Dras. He touched her arm. "Hey," he said, "don't leave me."

Rosalyn's heart sank. She did her best to cover her disappointment. "I don't have to decide right now," she said.

"I'm ... I'm still thinking about it. So, you win. For tonight. But only because you're drunk and I'm too tired to argue."

"Fair's fair," Dras said, holding up his hands in concession.

"But I'm warning you, Dras Weldon, Greensboro's going to have to get a whole lot more exciting for me to stick around."

The Strange Man entered The Rave Scene.

He moved with confidence across the dance floor, his hair wild, his smile playful, if not superficial. He stalked the patrons with casual coolness, his eyes marveling at the party lights—rich reds and blues and yellows swirling and dancing on the walls, moving to the beat. Everything was so loud, confusing. The people here were distracted or drunk or too busy partying to know that evil was walking among them. Salivating, he mused how easy it would be to kill them all.

Tonight. Before the sun comes up. By the time they realize what's happening, the doors will be locked. None will escape, and I will lick their blood from my fingers.

Their massacre will be glorious.

But no, no.

He had already decided. He would take this slowly, though the temptation to rush headlong into mayhem still warred within him.

The Strange Man moved among the young people, smelling their debauchery like pheromones. He took to the staircase and ascended to the heights of the club, where he looked down at them as they milled about mindlessly. They were his new people; they just didn't know it yet. They wanted what he was offering—to be disobedient, to sin, to indulge themselves and swear against a God who would expect too much of them.

His lips parted in a Cheshire cat grin. "Perfect."

Dras was having problems.

His brain was a mound of mush soaked in alcohol, and he couldn't make heads from tails no matter how hard he tried. Unconsciousness fought to take hold. He slipped time and time again from his stool, spared a cold meeting with the hard floor only by Rosalyn's quick reflexes.

"I'm taking you home," she said, straining to heave his limp body back onto the seat.

He moaned incoherently.

"Come on, Dras. Stay with me."

"I don't want to go home, Roz," Dras whined. "The night is young." Then, pulling from her grasp, he flung his arms into the air like a champion and crowed, "And so am I!"

He laughed at himself. A few onlookers took notice. Rosalyn's face burned from embarrassment.

"Have I ever told you you're a lousy drunk?" she blurted.

"On more than one occasion."

Rosalyn smiled. She couldn't help it. She loved him. He was a goofball and probably wouldn't amount to anything, but she loved him.

Realizing he couldn't possibly walk and knowing she couldn't drag him to the door, she decided they would have to hang around until Dras could manage something resembling a thought process.

Waving the bartender over, Rosalyn said, "Could you get him some coffee?"

Larry nodded, having witnessed this scene too many times.

Relieved that someone was cooperating, Rosalyn turned to Dras and said, "It's times like these when I wonder why I keep you around."

"Are you kidding?" he replied, barely able to keep his eyes open. "You'd fall apart without me."

His voice trailing off as if he were falling asleep, he rested his head on the counter. Rosalyn watched him. Maybe he was right. Maybe she needed him as much as he needed her.

He began to snore.

"Wake up, Dras."

He didn't budge. She slapped him. That did the trick.

"What?" He came out of his stupor just as Larry returned with black coffee.

Rosalyn scooted the steaming mug toward Dras. "You stay here. Sober up, OK?"

She was already moving into the crowd when Dras reached for her. "Where are you going?"

She laughed. "Dancing. What do I look like? Your mother?"

Dras watched her walk away, the small of her back exposed and her wide, curvy hips rocking snugly in her jeans.

He shook his head. "No, you certainly do not."

From his perch, the Strange Man watched the crowd. He was shrouded in darkness, the lights themselves careful to avoid him. In particular, he studied the beautiful girl leaving the bar.

She was exquisite, with reddish-brown locks that bounced on her shoulders and big, dark eyes. Her body was soft and her flesh pink. There was a definite strength in the way she carried herself. Tough and defined, she was different than the others. Perhaps there were girls here with prettier features—or maybe just better applied cosmetics—but she had an honest beauty about her, a rare trait. He had not seen such confidence and allure in ages.

Not since…

He paused, the arrogance on his face vanishing as he remembered with terrible clarity a similar captivation. He thought of a girl from his past—the one whose memory plagued his steps, even after all these centuries. His curse had begun the moment he set eyes on that despicable child. He'd fallen into her trap, moved by her innocence.

His weakness had cost him everything.

As the memory resurfaced, his heart filled with utter hate.

He watched as the dancers gravitated toward this beauty everywhere she went. Men fought for her attention. She laughed and danced with them, giving each a turn.

The Strange Man fought back the uncontrollable rage and raw desire he felt. All at once he loved her and hated her, wanted to murder her, wanted to make love to her.

He ought to know her name. Having kept his eye on Greensboro for some time, there weren't many things within its boundaries he didn't know. What did it matter? He had seen enough. He would have her for himself, one way or another.

Like a ravenous wolf, the Strange Man stalked the crowd from on high, still following her, unable to look away. Lost souls were everywhere, souls ready for harvest, but his eyes remained fixed on the girl with the auburn tresses and the big, dark eyes. Enthralled, he watched her dance, detesting her for captivating him so.

Suddenly, a blonde girl clumsily stumbled against him, breaking his concentration. His image shuddered. Like a television set with bad reception, his handsome features flickered and dimmed, revealing a hideous, gruesome visage beneath the smiling façade, uncovering his true nature.

Now the Strange Man's face was pale and bald, his yellow eyes prominent, even in the shadows. A ghastly green-toothed grin stretched tightly across black lips.

The blonde looked up to apologize and saw the awful truth. For one moment, as the Strange Man fought to regain his illusion, she saw him as he truly was. Her eyes widened and her lips trembled, as if her mind were giving way to madness.

The Strange Man regained control, restoring his handsome face.

He leered at the blonde.

The girl backed away, terrified at the incomprehensible thing before her. The Strange Man took a step in her direction, when suddenly a voice called over the din.

"Lindsey! What's with you? Are you coming or what? I'm already late enough as it is!"

Lindsey turned to her boyfriend, TJ Walker, who was waiting impatiently at the top of the staircase. She backed away from the Strange Man, afraid of what he would do. He smiled, coolly placing a finger to his lips.

"Shhh," he whispered. "Our little secret."

Stifling a gasp, Lindsey continued backing away.

"Hurry up!" TJ shouted.

Lindsey broke from the Strange Man's hypnotic glare and ran to TJ, who dragged her down the stairs, pulling her through the crowd to the exit.

All the while from the top deck the Strange Man watched, winking and flashing a creepy sneer when Lindsey cast one last look his direction.

Rosalyn swayed to the music. She felt the vibes tonight, despite having to babysit Dras. These days it seemed that babysitting was all she ever did as Dras slipped further into childhood. The more she mulled over their conversation, the angrier she became, angry that he so stubbornly refused to leave Greensboro. She had catered to him long enough. Inevitably she would have to decide what she wanted to do with her life. She could make the difficult first step of moving forward, away from the past, or she could remain chained to Dras and Greensboro forever.

Gotta decide soon, Roz, she told herself. But not tonight. Not tonight.

Tonight she'd dance. She'd save the hard decisions for tomorrow.

The Rave Scene was more crowded than usual. Probably had to do with the storm. The lightning and thunder had everyone's blood pumping. Rosalyn found herself surrounded by people, some she hadn't seen this far out in a while. One, in fact, she had never seen, a stranger on the level above her.

Her eyes fixed on him, and for a moment her heart skipped a beat. Who was he? Whoever he was, he was gorgeous! With mysterious, dark eyes and a charming, boy-next-door smile, he was a mixture of every romantic fantasy she'd ever had.

"Wow," she mouthed silently.

It wasn't like Rosalyn to be swept off her feet. She was a hopeless flirt to be sure, but that was all part of the game. When it came to romance, she had lived dangerously, teasing but never giving her heart away. But this man—so beautiful and full of charisma—was different. This time she was certain: it was her turn to fall.

As though he could hear her thoughts over the suffocating noise, the man was staring down at her. Embarrassment overwhelmed her. She turned away, feeling her face burn red.

At the bar Dras was still lying facedown on the counter. She rushed to his side, pushing past the people in her way.

"Dras," she said, nudging him. "Wake up."

The nudge shoved Dras off the stool. He collapsed with a thud. Rosalyn groaned in aggravation. Hoping the incredibly handsome man hadn't seen this little incident, she turned to look.

Expecting to see him fifty feet away and on the second level, she jumped when she saw him standing directly behind her. She yelped with surprise, then laughed to cover it up.

"Uh…Hi…Sorry," she said, feeling like an idiot.

She couldn't help but glance up at the deck where she'd seen him standing only a second ago. How did he move so fast?

The man, his full lips separating to reveal a heart-melting grin, looked down at Dras crumpled in a heap on the floor. "Looks like your dancing partner is out of order."

He's so hot! Rosalyn thought, hoping she hadn't said it out loud. In the morning she would scold herself for allowing herself to be reduced to a giggling schoolgirl. But morning was hours away. For now, she giggled. "Yeah. Can we say 'rehab'?"

She cringed. *I'm such a dork.* She wanted to smack herself.

With a wave of his hand that made her want to take him home, the man said, "Dance with me."

Yes! Yes! YES! Aloud, "Uh…sure. OK."

He smiled and took her hand. At that moment he could have led her anywhere and she would have gone. He was so perfect. She gazed at him in awe, all her concerns about Dras, Vermont, and the future vanishing. All she knew was that this couldn't be for one night only. No, she couldn't let this one get away.

The man slid his arms around Rosalyn's waist and led her in a slow dance, though the music had a quick tempo. Rosalyn found herself falling into his dark eyes. His half grin touched every nerve in her body. She could have sworn the whole room stopped just to watch them. *It's like everything works for this guy.* Even the lights overhead seem to fawn on him, always showering him with beautiful color. *He is so perfect.*

The man smiled at her, holding her in his sway without speaking a single word.

Rosalyn's mind began to feel sluggish and dreamlike. *This is so great. I wish Dras could see this.*

"Hey, Rosalyn!"

The romantic violins in Rosalyn's head twanged abruptly to a halt as she was yanked out of her trance. She and the man looked in the direction of the interruption, where they saw Dras standing on the bar twirling his coat over his head like a drunken stripper while a very agitated bartender tried to pull him down. Dras was crowing and dancing for all he was worth. A few of the customers threw loose change at him and offered him dollar bills. While Dras was giving the performance of his life, Rosalyn, on the other hand, was muttering, "I'm going to kill him. I'm going to kill him."

She turned to her dance partner, trying to mask her feelings of total humiliation. "I really need to take him home before he hurts himself," she said.

The man offered a forced nod. "Of course."

Bemoaning missed opportunities and reluctant to leave, Rosalyn went to help Dras. Her loyalties were to him first.

The Strange Man watched her go.

"Dras, work with me," Rosalyn grunted, straining under her friend's dead weight as she helped him down from the bar.

Dras braced himself against the counter as bartender Larry looked on, his arms crossed, shaking his head with disgust.

"Thanks, Rosalyn," Dras moaned. "I don't know what I'd do without you."

Their eyes met. A smile passed between them. And for an instant it was as though they were the only two people in the whole world.

That's when the Strange Man saw it—that force, that binding energy that kept the girl immune to his spell.

Love.

He *hated* love.

It was clear to him now. As long as the boy remained, the girl would forever be bound to him. However, if the boy were somehow to be removed from the situation... *The girl would belong to me.*

The Cheshire grin formed on the monster's lips as his mind swirled with detestable possibilities, all his grand desires for the town and its simple people fluttering away. He would carry on his work, yes, but it could wait awhile. Right now, all he could think about was the girl.

She was beautiful and powerful, and now that he saw the love she and the boy shared, he wanted her all the more for himself. Jealousy burned in his wicked, twisted heart, and a fire welled up inside him, the pressure mounting to a boiling point before he finally unleashed it in one glaring, vengeful stare.

From across the room, the idiot boy caught the full force of the fierce look and found it so powerful that he stumbled and fell backward off the counter. A few patrons applauded and cheered his antics. For now, the Strange Man accepted the amusement as a small offering and smiled darkly.

He would deal with the boy soon enough. For now, he had other matters to attend to. The blonde—Lindsey—had seen his true nature.

She must be dealt with.

CHAPTER FOUR

A T A QUARTER past two in the morning, Lindsey McCormick pulled up to the Walker house. Her teeth chattered, and her insides felt hot and squishy. She didn't know how she knew, but she was certain that she had just witnessed true evil at The Rave Scene.

The storm blustered in full effect, blowing sheets of hard-hitting rain against her tiny car, threatening to overturn it. She wrapped her fingers tautly around the steering wheel, her arms unusually stiff. She drove TJ home, even though all she could think about was going home and crawling into bed with her mom and dad like she used to do when she was little.

TJ lounged in the passenger seat, one muddy Converse propped up on the dash, his hand on his forehead rubbing at the beginnings of a hangover. Lately he seemed detached, and Lindsey wondered if it was over between them. He wasn't the best boyfriend, but right now he was the only one she had, and rocky relationship or no, she wanted to tell him what she'd seen.

She'd hoped by now her queasiness would have worn off. Instead, it had grown stronger with each passing moment, as if the man—no, the monster—she met at the club was coming for her.

Oh, God. She trembled.

TJ waited for her to pull to a complete stop. He blew out an aggravated sigh. "Man, my mom's gonna be all over my case."

He was twenty-three and fully capable of living on his own, but after a high school knee injury doomed his chance at a football scholarship, he took to drinking in excess and feeling sorry for himself. He was pretty much a wreck of a person, and Lindsey knew she was not the first naïve girl to think that all he needed was the love of a good woman. The former star quarterback seemed content to live the rest of his days in his mother's house, reminiscing about his glory days and wasting away to bitter obscurity.

Any other night, Lindsey might have encouraged him to find his own place where he wouldn't be under his mother's rules and could live freely. But this was not any other night. Tonight, Lindsey had faced the devil in the flesh.

TJ groaned, "What's with you, anyway?"

Lindsey turned to him, her face pale, her lips quivering, and stammered, "I...I saw someone at the club tonight."

TJ sat up a little straighter, suspecting he was about to hear a confession of infidelity. "Who?" he barked. "It wasn't that spaz Weldon, was it?"

Lindsey had dated Dras Weldon before TJ and had often wondered what her life would be like, had she stayed with him.

"No," she cried, shaking her head. "I need you to listen to me. It was a...a *strange* man. I've never seen him before."

TJ backed down. "Oh."

"I bumped into him, and when I did..." Her voice trailed off. She was hoping that saying it out loud would somehow make what she saw appear ridiculous. "He...he changed."

It didn't.

By speaking it, she gave shape to her fear, and now more than ever she could feel its cold presence. Her hands were growing numb. She loosened her grip on the steering wheel.

"Yeah?" TJ said, disinterested.

"He was like...the bogeyman."

TJ snorted. "You're crazy."

Lindsey began to weep. "Listen to me, TJ! I saw him! He was like the devil. I saw his eyes. He wasn't"—she was suddenly embarrassed, but she had to finish—"he wasn't human."

"The devil, huh?" TJ laughed. "Like God and Jesus and all that junk your dad believes, right?"

It sounded crazy. Lindsey knew it. She wouldn't have believed it herself, had she not seen it with her own eyes. She'd been raised in a good Christian home but had never believed in the things Rev. Jack Weldon talked about on Sunday mornings. They all seemed so far-fetched. Things like God and Jesus and virgin births. Things like the devil.

Yet, after what she saw tonight...

"You don't believe me," she said in a tiny voice.

"You're right. I don't," TJ huffed. "Look, Linds, your old man is holding on to some stupid old book that was written by a bunch of dumb fishermen. They're just stories."

TJ placed his hand on the door handle.

He's leaving me! I'll be all alone!

"Get a clue, will ya?" TJ pulled the handle. The door swung open, letting in the storm. "Watch the news or something, 'cause God and Jesus? They're on the way out."

"Don't leave!" Lindsey shouted, groping at his sleeve.

He pulled free. "Call me later," he said, slamming the door.

Lindsey watched in shocked horror as her boyfriend pulled his jacket over his head and ran to the front door of his house.

"No..." she whimpered.

She sat still for a moment, terrified and unsure of what to do next.

Then out of the corner of her eye she caught sight of a face in her side mirror bathed in the blood-red glow of her taillights. The eyes glimmered like those of a cat. She screamed. But just as she did, the creature—the same awful thing she saw at The

Rave Scene—ducked out of view. She spun around, looking through the rear window, but she could not see the Strange Man.

He found me!

Her heart leaped into her throat, and she wanted more than ever to go home, to see her daddy and listen to him tell her that there was no such thing as the bogeyman. But Lindsey knew the truth now. There *was* a bogeyman. And he was after her.

She pressed the accelerator to the floor, and the tires squealed as she took off. She sped through the deserted streets of the rain-soaked town running red lights and hopping corners. At times the wind blew so hard she had to fight to keep the car on the road, but she was determined to get home. To see her mom and dad.

Fear surrounded her in the darkness, and Lindsey thought of all the times she blew off her parents' concerns about the way she lived. After high school, her life became a revolving door of boys, friends, and booze. She maintained good grades in college and thought that what she did with her free time was of little consequence. But her father was a religious man, if not a firm fixture at the local church, and he was constantly chiding her, saying he'd taught her to behave better. She didn't listen. Lindsey wasn't sure if she believed God existed or if there was any such thing as absolute right and wrong. After all, she reasoned, Dras Weldon was a preacher's kid, and he never believed all that stuff. As for Greensboro, it was a "churchy" town. All the God-talk was part of the scenery, never something to be taken seriously.

But tonight she had seen the devil, and she couldn't deny it. And if he was real, maybe God was real too. And maybe He'd forgive her for not believing in Him and keep her safe from the thing that was chasing her.

Wet mascara staining her face, Lindsey cried out, "Oh, God, I am *so* sorry. You were right. You were right all along. Please, Jesus, don't let him get me...Don't let the bogeyman get me."

Still sobbing, a sense of peace washed over her. She held her breath, waiting for some sign that God was with her, that she was going to be OK.

Her thoughts were interrupted when she glanced in the rear-view mirror and saw headlights. Someone was following her. She drove faster, catapulting through a deserted intersection and landing with a terrible, spark-sending *crunch*. The turnoff to her parents' subdivision was just ahead. She strained to see it through the torrential downpour.

As she drew closer to safety she glanced in her rearview mirror—then shrieked. Waiting for her, blocking the entrance to the subdivision, was a mass of dark shapes shimmering under the arc sodium streetlamps.

Lindsey swerved to avoid them and sped on, crying hopelessly, the path home fading in the distance while the pursuing headlights kept pace.

The interior of the car grew icy cold. Palpitating breaths escaped her body in frozen puffs. Her teeth chattered, her mind grew dim, her thoughts numb. On she drove, watching as the lights of Greensboro dwindled in number. She was heading toward the North Woods. Her heart hammered, fighting the cold that threatened to quench her life. She pressed down on the accelerator, steering toward the woods compelled by the strange chill that clutched her flesh and encircled her with death.

Long, curvy roads emitted from Greensboro like the tentacles of an octopus. The windshield wipers squeaked as they raced back and forth, clearing the glass so Lindsey could see. Through the side windows she saw the dark woods and angry storm whip by her in a blur. Tears rolled down her cheeks.

She tried unsuccessfully turning the wheel to the right and to the left to keep from going into the North Woods. As a child she'd heard stories about goblins in the woods. As an adult she'd banished such notions from her rational mind. Tonight, however, she would believe anything.

The warm lights of Greensboro were gone. Out here there was only darkness and the occasional glimpse of something blacker than black flapping next to her, herding the car toward the woods.

She couldn't get away. She wept and wailed, giving in to the terror. Paranoia forced her to look at the headlights in the rearview mirror. No matter how fast she drove, the pursuing headlights kept a steady pace, fixed at an unwavering point behind her.

The honking of an oncoming car brought Lindsey's eyes back to the road. She yelped in panic and avoided a collision by jerking the wheel, steering the car back to her side of the divider as the headlights of the oncoming vehicle flooded her car.

She checked the rearview mirror again. That's when Lindsey realized the two glowing orbs following her were no longer headlights. They were eyes.

Someone was in the car with her.

In the backseat.

Lindsey screamed herself hoarse. It was too late. The monster she saw at The Rave Scene, the Strange Man, hissed and lunged at her. With tapered talons he gripped her throat. She coughed, gasping for breath. The car started to veer. Pools of green mist glowing with ethereal light swirled around her ankles. Her knee wedged between the steering wheel and the seat, pinning her foot to the accelerator. The temperature in the car dropped precipitously, forming icy spiderwebs on the inside of the windows.

So cold, Lindsey thought, sinking into a pool of unconsciousness, but not before she saw his ghastly features in full detail in the rearview mirror. His once dark eyes blazed and stared at her like burning suns sunken deep in a grinning, chalky-white skull. So transfixed was she, Lindsey wasn't aware that her car had left the road, catapulting over the edge of a bridge, and plunged into the murky depths of Greensboro Park Lake.

Water beat against the frozen windows of the car, wanting in. Jerked back to reality by the impact, Lindsey screamed, filling the car with cries of fear and panic. The monster started to laugh, a shrill, wild, high-pitched lunatic's laugh. He squeezed her throat with his bony hands, his long nails drawing blood. She tried to pry his fingers loose. The struggle succeeded in freeing her trapped legs. She kicked desperately at the front windshield.

The intensity of the monster's shrill cackle cracked the glass. Water poured into the car, first through small fissures, then gushing as the glass gave way. Lindsey shrieked as the lake burst through the windshield. Somehow she managed to break free from the monster's grip.

Escaping through the gap where a windshield had once been, Lindsey swam free of the car and fought her way to the surface. She expected the Strange Man to be waiting for her, but when she surfaced, her attacker was nowhere in sight. The only thing disturbing the calm waters of the lake were the bubbles of the drowning car.

She looked around frenetically, unable to believe she was free. There was no sign of the Strange Man. She cried—this time in relief—and swam toward the bridge.

Her ordeal wasn't over. Behind her, the monster surfaced from the wreckage. As he floated to the surface he emerged from the dark waters until finally he stood on the water.

"Oh, Lindsey?" he said in a singsong voice.

She spun around and saw him floating toward her. Wringing his long, skeletal hands, he hovered closer, the tips of his pointed shoes dragging across the water, leaving ripples in their wake.

Lindsey screamed. She splashed harder, fighting to swim away, but the lake was becoming thicker. Gooier. *He* was changing it, corrupting it with his darkness, turning it into a clinging paste.

"*Help!*" she cried, her voice growing raspy as the sludge that was once water tightened its grip on her lungs. The more she struggled in the mire, the more entangled she became, until at last the Strange Man caught up to her.

The monster hung in front of her for a moment, watching her squirm. He cocked his head in amusement as his prey fought to escape the inevitable.

"Oh, child," he said, "it's unfortunate that you bumped into me earlier."

"I...I didn't mean to," Lindsey cried. "I'm sorry! Please let me go. I won't tell anyone I saw you!"

The Strange Man waved off the apology. "There, there. These things happen. But it doesn't change the fact that my friends and I have plans for your little town, and to be exposed this soon is simply unacceptable." Smiling, he said, "You understand."

With outstretched talons he plucked the girl from the sticky entanglement. He held her with one hand, raising her eye to eye with him. His burning eyes peered into her soul.

Lindsey's cries were but a whimper now. "You...have friends?" she asked, her voice quivering.

His sickly smile stretched wider. "Oh, yes. Would you like to meet them?"

Without giving her time to ponder her fate, the monster turned her so she could see the hungry shapes under the bridge, the ones that led her out of Greensboro. Lindsey stared in horror as the growling things scurried in the darkness, animalistic things blacker than black and darker than the darkest night twitching like shadows that had come to life, clamoring over themselves in their eagerness to devour her.

"Oh, God..." she breathed.

The Strange Man snarled. "What do you know about God?"

He fed her to them.

As Lindsey disappeared into the shadows, as the twitching things destroyed her body, the Strange Man lifted his face defiantly to the pelting winds and rain and released a savage roar.

CHAPTER FIVE

DRAS DIDN'T REMEMBER much from the night before. He got home all right, though he didn't know how. He awoke on his couch in his apartment with his shoes off and a quilt pulled to his neck.

At first he thought the loud ringing in his head was his trusty alarm clock waking him to a brand-new day, but he was merely suffering from the splitting migraine of a hangover. He sat up abruptly, shaken by the memory loss of how he got from Point A to Point B, then discovered quick and sudden movements fell into the "not a good idea" category. He winced and rubbed his temples. Once the pain began to subside, he found the strength to let out one pitiful moan.

With bed hair and morning breath, Dras swung his feet over the edge of the couch and braced himself to stand like a young colt trying to find its balance. A colt would have had better luck. Dras stumbled and slipped back onto the couch. Taking his failure as a sign, he sat there for a moment, letting the seconds tick away, just breathing, trying to find his balance again. In no time boredom set in, so he attempted the graduation from the couch to the walking world once more. This time he was better prepared. He made it to his feet, scratched his stomach, then slowly shuffled around the apartment, navigating his way through the piles of dirty laundry, empty beer and soda cans, and discarded comic books.

He yawned and sighed, dubbing the morning long and hard. He was unable to recall what morning it was exactly. In fact, he wondered if it was morning. He shook it off, though. Not important. All he knew was that the sun was up, and so was he, and he wanted food.

Dras meandered into the kitchen and opened the cabinet. He pulled out a box of Frooty-Os and rinsed a bowl from among the dishes in the sink. He poured the cereal. It filled only one-eighth of the bowl. Discarding the empty box, Dras dug in his cabinet again, this time finding a box of bran cereal. Shaking it, he discovered it was almost empty. *I really gotta get to the store this week.* Shrugging, he dumped the bran cereal in with the Frooty-Os. Now all he needed was milk.

Still trying to remember what day it was, he opened the refrigerator and rescued the milk from the cold clutches of the appliance. The minute he screwed off the top, the smell of the milk hit him. Checking the expiration date, he discovered it was only ten days past. With a sigh, he set the milk back in the refrigerator in the same spot he found it, wondering how many times he had done that already.

Dras scrounged some more in the refrigerator and spotted the orange juice. He reached for it, reasoning that it was nutritious and part of a well-balanced breakfast. He poured the orange juice into his bowl of Frooty-Os and bran cereal, pulled out a plastic spoon that changed colors depending on temperature, and proceeded to eat his sensible breakfast.

After a thorough tooth brushing, still trying to get the awful taste of his sensible breakfast out of his mouth, Dras moved into the bedroom. The next step in his morning ritual was to get dressed, and he supposed obliging wouldn't necessarily kill him.

He entered a room that could have easily belonged to a twelve-year-old judging by the quantity of model monster kits and action figures lining the dusty shelves. He took a quick glance at his alarm clock, curious to see how early it really was.

Ten-thirty. *Not bad.*

Passing by the computer, he caught sight of a yellow sticky note posted to his terminal.

BETTER NOT BE LATE FOR CHURCH AGAIN. JEFF WILL
HAVE A FIT. —ROZ

In a moment of clarity, he realized what day it was.
Sunday.

His eyes shot wide open. *Sunday! Already?* He panicked.

Tumbling across his bed, crashing into a closet full of wrinkled clothes, he searched for a reasonably clean pair of jeans. In a fevered rush he stripped off the pants he was wearing—which reeked of the alcohol he had spilled on them last night—and struggled to pull on a new pair. As his legs got tangled up in the pants and he hurtled to the ground, a single thought ran through Dras Weldon's mind: *It's going to be one of those days.*

"He is a hungry lion. A murderer, the Scriptures say. He is Satan. The devil. The eternal enemy of God Almighty. And today, he is after our children."

Rev. Jeff Weldon stood boldly in the pulpit, dictating his convictions with clarity to his congregation. His athletic build was obvious even in a suit and tie. Jeff had a brown-haired, all-American look, that trustworthy clean-shaven appearance that people expect in a preacher. Only a slightly crooked, once-broken nose gave any indication that possibly he hadn't always followed the rules. His green eyes scanned the pews, focusing momentarily on familiar faces. He had important things to say this morning, if he could only convince them to listen.

The congregation of the Good Church of the Faithful sat in silence, waiting for their pastor to continue his sermon.

"The devil is on the streets stealing our kids. We, as a community, have let our children out of our sights because we've been too busy with our own lives—with our careers, or the things we do for fun or, yes, even with all of our church activities. We have locked ourselves up in the safe tower of this church building and have not given the lost of this community a second thought."

Some of the elders folded their arms defensively. Jeff pushed onward. An occasional amen fueled his fire. He knew he was treading dangerously close to meddling with the deacons' long-standing way of doing things, but after seeing the storm last night and feeling a terrible sense of foreboding, something in his heart told him that the time for pleasantries had passed. Something was coming to Greensboro. Something dark and deadly. The people needed to be warned.

"We've lost sight of what God has called us to do!" Jeff boomed. "We must teach our children the true ways of God and not just church traditions. We must introduce them to the Lord Jesus and encourage them to have a relationship with Him, not just religion. It is not enough to know about Christ; they must know Him personally and follow Him personally in order to find the peace that comes from knowing God. But"— his voice trailed off, knowing he was about to elicit more dirty looks from some of the elders—"if we're to teach them, then we need to know the truth too."

As he often did, Jeff looked to the front pew for a supportive smile from Isabella. Knowing she was by his side no matter what gave him the courage to preach what was on his heart despite the controversy it might cause. Today, as always, her dark eyes met his with encouragement, and the nervous twitching in Jeff's stomach momentarily subsided. He was ready to get down to business.

"Let me ask you something, church," he spoke conversation-ally, setting aside theatrics, and stepped to the side of the pulpit to make a more personal appeal. "Have you forgotten what it means to serve the Lord? Are you here this morning wanting to fellowship with Him? Or are you just here so you can check another item off your 'to-do' list? What does your faith mean to you? What has it cost you lately? Has it cost you *anything*? Have you had to sacrifice for the Lord? Can anyone even tell you're a Christian?"

He paused, hoping his barrage of questions made an impact. Some women exchanged uncomfortable glances. Several men adjusted their sports coats. Mostly the congregation just looked bored. The few teenagers who were in attendance snickered over private jokes and passed notes. Some of the older ladies cooled themselves, fanning blank faces with church bulletins. One of the deacons was fast asleep, his mouth open, snoring despite his wife's persistent elbow in the gut. Only Isabella and a handful of others remained focused and alert.

Why do I bother? Jeff wondered, his heart heavy.

"I'll tell you this," he said. "First Peter 5:8 and 9 tell us, 'Be of sober spirit, be on the alert. Your adversary, the devil, prowls about like a roaring lion, seeking someone to devour. But resist him, firm in your faith, knowing that the same experiences of suffering are being accomplished by your brethren who are in the world.'"

Looking steadfastly into the faces of the indifferent crowd, Jeff went on. "We took it hard when the highway moved. I know a lot of you lost your jobs, your homes. I don't think Greensboro will ever be the same. But, folks, we have to wake up. We've got to pull ourselves out of this apathy and learn to care again. The next generation needs us. There's still a war going on for their souls, and it's time we realized what is at stake. For our sakes and for our children's."

"Amen," old Leonard Fergus bellowed from the third row.

"Folks, the sad truth is," Jeff said, "evil comes for us all. And for some of us, it's already here."

Furiously pedaling his bicycle, Dras passed the large sign in town square that proudly declared:

Greensboro: A Nice Place to Live

He was rather ashamed to still be riding a bike at his age, but his current unemployed status made it rather difficult, nay, impossible, to keep up with car payments. The miracle that he lived in an apartment of his own could solely be attributed to the generosity of his parents. Well, at least when he wasn't squandering rent money on his G.I. Joe collection. Dras hoped Jeff never found out that particular piece of information. He would never hear the end of it.

It was a beautiful morning, all things considered. The trees blossomed with the life of spring, swaying in the breeze, rejoicing that last night's thunderstorm had retreated to the horizon. Folks were out in number surveying downed branches, scattered foliage that littered the streets, torn siding, and shingles. The destruction was mostly cosmetic, though, and did nothing to dampen the magic that filled the morning air as Greensboro's residents looked forward to a day of rest and family get-togethers. Everything seemed as it should be, and none appreciated that feeling more than Dras Weldon.

As he pedaled through town, praying his brother wouldn't notice his tardiness, he gazed at the familiar surroundings. Once upon a time Greensboro was the last stop in Maribel County on the way to the City. With its quaint little diners and old-time gift shops, it was a welcome break from the fast and furious world. But when the highway moved, things changed. As travelers began bypassing the little town on their way to the City, the quaint little shops that once attracted them died on the vine. Before long, Greensboro—the pride of Maribel County— all but vanished from the face of the earth, and Dras, like most of the people in town, missed the good old days.

To his left, he spotted the old ice cream parlor that his family used to visit every Saturday night when he was little. Now the windows were boarded up, and the sign permanently read CLOSED. He passed the vacant lot that was once the site of the card shop where he used to buy comic books. Though it was never confirmed, most folks believed the owners of the shop torched it for the insurance money. For Dras, the most heart-wrenching sight of all was the old movie theater, closed and in a state of complete disrepair. Anyone looking to enjoy a movie on the big screen these days had to drive to Russellville or the City. It seemed every street held sweet childhood memories that had been marred by the cold hand of change.

Why did the highway have to move? Why do things always have to change?

Oh, how he longed for the old days when he and Rosalyn were eleven. They would stay up late without their parents' knowledge and watch the old scary movies on *Midnight Matinee*. Dras missed being a kid, when it was OK to sleep until noon and watch cartoons and eat sugary cereal.

But things had changed, and the depressing tour of his long-gone favorite childhood places touched something in him. He remembered bits of conversation from the night before. Though he was pretty drunk at the time, he recalled Rosalyn telling him that she wanted to leave Greensboro.

Now Rosalyn wants to change too. What's in stupid Vermont, anyway?

He sighed. The thought of going through life without her was nearly unbearable. The world was moving on despite his reluctance to join it, and Dras knew that if he wasn't careful, he'd be left behind.

His future looming on the horizon, Dras pedaled into the church parking lot. Cars were parked everywhere. He was late, really late. He groaned, dreading the inevitable confrontation with his brother.

Dras crept through the back doors, out of breath from pedaling so hard. No one noticed him as he slumped into the back pew.

No one but Jeff.

At first, Jeff was just glad to see his brother. Even if he wasn't on time, at least he was in church. Then Jeff noticed Dras's sunglasses and how he hung his head, and he knew his brother had been out partying. Disappointment broke his heart.

Well, I made it, Dras thought, congratulating himself. Sure, his shirt was only partially tucked into his pants, and he could still feel the bed hair's curse upon him. But he'd made it to church, and that had to count for something. He just hoped Jeff would take that into consideration before giving him the third degree.

Dras's head still throbbed, and now he wished he hadn't rushed to get here. He'd moved too fast, and the world was spinning. The brilliant sunshine beaming through the ornate stained glass windows added to his suffering. His sunglasses could block out only so much light, and what reached his eyes added to his pain. Still, he was present and accounted for. *So take that, Reverend Jeff Weldon!*

Jeff paused in his sermon, and Dras knew he'd been spotted. He felt a wave of embarrassment flush his face. Thankfully the shades prevented direct eye contact. Dras squirmed, wondering if Jeff was going to continue his sermon or point him out to the congregation.

Hey, look, folks. There's my brother, the sinner!

Fortunately, Jeff continued preaching. It was probably a powerful sermon, Dras assumed. One that the congregation found useful, he was sure. However, once the words made it through the maze in Dras's brain, they lost something in translation. All Dras heard was, "Blah, blah, blah." He had no explanation for it. Maybe it was a birth defect of some kind, one that scrambled whatever his big brother had to say into incomprehensible garble.

As he mulled this thought over, he drifted to sleep.

CHAPTER SIX

THE MORNING HAD been rough for Franklin Whitaker.
The large tree in his backyard suffered a lightning strike during last night's storm, dismembering one of its sturdy limbs. The huge limb landed on top of Franklin's roof. Luckily, it caught just the corner and rebounded, so the damage done to the house was superficial. But it served to give him and his six-year-old son, Timmy, quite a midnight scare. Timmy refused to go back to sleep in his own bed and spent the remainder of the night tucked beneath his daddy's arm in a sleeping bag on the floor until the early Sunday morning light permeated their blinds.

Having assessed the damage, Franklin called a few coworker friends over and spent the better part of the morning removing the limb from his yard. Timmy watched from inside the house, sad that his Sunday morning was ruined.

In the Whitaker home, Sunday morning was special. Franklin had been reared in church, like just about everyone else in Greensboro, and in his youth Sundays had been filled with Bible studies and old hymns. But as he grew older, church became less a priority. He fell in with a rough crowd in high school and just after graduation married Tonya Harris, a party girl a couple years his senior who told him she was ready to settle down.

Shortly after Timmy was born, Tonya's old friends and habits caught up with her. Before long, she was using drugs and calling old boyfriends. She abandoned the family. Once again Sunday became important to Franklin, now a single father. It was his "Timmy Day," the day he set his burdens aside to spend time with his best friend, his little boy.

Timmy always had the rule of the day, and most Sundays he wanted to go fishing. He was only six, so he was no bass master, but it was time spent on the lake with his daddy, and that was what mattered.

Franklin noticed a disappointed Timmy watching the men who worked with him at the pest control company heave the downed limb into the middle of the backyard. For a moment, the boy's face brightened when the men loaded their trucks and drove away. But instead of going inside to meet his son, Franklin went to work cutting the large limb with a chainsaw, converting it into firewood for the winter.

However, when Franklin looked up from his work and saw Timmy staring at him from the patio door, he remembered where his priorities should be.

Franklin brushed himself off and removed his gloves and goggles. Navigating around the remainder of the limb, he slid open the patio door and looked down at his boy. There was a forlorn look in the child's eyes. Franklin smiled at him.

"Go on. Go get your pole. I can do this later."

Timmy did not need to be told twice. He ran to his room to get his tackle box and pole.

Ten minutes found them pulling up to Greensboro Park Lake in Franklin's truck. Timmy kicked his little legs, barely able to contain his excitement. Timmy Day had been saved!

The Whitaker men hopped out of the truck, and Franklin moved for the bed, where their poles and tackle box lay scattered.

Noticing his son's enthusiasm, he chuckled and said, "Why don't you go on down. I'll be there in a minute."

"OK!" Timmy ran down to the lake.

Franklin smiled. He thought briefly of his ex-wife and wondered where she was, what she was doing, and if she ever thought of the beautiful boy she left behind.

Juggling boxes and poles, Franklin clanked and clattered his way down to lake's edge.

"All right, Timmy. You ready?"

Timmy jumped up to meet his father, smiling proudly. "Look, Dad! I already caught two!"

Franklin thought the boy was joking. Timmy had never caught a single fish in his young life, let alone two. Besides, he didn't even have his pole. But when Franklin looked down at him, he saw the boy standing proudly, chest puffed out, his toothy grin beaming in the Sunday morning light, and holding a fish in each hand.

Bewildered, Franklin said, "How...?"

Then he saw the lake behind his son and froze in fright.

CHAPTER SEVEN

CHURCH WAS FINALLY over, and Dras had managed to nod off only four times, a personal best. Much of the credit belonged to Isaac Monroe, who sat in the pew directly in front of him and felt compelled to shout, "Amen," at regular intervals, each time startling Dras awake and adding to the physical and emotional pain of his hangover.

People stepped into the aisles, and Dras watched as they broke into groups for conversation. As he made his way for the exit, dodging kindly old people, he overheard some of the ladies whispering.

"I heard Lindsey McCormick never came home last night."

A gasp. "Oh, really?"

"Her mother called me this morning to see if I'd seen her. You know, I live next door to the Walkers, and she's been dating that boy."

Dras froze at the mention of Lindsey. He'd sort of dated her last year until she thought it would be better for both of them if they saw other people. Then she started dating that knuckle-dragger TJ Walker, who used to pick on Dras in high school.

Wasn't Lindsey at The Rave Scene last night? He vaguely recalled seeing her, the aftereffects of alcohol clouding his brain rather effectively. A chill ran down his spine. *How creepy. I might've been one of the last people to see her.* Sadly, he remembered her and hoped that, wherever she was, she was OK.

Choosing not to think about it anymore, Dras pressed on. He could see open doors ahead of him and smell the fresh air outside beckoning to him. *Freedom!* He was almost there. Only one thing stood between him and the rest of his Sunday—Reverend Jeff Weldon.

As he did every Sunday, Jeff stood at the front doors, greeting and fellowshiping with the church members as they left the service. Dras found himself pulled into the line. He watched as, one by one, Jeff shook people's hands or gave old ladies hugs. The line dwindled, and soon Dras would be face-to-face with his brother.

He considered breaking rank and sneaking out a back door, but when he turned, Miss Jenkins stood behind him, blocking all hope of escape. She offered a sickly-sweet smile, which he simply returned.

As the line moved forward, his anxiety grew. Dras turned again to the little old lady and tried a new tactic. "I'm in no hurry. Why don't you go ahead of me?"

Miss Jenkins continued to smile but did not budge. The line kept moving, and Dras's time was coming fast. Everything began moving in slow motion. Dras suddenly had a mental image of being seconds away from the edge of a waterfall, then crashing into the rapids below. All he wanted was to claw his way back to safety and away from the edge.

Jeff was shaking the hands of the couple in front of him. Dras forced his way behind the little old lady and nudged her in front of him—a little too hard.

Jeff caught the woman, and the two of them had a nice little laugh over the incident.

"How are you today, Miss Jenkins?" Jeff said.

"Oh, fine, dear." She gave her pastor the same stretched smile she had bestowed on Dras. Jeff bent over and gave her a little squeeze. Miss Jenkins adjusted her bonnet and, over her pastor's shoulder, delivered a blistering disapproving frown to

Dras, who could only smile sheepishly in response. When Jeff pulled away, her smile returned, accompanied by a giggle.

"Have a good day, Miss Jenkins."

His smile faded as he turned to Dras. It was that time again.

"You said you were going to start trying, Dras. You said you'd be here."

"What?" Dras cried. "I'm here, aren't I?"

He was wishing he'd acted upon the sneaking out the back door plan. *It would have been better. Too late now, though.* The brothers stood at a distance, playing their parts in an eternal face-off. Dras expected tumbleweeds to roll by at any moment.

He remembered his sunglasses. They didn't leave too much for Jeff to piece together regarding his hangover. He was caught. Not only did Dras show up late for church, but he was coming off a buzz to boot. He felt ashamed, knowing he had promised his brother he would do better for Mom's sake.

Why does the guy have to stand so tall?

Dras could feel the air tightening in the entranceway, despite the fact that the doors were wide open and not five feet behind his brother. The watchdog was on the warpath again, and Dras was in his sights.

"I'd almost rather you didn't come instead of coming like this," Jeff said.

Dras rolled his eyes. "Come on, Jeff. Loosen up. You're not Dad."

Dras knew his words cut deep. His brother idolized their father.

Jeff kept his cool. "You can't keep living like this, Dras. It's not good for your body, and it's not good for your soul."

Dras smirked. "Do we *have* to go through this every Sunday? Church is over. Your congregation isn't watching. You don't have to preach at me."

"Do you think I do this for show, little brother?" Jeff struggled to hold in his anger. "I'm trying to warn these people before it's too late. Time is short. Maybe one day you'll realize that."

He was clearly hurt. The pain was all over his face. Dras had considered apologizing, but after that little outburst the kid gloves came off. He waved his brother off.

"Yeah, yeah. I know all about the Ten Commandments. I'm a Christian just like you, remember?"

"I swear, Dras, someday..." he said, exasperated.

"You shouldn't swear," Dras replied, snickering.

Jeff didn't see the humor. "Do you really know what it means to be a Christian?"

"Yeah, waking up on Sunday and going to church to hear my brother shout at me for an hour about how I'm doing everything wrong."

"I'm not out to get you, you know? Neither is God. I just...I just want you to be OK."

"I'm fine," Dras huffed.

"Are you? That's not what Rosalyn tells me. She says your drinking's getting worse."

Dras stepped back. "Hey, pardon me for not wanting to settle down and grow old already, all right?"

Aware that people were looking at them, Jeff's voice became quieter, more intense. "You say you're a Christian? Act like it. Because if you think that just because you're my kid brother I'm going to keep covering for you, you're wrong. I won't tolerate this hypocrisy in my church from anyone. Especially not you. You know better, man. What's happened to you? You say you're just having fun, but it looks to me like you've just checked out."

Dras didn't back down. They were two bulls locking horns. Jeff's feelings didn't matter anymore to Dras, only the win. And no way was Jeff going to get the last word. No way, no how.

Dras looked him square in the eye and gritted his teeth. "It's *my* life. Not yours. *Mine.*"

Jeff didn't back down, either. "You're right. But have you ever stopped, even once, to think about who your life is affecting?"

Dras couldn't believe Jeff had just played the Rosalyn card. "Leave her out of this."

"It's not bad enough her mom's an alcoholic; now she's gotta clean up after you too? She needs you to show her the hope Christ can give her, Dras. Everyone else in this town has given up on her. Don't you give up on her too."

Dras shoved a finger in his brother's face. "Don't—" But he was too angry to finish the sentence. Determined not to let his brother get the best of him, he mustered all his Bible knowledge to argue his point. "Doesn't it say in Ecclesiastes to eat, drink, and be merry? Even Jesus turned water into wine."

"Typical, Dras," Jeff said, shaking his head. "Jesus wasn't a drunk."

"A *drunk*?" Dras shouted. "Is that what you think I am?"

"When are you going to grow up, Dras?"

"I think you're grown up enough for the both of us!"

By now, the church's remaining parishioners were beginning to take interest in the bickering brothers. Isabella spotted the two locked in their dance, but before she could intervene, she was intercepted by a dark, elderly man sporting a sweater vest and golf cap and supporting himself on a cane. Leonard Fergus was a deacon and one of the founding members of the Good Church of the Faithful. Jeff and Isabella had known him their whole lives. He was a mainstay in the congregation, and despite his age and the attitudes of his contemporaries, he loved it when Jeff shook things up with a hot sermon.

Isabella greeted him. "Hello, Leonard."

"Hey, Isabella," he drawled in his lazy, gravelly voice. "Just wanted to thank you for sending that casserole over. Haven't had a good woman cook me a meal in a while."

Isabella smiled while Jeff was shouting at Dras in the background about his responsibilities to the Lord. "It was no problem," she said. "Really."

Leonard noticed she was distracted and peeked over his shoulder at the dueling Weldons. He said, "Good to see Dras out this morning. I know Jeff worries about him."

Isabella nodded, her attention on Jeff and Dras. "Would you excuse me?"

Leonard tipped his cap and flashed an understanding wink. "You go on."

Isabella marched into the fray. Jeff and Dras were brothers, she reasoned, and neither of them was going to back down. The only sister to four brothers, she knew how stubborn boys could be. They were going to need an unstoppable force that wouldn't put up with their nonsense and who would set them both straight.

They were going to need her.

"Such a waste, that boy," she heard one lady remark in passing.

Out of the corner of her eye she caught sight of an elderly woman talking to two ladies in flower-patterned dresses. They spoke loud enough for her to hear.

"His father must be so ashamed of him. Such a good man, Jack Weldon. Too good to have a no-good son like that."

"You know he goes to that awful Rave Scene place, don't you?"

"He *does*?"

"He and that Myers girl."

"She's nothing but trouble. Trysdale Trash, just like her mother, if you ask me. Mark my words, nothing good ever came from *that* family."

Isabella smiled when she saw Leonard approaching the gossips. He tipped his hat and chimed, "Morning, sisters. Spreading the love of Christ, I see."

Looking like children caught with their hands in the cookie jar, the ladies huffed and walked away. Chuckling, Leonard strolled on.

With a smile that could light up a room, Isabella Weldon stepped between the feuding brothers and placed a loving arm around Jeff. She nodded at Dras, feigning innocence as to the state of affairs. "Hey, Dras. I didn't see you come in."

Uh oh, Jeff thought when he saw his wife approaching. *I know that look.*

To her church prayer group Isabella was known as "the Big Gun," and Jeff knew he was in trouble. When things were really bad, she was the one they called to save the day.

As Isabella greeted Dras, he took a quick glance around and saw a handful of gawking looky-loos. He felt instantly ashamed. He scolded himself for letting the situation get out of hand.

"I was a little late," Dras was telling Isabella. He had always loved having Isabella for a sister-in-law.

"Are you coming over to the house for lunch?" Isabella asked. "We'd love to have you."

Jeff had to bite his tongue to keep from saying something, and Isabella knew it. Her grip on him tightened. He expected Dras to accept her offer for no other reason than to watch him squirm.

"No, that's OK, Isabella," Dras said. "I've gotta go." He

adjusted his sunglasses and smiled his innocent, boyish smile. "See you later."

Feeling disappointed and frazzled, Jeff watched Dras get on his bike and pedal away. Isabella lovingly rubbed his back, and he began to cool.

"That kid's going to give me gray hairs, I swear," he said. "I'm sorry about that."

He spoke to Isabella, but his eyes were on Dras. His anger melted into compassion for his little brother, but the opportunity to reach him was gone again, for now, and he could only watch him go.

It seems I'm always watching him go.

"It's OK. Happens to everybody," Isabella said.

Jeff gazed at his departing congregation—his flock—and frowned. "But it shouldn't happen to me. I should be over this."

"What? For their sakes? Come on, Jeff. You're only human. They understand that. Besides, I'm sure they would agree that no one annoys us like our families."

He paused for a moment before releasing a sigh. "I just wish I knew what to say to him."

Isabella rested her head on Jeff's shoulder. "You can't convince him to do the right thing, Jeff. It's not your job. God only requires us to tell others about Him. It's His job to soften their hearts so they'll listen. It's just not Dras's time yet. But he'll come around. You did."

Jeff wanted to believe her, but he worried that some people could never change.

"I know," he said. "I was just hoping to spare him a lot of the mistakes I made."

"You just have to have faith."

Jeff gave her a modest kiss on the lips. Yet again, Isabella had saved the day.

"What was that for?" she asked.

"For keeping me sane."

She kissed him back. "That's what I'm here for."

CHAPTER EIGHT

O N THE OTHER end of town, Sheriff Hank Berkley had
problems of his own.

The tow truck had already pulled Lindsey McCormick's car from the murky depths of Greensboro Park Lake by
the time he arrived. The scene wasn't the circus he'd feared,
and he was glad for it. Until now, the McCormick girl's fate
had been only speculation and whispered rumor, but with the
discovery of her car, the investigation—and all the surrounding
media hoopla—would begin.

Mud and grime covered the missing girl's car. Water
continued to seep through the seams in the doors. The tow
truck's driver, one Metsy Buchanon, leaned uninterestedly on
the side of the crane, taking a smoke while he awaited further
orders. As Sheriff Berkley neared, Metsy nodded without a
word. Hank took a quick look inside the car and found it empty.
No sign of Lindsey.

When he looked up, Hank saw a game-and-fish truck parked
on the other end of the lake. Workers threw large nets into the
water, pulling in a whole harvest of fish. A whole harvest of
dead fish. There were only a few left in the water now, but the
back of the truck was piled high. Hank frowned at the strange
sight, then turned his attention back to his side of the lake.

Off to his right, the sheriff spotted Dane Adams, his loyal
deputy and hunting buddy, kneeling and talking at eye level to
a little boy. The boy's father stood behind him with a hand on
his son's shoulder. The boy was giving his account of finding the

dead fish. Hank held back, allowing the boy to finish without interruption. He watched the careful way his deputy spoke to the child. As the boy told his story, Deputy Adams listened intently, keeping his voice steady and calm when he asked questions. Finally, the boy finished, and Deputy Adams stood with a smile, giving the father a nod. The father patted his son on the shoulder proudly. They turned and walked away.

Deputy Adams removed his hat and wiped sweat from his brow. He released a long sigh. It was time for Sheriff Berkley to get some answers.

"What do we got here?" he asked.

Deputy Adams shook his head. "Craziest thing ever. That was Franklin Whitaker and his boy. They said they came down here this morning to do some fishing and found all the fish dead, just bobbing up and down. Game warden came down and said he ain't never seen anything like this and gave us a call to come check it out." Deputy Adams sighed heavily again. "That's when we found the car. Ran the plates. Belongs to Lindsey McCormick."

"What about the girl?"

"Gone, Sheriff," Deputy Adams said, almost apologetically. "I did find a few bloodstains inside the car, on the seat, so I'd say there was a struggle. But we've combed the lake three times, and we ain't found nothing but more dead fish."

Sheriff Berkley scanned the lake as the gravity of the deputy's words weighed on him. His heart sank.

"Do you think she survived?" the deputy asked. "Got out and got away?"

"It's possible, I suppose. But she never made it home, and I reckon that's the first place she'd go if she were able."

"Do you think she was kidnapped?"

"Or worse."

"Oh."

"Keep it to yourself for now," the sheriff said. "I don't want to get this town in a panic."

"Sure thing."

Berkley began to walk away. Deputy Adams called out to him. "Who would do something like this, Sheriff?"

The tired old sheriff shook his head. "I don't know...I don't know."

A car came to a screeching halt at the top of the nearby hill, and both officers turned to see a frantic man jump out, leaving the door wide open. His expression was full of terror. Both men recognized him.

"Ray McCormick?" Deputy Adams mumbled, confused. "He shouldn't be out here."

"My daughter!" The man ran down the slope toward the lake. "Where's my daughter? Is she here? Is she OK?"

"Stay here. I'll take care of this," Hank said to his deputy.

Deputy Adams held back as the sheriff moved to intercept Ray McCormick before he reached the wreckage. From his position at the water's edge the deputy couldn't hear what was said, but he saw the sheriff shake his head and hold out empty hands. McCormick's hands began to shake. The deputy watched the emotional scene a moment longer before turning toward the lake.

"What's next?" he murmured.

CHAPTER NINE

ARRIVING HOME AFTER the church service, Dras felt pretty good about things. He'd managed to drag himself to church, albeit late, but no matter. Not to mention he always enjoyed a good fight with his brother. *OK, that's not true.* But it did feel good to get the last word in for once. He stepped a little lighter as he walked into his apartment to find the blinds open. Merciless sunlight flooded the room.

Dras winced in pain and shielded his eyes. He'd taken his sunglasses off. Now he wrestled them out of his back pocket and put them on again. He forced himself past the sunlight, its rays wreaking havoc on his senses, and rushed to close the blinds and spare himself any more misery.

Taking deep breaths, he tried to will his headache away.

"I thought I closed those before I left."

He *had* closed them. Just to avoid this very predicament, in fact.

How did they get open again?

A strange uneasiness washed over him. Someone had been here, in his apartment. And maybe...maybe that someone was still here.

He tried not to panic, tried to think of the smart thing to do. He froze where he stood, assessing the situation. At this very moment there could be a blind-pulling psychopath in his apartment. He slipped off his sunglasses and tossed them aside, scanning the now darkened room for something to use in his defense.

A baseball bat was barely visible behind the couch.

Slowly, so as not to make a sound, he maneuvered toward the bat. It wasn't easy maintaining his stealth while dodging empty beer and soda cans. But he did his best.

He reached the bat. Clutched it to his chest. Whoever was in the apartment with him was not getting out in one piece or, at least, not without a big knot on the noggin. At this point, it didn't really matter to Dras which. His main concern was survival.

The living room and adjoining kitchenette were clear, as far as he could tell. So he proceeded to the hallway. Anxiety swelled inside him. The situation gave him the creeps. When he was little, Jeff was always the one who investigated strange noises when their parents weren't around, but since Dras just managed to cheese *that* guy off, he knew he was on his own.

He tiptoed past his bedroom. Peeking in, he found it empty of any criminal blind-pulling element. He breathed a small sigh of relief.

One down.

He moved forward, slowly, to the next room. The bathroom. He took a deep breath. It was the only room left. It wasn't a big apartment, after all. He cocked the bat over his shoulder, ready to strike. This was it. If the killer were still here, he would be in this room.

Unless he's behind me!

Dras spun around, prepared to attack the spawn of Satan.

No one was there.

Without warning, a shadowy figure charged out of the bathroom and crashed into Dras from behind. Screaming for all he was worth and hoping the psycho killer wouldn't think less of him for it, Dras attempted to protect himself, succeeding only in flailing about and knocking a couple pictures of him and

Rosalyn off the wall. In the confusion, he lost his weapon and could only cry out as his attacker was all over him.

"Rosalyn?"

While she hadn't screamed like a sissy man, she did look visibly startled. Dras, however, was having a panic attack. She found it amusing.

"Chick!" he screamed, not out of anger, but more as a means of recovering from shock. "You scared me!"

"Sorry," she giggled. "I didn't think you'd be home so soon."

Still on edge, his nerves shot and his head hurting worse than ever, he panted, "I can't believe you pulled the obligatory predictable friend scare on me."

While Dras braced himself against the wall and tried to keep his heart from exploding, Rosalyn brushed the whole incident off. She smiled, poking fun at him. "I can't believe you fell for it."

Breathing deeply, Dras followed her into the living room. When Rosalyn noticed the blinds were closed, she crossed the room and pulled them open again. She repositioned a flower on the small end table so that it faced the sun.

Dras hadn't noticed the flower when he arrived, what with plotting the demise of the blind-opener. "What's that?" he said.

"A flower. I thought you could use something to liven up the place. It's a mess in here, Dras. When was the last time you dusted?"

"Dusted? You're supposed to dust?"

Rosalyn rolled her eyes and patted him on the chest on her way to the kitchen. Dras supposed he could live with the light for a while, just to make Rosalyn feel better; he just needed to stay out of the direct sunlight, lest he burst into flames.

Rosalyn began rummaging through his refrigerator without so much as an explanation. "So how was church?" she asked.

Dras groaned. "Oh, don't even get me started. Jeff is such a self-righteous jerk."

She laughed. "He's not that bad."

"Oh, no…" Dras drawled dramatically. "Jeff's a *great* guy. He's forthright and honest. Sincere and kind. He's a wonderful husband to Isabella, and he'll make a terrific dad one day. He's dependable and responsible and everything that a parent could want in a son and blah, blah, blah."

Rosalyn tried hard not to laugh at Dras's tirade. "Not feeling jealous, are we?"

"Hey, you try living up to that kind of reputation. Everyone looks at me, and I'm just the screw-up little brother. You know what that can do to a person?"

"Um, hello?" Rosalyn chimed, raising a good-natured hand. "Trysdale Trash over here, remember?"

"Sorry. I'm just grumpy."

"S'OK. I've forgiven you for worse." She turned back to the refrigerator.

But Dras wasn't finished. "I mean, I'm a Christian and everything, but you don't see *me* shoving it down people's throats. People can believe whatever they want to, right?"

"It's important to him, you know?" Rosalyn said. "Go easy on him. He's just trying to look out for you."

"Yeah, I know. I just wish he'd let me make my own decisions. I *am* a grown man."

Rosalyn raised her head and pointed at a He-Man cartoon magnet on the door of the refrigerator. With a wink, she said, "And it shows."

"Ha-ha. Funny." Dras watched her as she examined his leftovers. "Don't…uh…Don't take this the wrong way or anything, but what are you doing here anyway?"

Rosalyn popped out of the refrigerator. "Hello? Lunch?"

"Oh. Right."

Finding nothing worth eating in the refrigerator, she grabbed Dras's last two microwave meals from the freezer. "Did you forget?"

Dras thought a moment. "Apparently. I must've really gotten thrashed last night."

Wondering exactly what he had done last night after water-logging himself at the bar, he watched as Rosalyn wrestled with the cardboard boxes to get to the meals inside. "Tell me about it," she sighed. "It took us half an hour to get home because I had to keep pulling over so you could throw up."

Dras's face flushed, and he had the urge to dig his toe into the carpet. He felt bad. He didn't like it when he got sloppy drunk. Rosalyn didn't like it, either. He felt doubly bad for that.

"Sorry," he muttered.

Rosalyn shrugged. "I'm used to it by now, Dras. I just think you need to lay off the stuff for a while. Let your liver recover before it goes another round with Mohammed Dras. You only have one of those things. The idea is it's supposed to last you a lifetime."

He smiled. He always found it funny when she hid her concern behind sarcasm. It killed her to admit she worried about him. Of course, that wasn't going to stop Dras from rubbing it in.

"Ah, Roz. I didn't know you cared."

Walking past him to put the frozen dinners in the micro-wave, she gently slapped him on the face. "Restock your fridge. I can't even find the ketchup."

She pushed the microwave's buttons and waited for the precious "ding." Dras opened the refrigerator. He stuck his head inside.

"It's right by the green Jell-O," he said.

"Dras, that Jell-O was red when you put it in there."

"Oh."

He took a step back, just in case the gelatin dessert had grown sentient with age. He could have removed the bowl and rinsed out the alien entity, but the thing growing in his refrigerator seemed unimportant all of a sudden. Talking about last night's drinking binge reminded him of what he'd heard at church.

"Hey," he began, a bit uncomfortably, "you remember Lindsey McCormick?"

Rosalyn laughed. "*Do* I. She was all you talked about for six months. I thought you were going to lose it when she dumped you for TJ. Why? Did she say something to you last night at the club?"

"No, I...I heard somebody talking about her this morning, and...it just got me thinking about her."

"The one that got away, huh?"

"I guess."

He wanted to say more, to tell her that Lindsey had disappeared and that he was worried about her. But before he could say anything, Rosalyn made an announcement.

"Well—" she smirked as she leaned on the counter, still waiting for the microwave to do its magic—"while you were trying out for Chippendale's last night, I met someone."

Dras closed the refrigerator door and faced her. Pieces of images from the night before were coming together in his mind, and he felt concerned but didn't really know why. "It isn't that creep I saw you dancing with, is it?"

Rosalyn defended her mystery man. "He's not a creep. You don't even know him."

Dras cocked an eyebrow. "And you do? What's his name?"

Rosalyn hesitated.

Dras laughed. "What, you haven't even asked Mr. Perfect's name?"

"We're not that far in our relationship yet," she blurted. "We're taking things slow. We've both been hurt."

Dras snickered. "Slow? No wonder you failed your driving test the first time, Roz. Allow me to clarify—"

He began in an instructional tone, as if explaining the vast mystery of the cosmos. "Slow actually involves movement—"

Rosalyn folded her arms, ready to take her lumps.

"Making googly-eyes at each other constitutes a standstill."

"I didn't make *googly-eyes* at him." She grinned shyly and tucked a loose strand of hair behind her ear. "You're overreacting. Besides, you can laugh all you want, I think he's…mysterious."

Dras shook his head. "I'm not buying it. Admit it. You fell, and you fell hard."

Although he joked, Dras waited for her answer with an unexpected and uneasy anticipation. He didn't know how to explain it, but there was something wrong. Something that left a strange, crawling sensation in his stomach.

Then when Rosalyn turned away to think about what she would say next, Dras *knew* something wasn't right. Something—someone—had come between them. He didn't know what he was feeling.

Am I…jealous?

Just when Dras thought he would pop from the suspense, the microwave dinged. Rosalyn took the opportunity to avoid eye contact with Dras and went to tend to the microwave dinners.

It was an odd moment. *But it shouldn't be*, Dras thought. *It's not like she's never dated anybody before.* Still, he couldn't shake the feeling that the stranger from The Rave Scene would be the one to take her away from him. One thing was certain. The fear inside him was too serious. Too real. He laughed it off, just to feel safe again.

"I knew this day would come," he said.

Rosalyn couldn't look at him. She was quiet. Dras knew she felt the strange distance creeping between them too. It started with her wanting to get out of Greensboro. They'd been inseparable for a lifetime, but now it seemed events were conspiring to pull them apart. It scared her. At least, he hoped it scared her. It scared him too.

"What day?" She tried to sound interested, though he could tell she wished the whole conversation would just go away.

In an effort to lighten the mood, Dras clasped his hands to his chest dramatically. "The day I watch my little girl grow up."

Rosalyn faced him. Despite the smiles, there was worry on their faces, and they knew the joke carried more truth than either of them cared to admit.

Rosalyn faltered, then gave Dras an annoyed look. "Stop."

The seriousness broken, Dras decided to switch the comedy to full tilt, just to be sure they made it out of this unfamiliar territory. He threw a hand to his forehead, really laying on the melodrama. "One day, you won't even need me," he moaned.

Rosalyn couldn't help but snicker. She took the dinners, handing one to him. She looked into his eyes with sincerity. "Are you kidding?" Her tone was soft and real. "I'd fall apart without you." Then, as she'd always done when she couldn't put into words how much he meant to her, Rosalyn gave Dras a quick peck on the lips.

It was just a silly gesture. She'd done it hundreds of times before. But this time—

They parted. As they did, Dras looked back at her, smiling at first. She was trying to smile too. But something felt awkward to both of them, and their smiles faded. They just stared at each other.

Dras panicked. *Whoa! What just happened?*

It was too close. Too intimate. A part of him that had never spoken up before suddenly wanted to kiss her again. Rosalyn blushed, averted her eyes, and went to sit at the table and eat.

Dras could only stand and watch her, baffled, the imprint of her soft, warm lips still lingering on his.

What's happening to us?

It was late when Rosalyn arrived home that evening. The sun had set and the moon had come out to play. She and Dras finished their quiet lunch without further incident and popped in one of his old movies. For the afternoon's viewing pleasure, Dras chose the classic 1987 slasher bonanza *Groundhog Day Part XII*. He made popcorn, Rosalyn made snide remarks, and everything seemed as routine as it could be.

Still, the kiss was on her mind.

She left Dras's apartment that evening with a sense of incompleteness. The kiss was sweet, innocent, friendly, routine. However, when she pulled away from Dras, something tugged at her heart. Something undefined but powerful. Rosalyn knew they had to discuss it. It was too strange a moment to just push aside and forget. They had to talk about it, to find out whether or not it was something that should happen again.

She *wanted* it to happen again.

Nevertheless, when she got home, Rosalyn did her best to shake off the feeling. It was not something she wanted to deal with right now. After all, getting involved with her best friend would just be asking for trouble. Sure, she loved Dras. He was her soul mate. They both knew that. Maybe it seemed obvious to everyone else that they should pursue a romantic relationship, but she was afraid of things not working out and losing what they already had. It sounded like a trite excuse, but it was the honest truth.

Dras is all I have left.

The thought terrified her.

Following the last big fight with her mother years ago—the one that led her to move away from home—Rosalyn didn't feel like she could go back again, and avoiding her mother meant she didn't see her kid sister, Annie, as often as she'd like. Granted, she could visit her without moving back in, but that would mean having to see their mother too.

Ugh. Not in the mood. Ever.

Dras was the only thing she allowed herself to care about these days.

If something were to happen to him, if I ever lost him...

She tried to tell herself her fears were unfounded. Here they were, safely tucked away in Greensboro, where nothing ever changed. She figured that soon enough she would give up her hopes of going to Vermont and that she and Dras would stay just as they were for their entire lives.

Maybe Dras is right. Maybe things don't need to change.

Rosalyn entered her apartment, locking the door behind her. As she dropped her keys on the table next to the door, she passed a wall filled with pictures of her and Dras—pictures of them when they were little, in grade school, in high school, and more recent ones too—a pictorial history of a lifetime together. There was not a single picture on the wall without Dras's goofy grin in it. He was always there, a part of her.

She frowned and thought of Vermont.

What am I going to do?

That night, as Rosalyn slept, an eerie green mist began to ooze through the window she left open. In the quiet town of Greensboro, people could open their windows and allow the breeze to soothe them to sleep without the fear of intruders.

But things in Greensboro were changing.

The fog rolled across the floor, pooling beside her bed. Something emerged from the cloud, something hideous and grotesque. It pulled itself together into a corporeal form.

The Strange Man.

Stepping out of the mist, his green sneer wide and dripping, he sat on the edge of Rosalyn's bed and watched her sleep. The twitching, creeping, crawling shadow things hid in the darkness and clicked and whispered behind him. He spoke to them as he gazed upon Rosalyn's sleeping form.

"Lovely, isn't she?"

Tapered talons outstretched, the Strange Man reached for his prey, keeping only a hairline's width of distance from physical contact with her smooth skin, following the curves of her face and shoulders, studying every line, every detail of her lovely form. He smiled fondly as he looked upon her with lustful eyes.

His eyes roamed to the nightstand beside Rosalyn's bed, where there stood a single picture of the girl with the Weldon boy. It was a newer picture, taken last Christmas, with the two of them caught laughing. The Strange Man plucked the picture from its perch and gazed at it, seething at their captured happiness.

A disgusted snarl formed across his blackened lips as he turned to face the legions of hungry things in the darkness. The shadows began to chatter wildly, erupting in excitement and hunger. They were clamoring over each other, ready and willing to do their master's bidding, and he was ready to send them.

"Watch the boy closely," he commanded. "It's almost time to have a talk with him."

The glass of the picture frame splintered.

Suddenly, Rosalyn awoke with a start, her eyes wide, sweat beading on her back. Waiting for her in the waking world was an awful feeling that someone was watching her. Yet as she looked around the room, she found she was alone. Then she noticed that the picture of her and Dras had fallen to the floor. She picked it up, puzzling over the crack in the glass that had spidered over Dras's face.

She put the frame back on the nightstand, making a mental note to buy a new one on her next trip to the store. She took a deep breath to calm herself and noticed that the window was still open. Now it somehow seemed risky to leave it that way. Cautiously and defensively, still looking around to make sure that she was, indeed, alone, Rosalyn got out of bed and moved to the window. She shut it securely and took one last look around the dark corners of her room, just to make sure. She convinced herself that everything was safe, crawled back to bed, and fell asleep.

Outside her bedroom window, watching Rosalyn snuggle beneath the covers and nestle into her pillow, hung the Strange Man, his lips curled with delight.

"Soon, my love."

And then he was gone.

CHAPTER TEN

DEPUTY DANE ADAMS led the hunt for Lindsey McCormick in the North Woods late Tuesday afternoon. The sticky heat soaked his clothes and matted them to his bulky frame. He stopped at regular intervals to catch his breath and wipe his drenched face with an equally drenched handkerchief.

"Whew." He exhaled, trying his best to bolster the morale of the men Hank placed in his charge but unable to deny his humanity. He was hot, his legs felt like lead weights, and his thoughts drifted to a scene in which he was splayed out on his front porch sipping a cool glass of his mother's sweet tea.

Behind him Deputy Roy Miller, an eagle-eyed retired Marine—retired, never ex-, because no one ever stops being a Marine—remained steadfast and alert, his gaze constantly shifting across the wooded landscape despite the perspiration rolling down his face. He was a gruff, take-no-prisoners kind of guy but had a cool head and fair heart. The other men looked up to him and followed him, no questions asked.

As Dane took deep breaths, he took stock of the former military man, who was hunched low, patiently scouting the terrain, the other deputies following his lead.

Wish I could be like him.

But Dane was about a hundred pounds shy of "being like him," despite the good five years he had on Miller in age. Miller was a man's man, and to his chagrin, Dane realized he was closer to being a mama's boy.

"Need to take a break?" Miller asked him, gauging the heavyset man's fatigue without condemnation.

The other men were looking at Dane. He made himself stand taller. He shook his head. "Nah. Let's keep moving."

Deputy Hollis, a gangly, baby-faced young man, shined his flashlight into the dark recesses of the glen. "You really think we'll find that McCormick girl out here? We've been at this for days. You'd think we'd have found something by now."

Hollis was new to the force and idealistic enough to think they were still looking for a missing girl, when, in fact, every man here knew that Lindsey was probably dead.

They were out here looking for her *body*.

Everyone thought it; no one wanted to say it out loud.

"What's wrong, Hollis? Scared?" another deputy, scruffy-bearded Carter Ross, quipped. He held his flashlight under his chin, shining its light upward, casting distorted shadows across his mustached features.

"Of course not," Hollis sputtered. "Sun's just going down, and it's not safe in the woods after dark, that's all."

"Oh, come off it, Hollis," hollered Deputy Ortiz, bringing up the rear. "We've got flashlights."

"And guns," Deputy Ross quickly pointed out. "I think you're just remembering all those old stories, kid."

Ortiz and Carter snickered. Dane stepped between them.

"All right, all right," he said. "That's enough. Just small town superstitious hokum, Hollis. No bogeymen out here."

"I'm not afraid!" Hollis defended himself hotly. "I never said anything about a bogeyman!"

"Nah, but you were thinking it," Carter teased.

Hollis grumbled something, squinting into the blood-red sun as it began its downward dip into the western horizon.

"Hey, hey," Deputy Ortiz called out to the others. "How'd you hear those old stories anyway?"

"What do you mean?" Miller asked, his eyes never wavering from the search.

"Well, you know, all those stories get told a bit differently, right? My uncle's the one who told me about the bogeyman. He told me he hid under my bed and was gonna pull me under if I got out past my bedtime. How'd you hear it, Miller?"

Miller huffed, finding the conversation counterproductive to the job. "My dad said something about his gramma telling him about it. He never believed it. I didn't either. Like Dane said, it's just old wives' tales."

"It was the closet for me," Carter said. "I heard some friends at school tell the story. They said the bogeyman hid in your closet and scratched on the door, trying to get you to let him out."

Hollis's eyes widened into perfect circles. "Could...could we quit talking about this, please?"

"Just passing the time," Carter said.

"Hollis is right," Dane said. "We're not out here to tell camp-fire stories."

"How'd you hear it, Hollis?" Ortiz asked, ignoring Dane.

Hollis blushed. "My...my sister told me. All of her...her friends were at the house for a...um, sleepover, and they told the story."

"Your sister invite you to her sleepovers often, Hollis?" Miller chuckled. The group followed suit.

Hollis slumped, trudging through the forest. "No."

"So what'd she tell you?" Ortiz asked.

Adjusting the collar of his uniform, which suddenly seemed awfully constricting, Hollis said, "She...she said he was this tall man, dressed all in bluh...in black, with a top hat and a cane. And he…he's supposed to have this crooked neck, like it's broken, right? And…and he's always smiling. Real big, like he's about to eat you. She said he used to live in Old Greenesboro, buh…back before the place burnt down, and that he took all the little children and turned them into monsters, and now they're like his slaves, you know? My sister said that he's always looking for more bad kids to…to turn into slaves."

A hush fell over the deputies, each one finding the detailed description frighteningly real. It was Miller, ever fearless, who broke the silence. "Gee, Hollis, no wonder you're so afraid."

The deputies broke into a chorus of laughter. Hollis turned beet red.

"I'm…I'm not afraid!"

"Hey, Hollis, your sister still table-dancing in the City?" Ortiz asked.

"Shut up," Hollis snapped, aiming his flashlight at the deputy. "You guys are being dumb."

Suddenly, Dane went rigid. "Wait!" he whispered. "You hear that?"

Carter nudged Hollis, hoping to spook him. He received an angry punch on the arm in return.

"Shut up!" Dane hissed. "I heard something. Out there." He indicated the location with his flashlight beam.

"Want me to take point?" Miller asked.

Take point. Dane wished he'd said something military like that. He hitched up his pants. "I'll take point," he said. "Stay close, though. All a'ya."

"All right, everybody. Listen up!" Earl Canton, a boisterous man with a beer belly, mean eyes squinting from underneath a ball cap, and a dark mustache that grew into his sideburns, stood in the bed of his pickup truck, his booming voice echoing over the small crowd. Men loaded up for the night with canteens and energy bars, rifles slung on their backs, and flashlights in hand and murmured amongst themselves as their leader called them to attention.

"It's going to be a long night," Earl declared. The whispering ceased, and every man nodded, mentally preparing himself for the task ahead. "But we've got a lot of work to do, and I mean to see it done."

Off to the side, a handful of women—the wives of the men—set up shop at a foldaway table, filling up Thermoses with coffee and setting out fresh-baked cinnamon rolls. Earl noticed most of the men had their eyes on the sticky treats right now, but he was confident he'd be able to trust them to fall in line once their stomachs were full.

He disapproved of halfhearted commitment but knew they lacked focus because they hadn't suffered as he had. They hadn't lost someone. They hadn't lost a son.

Charlie.

Earl had warned his boy not to go into the North Woods. But Charlie had just turned eighteen. He said he was a man and didn't need to listen to his father. He went drinking with his friends then into the woods to dive off the cliffs into the swimming hole.

It was the last time Earl ever saw his son.

Charlie dove headfirst into shallow water. Broke his neck. Earl hated the North Woods for what they had taken from him. But then, the North Woods was just one item on a long list of things that Earl hated these days.

When he heard Lindsey had gone missing, Earl resolved to find her alive, desperate to spare some other parents the pain of losing an only child. Maybe a part of him—deep inside—was still trying to save Charlie. Earl Canton was not the kind of man to reflect on such things.

He was a man of action.

"I want three groups," he ordered. "Everybody keep their walkies on. We don't need to lose no one else out here."

"Why don't we come back in the morning, Earl?" skinny Milton Wilbanks whined. "Ain't safe out in these woods at night."

"The sheriff and his boys got all day to find this girl, and they didn't get it done," Earl barked. "So we step in while they're off watching Wheel of Fortune and stuffing their faces with Doritos. You read me, Milton?"

Milton conceded, taking a bite of cinnamon roll.

"They give up on her when the sun goes down," Earl ranted. "I don't believe in givin' up until the job's done. One way or another."

"Maybe they're afraid of the bogeyman," quipped Linus Branch, a young man in a worn John Deere hat.

Instantly, Earl was in his face. "You wanna turn back?"

Linus reddened. Milton gulped hard.

"We ain't got no room out here for cowards," Earl shouted. "Lindsey needs brave men looking for her. You in or out?"

Linus stuffed his hands in his pockets and looked at the tops of his scuffed work boots. "Aw, shoot, Earl. You know we're in. I was just funnin'."

"Yeah," Earl snapped, "a lot of fun. Now let's move out."

"Hold it right there."

Deputy Dane Adams and his band of deputies emerged from the tree line. Miller and Carter had their guns out. They silently slipped them back into their side holsters when they saw the commotion was just Earl and a few frightened locals.

"Blast it, Dane," Earl barked, removing his ball cap and slapping it against his jeans. "We're all armed out here. You just about got yourselves shot."

"Could say the same for you," Dane said. "What are you folks doing out here?"

Earl gave a half laugh. "Ain't that obvious? We're doing your jobs for ya."

"I don't remember Hank deputizing a single one of you," Dane said.

Earl hopped down out of the truck. The crowd parted as he went belly to belly with the deputy. "Way I see it," he began, making sure everyone could hear him, "we're doing you a favor, Deputy. You want this girl found, don't ya?"

Dane, a head shorter than Earl, kept a tight focus on him. "You bet I do. But we don't need a bunch of yahoos out here with rifles and itchy trigger fingers. Now, you all go on home. Let us handle this."

"'Cause you've been doing such a bang-up job at keeping our kids safe, huh, Deputy?"

"Cool it, Earl," Deputy Miller said. A reverent hush fell upon the crowd.

Dane felt the tips of his ears burning, embarrassed that he couldn't command the same respect.

Earl faltered, just a bit, in Miller's presence. "We're just trying to help, Roy. Besides, Stevenson said the law wouldn't have no problems with some concerned citizens organizing a neighborhood watch."

Dane scowled. "Well, *Deputy* Stevenson ain't sheriff yet, despite what he might think. Hank's still the law in Greensboro, 's far as I'm concerned."

Earl sneered. "Then you run back and hide behind ol' Hank Berkley and send *him* out here to shut us down. Until I get it from him, I'm taking my guys into them woods to find Lindsey

McCormick. You stop us, Deputy, you're just hurtin' the girl's chances at getting home. You wanna be responsible for that?"

Dane backed down to Earl Canton's bluster. "Fine, Earl. Have it your way. But Hank will be back out here, and he'll tell you the same."

Earl grinned, pleased with himself. "All right, boys. You heard 'im. Mount up. It's time to go."

Dane and the deputies watched as Earl's men took their flashlights, rifles, and Thermoses and headed into the North Woods. Earl stood facing Dane, the clatter of his search party rustling behind him.

"You all have a good night now," Earl said quietly to Dane. He grabbed his gun and followed his soldiers into the woods.

With the sound of their boot steps fading, Miller took a step to Dane's side, eyeing him hesitantly. "You sure that was a good idea?"

Dane didn't answer. Eyes downcast, he headed for home.

CHAPTER ELEVEN

SHERIFF HANK BERKLEY poured himself a fresh cup of coffee, took a sip, and burned the tip of his tongue. He spit the offending brew out of his mouth.

"Ack!"

The sun had set on another unsuccessful hunt for the McCormick girl. Dane Adams and his band of deputies had walked through the station doors sullen and exhausted. After dismissing his men, the deputy lowered his heavyset frame in the creaking wooden chair opposite the sheriff.

"Nothing," Dane said. "We got nothing."

Hank nodded. "Figured as much."

"Ran into Earl Canton out in the North Woods. He's got a few boys out there doing their own search for Lindsey."

Hank rolled his eyes. "That's all we need. If we're not careful, that ol' boy's gonna have this whole town in a tizzy."

"He's just worried, Hank. Whole community is."

Hank didn't need Dane to tell him that. The sheriff had a teenage daughter of his own. To think that it could have been her car he hauled out of the bottom of Greensboro Park Lake—

"Well, I'm not ready to start a panic over one missing girl and some dead fish," he said.

Despite the local press's accusations that the Maribel County Sheriff's Department was doing a less than stellar job, Hank had done all he knew to do. He'd shut down the park immediately after Timmy Whitaker's grisly fish discovery, fearing that the water was contaminated. That angered a lot of people, including the mayor. Summer was just around the bend, and folks were lining up to enjoy their vacation time at the lake. In a town the size of Greensboro, recreational activities were hard to come by, and when the local law shut down one of the few bastions of play, every hackneyed writer wanted to send a letter to the editor of the local gazette to rattle the cages. The station had received some heated calls too, but Hank didn't care. His concern wasn't for their tans or barbecues. He just wanted to make sure the kids were safe.

"We'd better order a curfew." Hank said, rubbing his eyes and not quite suppressing a yawn. "Tell 'em nine o'clock. After that, let's keep the folks inside." The sheriff thought a moment and then pointed a chubby finger in Dane's direction. "That goes for The Rave Scene too. I don't want those kids out at all hours of the night. Not until we know if what happened to Lindsey was an accident or—" He debated on whether or not to say it. He didn't have to. Dane was reading his mind.

"Got it," Dane nodded dutifully.

Hank stood. "I'd better go find Earl. Tell him to leave the protecting of this town to the law."

"Good luck," Dane said, also standing. "You know Earl."

Sighing, Hank nodded. "Yeah, I know. See you at Smokey's later?"

"I'll be there."

Before Hank reached the door, Deputy Ryan Stevenson, a large oak of a man with icy blue eyes and a carefully manicured dark goatee, stormed into the station. He had TJ Walker by the scruff of the neck.

"Let me go!" TJ cried.

Dane stood behind Hank, slack-jawed, as the sheriff tipped back his hat. "Stevenson, what are you doing?"

"Found this one lurking about the Old Greenesboro

ruins," Stevenson reported, a hint of a malicious grin on his thin, cracked lips. "You said he was wanted for questioning, remember, Sheriff?"

"I already talked to you guys!" TJ's tone drew the stares of the other deputies.

Hank cocked his head to the side and placed his meaty fists on his gun belt. "Whoa, whoa, Deputy. I just wanted to ask him a few questions. I didn't mean bring him in like he was a criminal."

Stevenson, smirking, let go of the young man. "Sorry, Sheriff. My mistake."

TJ straightened his jacket, looking mightily offended.

"Why don't you come on in and have a seat, son," the sheriff offered.

"I'm not your son," TJ shot back, but obliged nonetheless.

TJ followed the sheriff back to his office. Stevenson brought up the rear. Dane caught view of the gawkers in the station and waved them off. "I told you all to go on home."

Huffing in protest, TJ dropped into the chair that Dane had occupied a moment ago. He folded his arms. Dane entered and closed the door behind him. Stevenson stood off to the side, stoic as usual. Hank eased into his seat.

"What's this about?" TJ asked, his words a bit slurred.

"Why were you at the ruins?" Stevenson asked, his tone official.

The sheriff shot a glare at the deputy. He'd overstepped his bounds.

TJ spun around to glare at the deputy himself, then turned back to the sheriff. "I was drinking. So what? A lot of people go out to those old ruins to drink."

"Or maybe you were hiding Lindsey McCormick's body," Stevenson countered coolly.

"Shut your mouth!" TJ spat. "I didn't touch her!"

Hank raised a hand. "Calm down, TJ. No one's accusing you of anything. We just have a few questions. After all, you were the last person to see Lindsey before she disappeared."

TJ remained defiant. "I've already told you everything I know. She dropped me off at my house Saturday night, and that was it. I don't know what you want me to say."

The boy looked upset. TJ was a local hero not too many years ago, and Hank hated himself for thinking TJ might have killed Lindsey. But at the same time, it would make the case simpler. As it stood, with a wrecked car, no body, and a lake full of diseased fish, it appeared that the mystery was a long way from being solved.

"We're at a dead end, here, TJ," Hank said humbly. "I was hoping that maybe there was something you might have remembered since we spoke last time. The accident had just happened, and you were understandably shaken. I thought maybe now that a little time has passed, you'd be thinking more clearly."

"Without all that booze," Stevenson sneered.

Hank shot him a dirty look.

Dane nudged his fellow deputy. "Quiet."

The sheriff returned his attention to TJ. "Is there anything else you can remember about Lindsey that night? Did she do or say anything unusual?"

TJ shifted in his seat. Hank thought he might be on to something. At least, he hoped he was on to something.

"Well—" the young man began. He looked either way, as if fearful of spying eyes—"she was upset."

"What about?"

"She thought someone was after her."

"Why didn't you say anything before?"

"Because it was stupid," TJ laughed nervously. "She said—"

He grew quiet. The sheriff prompted him. "Who was it?"

"That's just it. She said it wasn't a man. That it was—" TJ lowered his chin and spoke into his chest, a little embarrassed. "She said it was the bogeyman."

Stevenson shook his head in disgust. "Told you. It's the booze talking."

TJ jumped out of his seat and turned on the deputy. Before he could act, however, Dane stepped forward, holding his hands out in a calming manner. "Easy."

"What did she say about the bogeyman, TJ?" Hank asked.

TJ continued to stare Stevenson down, but the hulking deputy kept his cool, taunting the young man with yet another smirk. Finally, TJ turned angrily to the sheriff. "She just said she saw him at The Rave Scene, all right? I don't know. I didn't see anything. I don't know what happened to her, OK?"

"OK, OK," Hank reassured him, afraid to spook him away before he got all his answers. "We're just talking here."

"Am I under arrest?" TJ demanded.

"No."

"Then I'm through." Without waiting for permission to leave, TJ Walker pushed his way out of the office and marched for the doors.

Dane looked to the sheriff, uncertain. "You want me to stop him?"

"Nah. Let him go."

Stevenson chuckled. "Kid's a punk. He doesn't know anything."

Hank turned on Stevenson. "Don't you have somewhere to be, Deputy?"

Stevenson continued to grin, as if he was untouchable. He walked out. Dane waited for him to be out of earshot before he turned to the sheriff. "I really hate that guy," he said.

"Just between you and me," Hank said, "me too."

"I'll get started on that bulletin for the curfew."

"Thanks, Dane."

"No problem." Deputy Adams nodded and turned to leave but stopped at the last minute. Cautiously, he turned back to face his friend and superior. "Uh...Hank? About what TJ said..."

"What about it?"

"You think there's any truth to it? The bogeyman?"

Hank averted his eyes and smiled, his cheeks reddening. "Don't you start on me now."

Dane checked to make sure no one was listening in on their conversation. He explained, "I'm serious. I've heard talk. Some of the old-timers—"

Hank leaned back in his chair, the springs straining under his weight. "Every kid who's grown up in Greensboro over the last hundred years has heard stories about the bogeyman. Every town's got its ghost stories. You willing to build an entire investigation around it?"

"Miss Jenkins said she saw strange shapes out in the woods behind her house two nights ago."

The sheriff chuckled. "Miss Jenkins has also been known to make moonshine in her shed."

Dane reconsidered. "Yeah." He paused, then added, "It's pretty good too."

Hank had never laughed so hard.

As mysterious and eerie as an ancient mausoleum, the rickety shack sat soundless and settled under the overhanging branches of the surrounding trees. The words KEEP OUT were spray-painted in black on the dingy front windows, and the door stood partially open.

Earl Canton leveled his flashlight at the creepy shack, his mind conjuring images from every horror movie he'd ever seen and screaming at him that further investigation was a bad idea. But he was determined to prove that blunderbuss Dane Adams and his precious Sheriff Berkley wrong and find Lindsey McCormick himself. Earl imagined riding into town in the back of his truck, coming home to a hero's welcome with a weak but grateful Lindsey at his side.

Yeah. That'll show you, Hank Berkley. You didn't do a lick of good keeping my boy out of the North Woods.

"It came from there," hard-faced farmer Burt Simmons whispered, slowly bringing his rifle to bear. "I heard something coming from that house."

Earl nodded, the men in his group shuffling in the leaves behind him. "Could just be a wild animal, Burt. No need to get all jittery."

"Hey, look," Linus said, staring aghast at the thin trees that stood like sentinels beside the shack. "Trees are all dead."

Sure enough, the trees surrounding the shack were withered and dead. As he looked closely, Earl noticed there was also a perfect circle of dead grass at their feet, surrounding the house and the decayed trees.

"That's strange, isn't it?" Milton shivered. "What do you suppose are the odds of that?"

"Bad soil," Earl muttered, advancing slowly.

"Maybe we should call the sheriff," Milton whined.

"Shut up, Milton," Linus reprimanded in a harsh whisper.

"Too late to go back now, ladies," Earl said. "Let's just check it out, nice and easy." Turning to Burt with a dip of his head, he said, "You and Linus take the back. Me and Milton on front."

"Got it," Burt acknowledged.

"You think someone lives out here?" Milton watched Burt and Linus move toward the rear of the house. He was clinging to Earl.

"Who can say?" Earl replied, his heart pounding as he neared the door. "Lot of old houses out here. Could be a fine place for a squatter."

"What about a killer?" Milton said.

Earl eyed the young man, not appreciating his doomsday talk. "Just cool it, will ya? Stay alert."

"You don't have to worry about that," Milton mumbled, gripping his rifle with two shaky hands.

Earl stepped onto the porch, the boards beneath his feet creaking under the strain. He closed his eyes momentarily, biting his tongue to hold back a curse. There was a bulging black trash bag against the open door. A quick look inside revealed the bag was full of empty beer cans and bottles. "Must be recycling 'em," Earl noted. "Not typical behavior for a knife-wielding maniac, is it?"

Milton whimpered.

Giving Milton a look that said, "You run off and I'll kill you," Earl leveled his rifle and used the barrel to slowly push open the door.

Instantly, he was bombarded by the smell of rotted meat and the sound of buzzing. Sure enough, a swarm of flies clung to the walls and the floor, swirling about, forming a black cloud.

Milton gagged and held his hand to his mouth. He let his rifle hang on his back and lifted his flashlight, shining it furiously, as if its beam could repel the terrible smell. "What is that?"

Earl knew. He'd hunted for years and had come across enough small game to know the smell.

"It's a body," he said, nearly staggering from the awful stench.

"Animal or human?"

Earl feared he'd found Lindsey. It'd be a quick end to the mystery, and the McCormick family could finally start to heal—but Earl didn't want to find Lindsey. Not like this. Not in a boarded-up house, surrounded by flies. Not dead, like Charlie.

Why can't I save anyone?

He'd seen Lindsey with that Walker boy a couple of times. She was pretty, full of life and excitement. He didn't know her, but he was pretty sure he would have liked her, maybe even as a daughter-in-law, if Charlie had still been around. Earl wanted to remember her like that. Not as a bloated carcass left in an abandoned shack, serving as a week's worth of dinner for a bunch of bugs. Ray McCormick didn't deserve that for his family.

No one does.

His heart hardened, angered that God would allow parents to outlive their children. He rounded into the living room and took in the full view of the bloodied mess before him.

It didn't appear to be Lindsey, or even female, for that matter.

Milton held back, covering his nose and mouth as best as possible against the horrid smell, shining his flashlight at the remains. Earl ignored the nausea that was building in his gut and forced himself to carry out the job. He knelt and carefully peered over the shoulder of the slumped form, checking the face with a smaller pocket light.

Earl reacted suddenly, jerking back. "Ah!"

"What is it?" Milton asked excitedly. "What did you see?"

Earl couldn't bring himself to say. He was ready to be rid of the creepy place and back in the brightly lit town where monsters didn't lurk. Not out here in the blasted North Woods with death.

Burt and Linus entered through the back door, both of them responding to the sight and stink just as Earl and Milton had.

"It's not Lindsey," Burt said after getting hold of his stomach.

"No," Earl confirmed, shaking. "Looks like Eldon Granger. What's left of him. He's been living in these woods ever since the highway moved."

Burt took a deep breath, then leaned over the body, studying it. Earl marveled at the man and how he could examine the remains so calmly.

Burt shook his head. "Lord Almighty."

"The Lord ain't got nothing to do with this," Earl said bitterly.

"He's been skinned!" Linus hollered.

Burt stood, wiping his hands on his pants. "Coulda died from a heart attack, stroke, starvation, any number of things. After that...well, I think the animals got to him."

Earl shook his head. "No...do you see his eyes? This man was scared to death."

"Scared by what?" Milton asked.

Earl hoped he'd never find out.

CHAPTER TWELVE

BY THURSDAY, THE nine o'clock curfew had inconvenienced enough people that all the wild speculations about strange occurrences took a backseat to the outcry to lift the nighttime ban. Even Earl and the search party's discovery of Eldon Granger's body did little to raise suspicions any longer, and the authorities, newspaper, and public majority were quick to dismiss the incident as a result of natural causes. Life was moving on in Greensboro. Lindsey McCormick's tragedy was old news, and the town was already beginning to forget her.

Ray McCormick, however, could not.

When Dras saw him on Thursday afternoon, Ray was stapling Missing Person signs with his daughter's senior picture outside the grocery store entrance.

Dras had stopped by for peanut butter, detergent, and some much-needed fresh milk. As he exited the store, he couldn't help but stop to look at Lindsey's frozen image staring back at him from the poster. He wondered what happened to her and still dared to hope that she was OK.

Maybe if I'd said something to her that night at The Rave Scene. Maybe I could've somehow...No. Don't be stupid. You couldn't have done anything. Bad things just happen. That's all. It's not your problem.

"Oh, hello, Dras," McCormick said as he finished placing his latest poster. "I didn't see you standing there."

Dras smiled back. "Hey, Mr. McCormick."

Dras saw deep sadness in the man's eyes. He felt bad that all he could offer was "hello." He ventured further, "I'm sorry to hear about Lindsey."

And he was. Dras knew Lindsey. He loved her once. *Well, something like that.* At the very least he had cared about her once upon a time, and he still wondered now and then what would have happened if things had played out differently between them.

Ray only nodded in response, and Dras could see the subject was too painful for the man to continue.

"How's your father doing?" Ray asked, changing the topic. "I heard his health was getting worse."

Dras flushed. Of all the subjects in the world that Ray McCormick could have brought up—

"Yeah, he's not doing too good. I..." Dras shifted uncomfortably, careful to avoid eye contact. "To tell you the truth, Mr. McCormick, I don't really get by to see him much." He chuckled to take the edge off his guilty conscious. "Sick people, you know? They give me the creeps."

Ray offered a quiet nod, as though he would have agreed with Dras once. However, current circumstances had left Ray McCormick with a painful reminder, a hard-earned piece of wisdom that he now shared with the boy. "You should probably go see him, Dras, while you can. You never know how long you have to be with someone. You know?"

Ray held back a sob and swallowed hard. Dras looked again at Lindsey's picture on the Missing Person poster. She smiled back at him, as if from beyond the grave.

"Yeah," Dras replied.

The two stood there in an awkward silence for a moment until Ray moved to go. After all, he had more posters to put up.

"Well, I'd better get back to work."

"OK. See ya, Mr. McCormick."

"All right, Dras. You stay out of trouble."

"I'll try."

Ray walked away, carrying with him his stack of Missing Person posters and his stapler, wandering from one storefront to another, looking for his daughter.

Dras took his groceries in the other direction, trying to erase the thought that Lindsey McCormick was really gone, unable to process that she might actually be dead.

Dead.

The notion seemed impossible to him as he rolled it over in his mind: *Dead. Death.* That was something that happened to someone else. Not your ex-girlfriend.

Not your father.

Finally Dras understood why the thought of Lindsey being dead bothered him so much. Because he knew that if death was here, if it had already claimed someone from his life, it could just as easily claim another. And that someone would probably be his father. Jack Weldon was in bad shape, and there was really no hope that he would get any better, short of a miracle. He was just sick, and things kept going wrong. But Dras didn't know what he'd do if—

Jeff was always better at handling the situation. He hadn't talked to Jeff since their fight after church on Sunday, but he knew Jeff had probably gone over to the house at least twice since then, just to check up on the old man. Jeff. The faithful son. He put Dras to shame, which further served to keep Dras from going to see his dad as often as he should. He did call every once in a while. Yet regrettably, the phone calls usually ended with a request for more money. And his parents always gave.

If something happened to his dad, who would bail him out of

trouble? Who would be there when he got some confusing bill statement that he didn't understand? Who would be there when he was running short on cash and the anxiety of not paying his rent kept him up at night?

Who will be there to be my dad?

He felt like he needed to cry or talk to someone who'd understand, but he wouldn't dare talk to Jeff about it. He was much too proud, and besides, he knew Jeff had his own problems to deal with and didn't need his little brother crying about missing his daddy. Dras hated him for being so strong and never needing help. He hated Jeff for never crying and for always knowing what to do. He hated him because he could never be him. He could never be that strong. He could never be the kind of man his father would respect.

Never.

It wasn't that he didn't believe in the Bible like Jeff and his dad; he did believe that there was a God up in heaven and a devil below and Christ somewhere in the middle trying to save souls. *Sure. Why not?* It was just that those things weren't his whole life. He didn't understand why his brother had to take the church thing so far.

His lack of church involvement was stacked upon the already too-high pile of things Dras had left undone in his life. He was unemployed, broke, lazy, and now there was this new feeling that he had let Rosalyn down too.

He knew she wanted to go to Vermont. Heck, he knew she needed to go. She was too good for Greensboro. She was everything to him, and what had he ever given her in return?

Nothing. Not one stupid thing.

A heavy sigh escaped him.

He and Rosalyn were coming to a crossroads, and Dras foresaw with sickening clarity that he was going to have to make the decision to let her live life without him or keep her in Greensboro and watch her wither and die.

Can I make that decision?

As he passed another picture of Lindsey, Dras felt an unusual chill in the early summer air. He shuddered and continued to push the cart that he had commandeered from the grocery store parking lot on his sad walk home.

This is too much.

With twilight settling, Dras didn't see much reason in forcing the day to go on any longer. He decided to rent a scary movie from his good friend Dave at the video store, preferring to deal with the horrors on the screen rather than the horrors in real life.

While Dras struggled to decide between an early 1980s camp slasher and something from the vampire film family, Dave reclined behind the counter, slurping a sour apple slush and reading a guitar magazine. Dras's fresh milk currently occupied space in the video store's frozen treats cooler, drawing curious gawks from the very limited clientele. Unable to decide on his entertainment for the evening, Dras called for assistance.

"Dude," Dras began, across the near empty store in a tone the president might use to begin the State of the Union address, "I need a professional opinion." He lifted up two faded VHS boxes. "*Garden Tool Massacre* or something with vampires?"

Dave shrugged and turned a page in his magazine. "What man can choose another man's movie? I don't have that kind of power."

The clerk took a long, disinterested pull on his slush's straw.

Dras slumped and decided. After taking his prize to the counter, he fished around in his Velcro wallet for cash. "You know," he sighed as Dave mindlessly punched the keys on the register, barely acknowledging him, "what is it with people wanting to leave this town? What's wrong with Greensboro?"

"That'll be a dollar fifty," Dave droned, his attention still fixed on the guitar magazine.

"And what's in Vermont, anyway? I mean, seriously. Or is it just me? Am I too boring? Too predictable?"

"I don't know, dude," Dave said, sitting back down and propping his feet back up behind the counter. "I just work here. The movie's due back on Tuesday."

"Yeah, yeah," Dras said. "I know the drill."

"Catch you next time."

Dras grabbed his movie, retrieved his groceries, and headed for the door. "Nice talking to you, Dave."

Dave raised two fingers in a halfhearted farewell wave, then flipped another page.

Once he was outside the video store, Dras's thoughts swirled as the proverbial rug seemed about to be pulled from underneath his stable life. *Lindsey, Dad, Rosalyn, Vermont.* With such notions too burdensome for his mind, he chose comfortable denial instead. With groceries and B movie in tow, he headed home to nestle himself amidst his couch cushions and pretend that the world was simpler and more pleasant.

He walked homeward surrounded by the silence of a town preparing to shut down. It was almost nine o'clock, the hour of Sheriff Berkley's curfew. Whether because of the curfew or just the general mood of Greensboro of late, Dras wasn't sure, but the streets were quieter than they used to be, and Lindsey's disappearance seemed to have brought a gloom that hovered over the town. The air was colder, the dark blacker, and he could not help but take cautious glances over his shoulder.

Why, he didn't know. If there was some crazed killer on the

loose in Greensboro, Dras was fairly certain he was an unlikely target.

Nothing special about me, he moped. *No job. No life. I'm a shame to my family. My only friend wants to move away. Yeah. I'm a real catch.*

Dras carried on in self-pity as he passed an alley, never noticing the thousand glinting eyes staring back at him. Watching him.

Arriving home, Dras got a phone call from Rosalyn, who needed a break from her college semester exam studies. She'd been cramming hard all week, but that hadn't stopped the two of them from talking almost every night. Not once did they discuss the undeniable sense that they were growing apart. And, most assuredly, they did not discuss their kiss on Sunday, the familiar gesture that had suddenly seemed new and different.

Instead, there was an unspoken mutual consent to avoid such topics and the dialogues they would bear. Though they did not voice their feelings to one another, it was evident in their quickness to discuss everything under the sun but what was bothering them that they had both decided it was better to ignore their problems and just try and enjoy the good times while they lasted.

To that end they turned to the same television channel and watched together as they chatted on the phone. It was a long-standing ritual between them, and why Rosalyn didn't just come over Dras wasn't really sure. It was just what they did.

"I've got to write an essay on moral relativism for my philosophy class," she complained as Dras slouched on the couch, eating cold, day-old pizza straight from the box it was delivered in.

He took a big bite and flipped through the channels before finally settling on the Home Shopping Channel.

"How can you *teach* a class on moral relativism? I thought the whole point was that you thought for yourself or whatever." He swallowed the stale pizza. "See, this is precisely why I left college. All that high-minded hullabaloo."

Rosalyn chuckled on the other end of the phone. "I think you're the only person in the world who would use the word *hullabaloo* in an actual sentence. Besides, I thought you left because you had sloppy grades, no employment, and your parents refused to spend any more money on your tuition."

"Ah, no." Dras raised a finger in protest. "That's how it would appear to the casual observer. But in truth, my decision was based on pure logic."

"Uh-huh," she said, patronizing him. "Just keep telling yourself that when you're manning the grill at Beefy Burgers."

Dras changed the channel. "Nah, they weren't hiring."

"Dras. A place like Beefy Burgers is always hiring."

"Well, they weren't hiring me."

There was a momentary lull in the conversation while Dras continued to flip channels. "What channel are you on?" he finally asked.

"Fifty-two." Rosalyn yawned. "Documentary on whales."

Dras turned to the channel and tossed the remote to the side, munching on pizza again.

"Hey," Rosalyn began, her voice hesitant, "speaking of employment, I went by Larezzo's today and picked up my schedule for next week. Turns out I work on Wednesday, so we can't go do that thing."

"No big," Dras muttered, not understanding why she sounded so dire in relaying a little bit of trivial information. Actually, he couldn't remember what "thing" they were going to do in the first place.

Rosalyn continued in the same careful tone, "Ray McCormick was there."

Now Dras understood. He finished chewing his bite of pizza and dropped the remainder of the slice in the box. Suddenly his earlier encounter with the man returned to the front of his mind. He felt the same sense that death was close and his family wasn't as safe from its sickle as he'd like to believe.

"Oh," was all he managed.

"He was hanging posters of Lindsey."

"Yeah, I saw him too."

"Did you talk to him?"

"For a minute."

Rosalyn became quiet. "I'm really sorry about Lindsey."

Dras shrugged, feigning indifference. "Why tell me?"

"Well, you know...you and her...whatever."

He appreciated her condolences but somehow didn't feel he deserved them. "Yeah."

There was another silent spell before Rosalyn ventured to rarely charted territory with Dras. "Did you love her?"

He'd expected the question to pop up at some point. With Lindsey's face everywhere and their past no big secret, he knew that someone would get around to asking him how he felt about her. In preparation, he tried to come up with a solid answer, but after having spent a lifetime trying to mask such feelings with a goofy grin and well-placed one-liners, he wasn't sure how he felt.

Besides, now there was an added uncomfortable sensation attached to discussing his dating life with Rosalyn. They were always able to talk freely about their crushes and flings, but after Sunday he didn't know if he really wanted to answer her question. In fact, he could almost tell by the sound of her voice that she didn't really want an answer, either.

The awkward moment was the closest they'd come to talking about their startlingly strange kiss. Dras felt anxious and sweaty. *Is this her way of starting that conversation? If we start it, where will it lead?*

Certainly nowhere Dras wanted to visit tonight.

He thought quickly and came up with, "I don't know. I thought I did, I guess, but…who am I kidding? There's only one person I could ever really love."

On the other end of the phone Rosalyn fell deathly quiet.

Dras cracked a grin and reached for his pizza. "Debbie Gibson."

Instantly the tension was shattered. Rosalyn groaned. "Here we go again."

Good. Dras relaxed, taking a bite of pizza. *Back to normal.*

"What?" he defended himself. "I'm telling ya, underneath that wholesome veneer, she's a—"

Rosalyn finished for him, having been on the other end of this ridiculous conversation for years. "—a smoking hot fox. Yeah, yeah, I know. And for the last time, it's *Deborah* Gibson now."

"She'll always be Debbie to me."

Rosalyn's voice switched back into study mode. "I'd better go."

"Yeah," Dras agreed, glad to end the night on an upbeat note. "I need to go too. I just rented a flick—"

"What's on the entertainment menu for tonight?"

Dras laid the pizza on his chest and reached across the couch to pick up the rental case, reading it to make sure he got the title right. "*She-Vampires From Mars.*"

"Oh, yuck!" Rosalyn cried, laughing at the ludicrous title. "How can you stand to watch that?"

"Hey, there was a time when you were right here with me, sister."

"Yeah, when I was *twelve.*"

"I guess I'm still twelve."

"Truer words were never spoken."

Dras sat up straighter, the pizza falling off his chest and landing on the floor. Nonchalantly he picked it up, dusted off the lint and dirt, and took another bite. Through muffled chewing, he asked, "You just gonna berate me all night, or are you gonna let me watch my movie?"

"Fine, fine. Don't let me separate you from your direct-to-video schlock."

"Don't knock it 'til you try it. That's all I'm saying."

"Later," Rosalyn drawled.

"See ya."

On the street below Dras's apartment, Ray McCormick stapled a Missing Person poster to another telephone pole. He paused after finishing the task, staring up into the smiling eyes of his lost daughter, and his heart broke for what felt like the millionth time.

A snicker in the darkness mocked his misfortune. Nearly dropping his stack of papers, Ray peered into the surrounding night, a chill caressing his bare arms and bringing goose bumps to the surface.

"Someone there?"

A quiet clicking, like a large insect scurrying, answered him. More snickers. A titter, a laugh.

Ray stepped back, bumping into the telephone pole. "Agh!"

he gasped, wheeling around and coming face-to-face with the lifeless smile in Lindsey's photograph. Laughter, snarls, and scratching noises filled the empty street.

Nearing panic and ready to tear down the sidewalk screaming, Ray clutched his papers close to his chest, about to make his break, when suddenly—

"Ray?"

A familiar car pulled alongside him. His wife, Caroline, leaned across the empty passenger seat.

"Ray, honey?" she asked through the open window, pushing long, curly tresses of dirty blonde hair from her face. "It's almost nine. Did you forget the curfew?"

Her question hung in the air as Ray listened for the bestial laughter he heard only moments before. But the horrible noises did not return. He and his wife were alone on the Greensboro streets.

"I..." he began, still shaken by the strange encounter, "I must have."

"Come on, honey. It's late. We can put up more posters tomorrow."

He was trembling as he got into the car. Caroline pulled away from the curb, and the sedan faded into the distance, the couple inside never seeing the cool green mist pooling beneath Dras Weldon's apartment window.

The sounds of hell's children picked up again, hooting and whooping, clicking and snapping, as a multitude of unspeakable evils gathered together, climbing as one bizarre black shape along the outside apartment wall. On the streets below, watching with calm, patient hatred, the Strange Man leered.

CHAPTER THIRTEEN

THE MOON HUNG high in the night sky, and while most people were settling in their recliners to catch the news or a movie, Jeff Weldon found himself huddled over the desk in his study at the Good Church of the Faithful, his nose deep in his Bible and commentaries, making notes. The late hour was beginning to affect his concentration, and his sermon notes were dwindling into unintelligible chicken scratch. Come morning he was certain he'd have no idea what he spent all night writing, and his time away from Isabella would have been in vain. He hated leaving her alone while he worked late into the evening to prepare his sermons and made a point to do as much of the work at home as possible, but the church study housed his father's and grandfather's commentaries and notes, two generations of wisdom that he considered far too priceless to keep at the house or shuttle back and forth. No, he felt they belonged here, on the study's shelves.

He picked up the phone to call Isabella and let her know he'd be at least another half hour. She'd be disappointed, he knew, and she'd try to keep the conversation light to let him know she was OK. He'd accept her graciousness, of course, and behave as though he believed her attempt to seem unaffected by his absence, even though he knew she wanted him at home with her. For his part, he wanted to be there with her too.

But duty calls.

He sighed, setting the phone back on the receiver, unable to bring himself to break the news.

Maybe I can get out of here a little earlier. I'm almost done. Almost done, then I can rest.

Jeff never wanted to be a preacher. Growing up, it was the farthest thing from his mind. In fact, the thought of following in his father's footsteps—indeed, taking over the very same pulpit—once seemed the epitome of a failed life in Jeff's eyes. But somewhere along the way he found himself drawn into the ministry. Maybe it was the chance to help people, to see lives changed for the better; maybe it was the chance to make his father proud. Either way, he joined the long line of Weldon pastors, eager to take up the family mantle and wave it proudly over Greensboro, upholding his good name. But in his heart, he didn't feel like a pastor.

Getting up in front of a congregation every Sunday morning was an anxious ordeal. Every single time he had to do it, he felt sick to his stomach, a mere heartbeat away from a panic attack. Looking out over the congregation week after week, seeing their blank expressions, filled him with cold-sweat fear.

Yet, he soldiered on. It was his job.

Maybe his father felt the same way all those years as the first pastor of the Good Church of the Faithful. Jeff never had the heart to ask him, terrified that he'd see disappointment in his father's eyes, so he kept his reservations mostly to himself, confiding his secret terrors only to Isabella. Her strength had sustained him for the last seven years, and he was thankful that at least one of them was confident he belonged as the pastor of the church.

But, as with all things in his life, Jeff only felt confident when he was prepared. So tonight, like most nights, he spent the better part of the evening at the church in his study, reading over the Scriptures, cross-referencing a dozen different commentaries, researching the original Hebrew or Greek, and occasionally dozing. The studying aspect of his job was his favorite. Aside from the security he felt when he properly prepared, he loved exploring history, reading about the lives of others who had struggled to serve the Lord. Even in his lowest moments, reading about the Old Testament prophets' peaks and valleys provided him with great encouragement and gave him the boldness to continue in his own journey.

He needed that boldness now more than ever.

If he said it once from the pulpit, he said it a hundred times: life was getting harder in Greensboro. At times he felt he could literally see the people's hearts hardening right before his eyes. They were losing the willingness to listen, the desire to grow.

What can I say to them to change their hearts?

He'd asked that question a lot lately. Every sermon he prepared, he began by writing those words at the top of the page, using it as a sort of a target.

What can I say to them?

Unfortunately, no matter how many notes he used to fill up a blank page, Jeff never felt he'd answered the primary question. He just didn't know what to say to the people to give them hope.

Dad would know what to say.

His heart broke, and he thought to pick up the phone and give calling Isabella another try. He needed to work harder, to prepare more.

Isabella will understand.

Before he could talk himself out of it, he grabbed the receiver and dialed home, knowing she would see "Good Church of the Fait" on the caller ID. At the first ring, he envisioned her sitting on the couch, flipping through channels in her pajamas with a disappointed slump in her shoulders, knowing she was about to spend another night alone. He felt terrible. But before he could reflect any longer on his lousy balance of husband-pastor responsibilities, Isabella answered the phone, her voice hopeful.

"Hey."

"Hey," Jeff said, rubbing his eyes.

"Another late one, huh?"

"I'm so sorry. I know I promised I'd be home by nine."

"It's OK," she said without emotion.

No, Isabella, it's not OK. "I'm almost done here, and then I can do the rest at home tomorrow."

"How's it coming?" she asked, turning the conversation away from potentially empty promises. "Are you getting it?"

Jeff was grateful to be talking about the work. He felt that even though they were apart they were working together. "Yeah, I think so. I don't know...there's just this feeling that I can't shake."

"Still thinking about the storm, huh?"

He was.

He told her on Sunday about what he'd seen climbing onto Greensboro's back, but he knew his words would not do the awful thing justice. There was something supernatural in that storm, and since that night, whenever Jeff stopped in his busy, mundane life long enough, he sensed it.

And it frightened him.

Something was wrong. He hadn't tried to articulate the full weight of it to his wife; he only told her that he felt odd and, the worst way Jeff Weldon could feel, unprepared. Isabella tried her best to be understanding and helpful, but Jeff realized it might be something he was supposed to deal with on his own. He was the pastor, after all. The shepherd of the Lord's flock.

If a wolf snuck in, shouldn't I be the one to fend it off? But what wolf? Where?

Too many vague questions and uncertainties. Too much for one night, anyway.

"Jeff?" Isabella said after his long silence.

"I'll be home in a bit, OK?"

Isabella hesitated, as if sensing his dread. "OK, baby. If I'm asleep, nudge me so I know you're home."

Jeff laughed, loose and loud, feeling a thousand pounds lighter. "Yeah, like that ever works."

Isabella chuckled too, and it felt good. For a minute it felt like they were still connected. They said their "I love yous" and hung up, but the guilt stayed with Jeff. He thought of Isabella, of her eyes and her lips and her hair.

Then he went back to work.

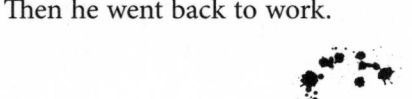

Running through the woods, pulled along a predetermined path as if a tether is tied to his stomach, forcing him onward. The drumbeats are louder now, the howling closer. A clearing in the branches overhead reveals a starless night sky. Only darkness remains, and that dreadful, inhuman shouting.

He knows he has to look, has to keep moving forward to see the vulgar happenings for himself, though he also knows that to do so will steal a small bit of his soul. But the urge is so strong, so primal.

As he ventures to the edge of the familiar yet alien woods, he sees the flickering firelight ahead. He is on top of them now, ready to bear witness to the unholy matter.

A second's hesitation—perhaps a desperate last plea by the sanity he would sacrifice—stays his hand from pulling back the foliage curtain. His pause lasts only an instant. The sick feeling in his gut forces him forward.

He pulls back the branches and sees everything.
"It's coming."

Jeff jerked upright, his face numb and wet on the left side. A small puddle of drool blurred the ink on the latest page of notes atop his desk. Blinking back his momentary disorientation, he realized he was still in the study at the church. He absently wiped his face dry, feeling nauseous. It was as if the whole world had shifted somehow, and nothing was what it used to be.

The dream held tight to his heart, beckoning him back to that awful forest. He stood, paced the study, and tried to shake the feeling back into his prickly hands.

What do the dreams mean? Why do I keep having them?

Jeff was never one for believing in prophetic dreams. More often than not, an apple was just an apple. But the frequency of his night terrors, the way their beginning coincided perfectly with last week's storm—

Jeff didn't believe in chance.

These dreams meant something. They evoked the same sense of animal peril that he felt when gazing up at the unnatural thundercloud rolling over his house.

Suddenly, he stopped in his tracks and mouthed the words, "...for I am surrounded by devils."

The quote came unbidden, like a ghost from the murky depths of his unconscious mind, a specter from his past. Possessed, he crossed the study, running his fingers along the spines of his father's old books, searching for one title in particular.

There.

Tucked away in a corner of the library he seldom consulted, Jeff found the old Bible his father had placed there years ago. At one time it had belonged to Everett Greene, the founding father of Old Greenesboro—Greensboro's preceding settlement. Only weed-covered ruins out in the North Woods remained of that bygone era.

Ruins, and this Bible.

Carefully—for his father had warned him since childhood to take great care with an aged book—Jeff removed the Bible from the shelf and lifted the cover to reveal the personalized inscription: "Give me strength, O Lord, for I am surrounded by devils."

The words were signed by Greene and dated December 1884.

It was late December of 1884 when all record of Old Greenesboro's population disappeared. God, what does it all mean?

"Burning the midnight oil?"

Jeff slapped the Bible shut—its pages coughing up a plume of dust—and stumbled to face the doorway, his heart slamming against his ribs. Leonard Fergus tipped his golf cap and hobbled in on his cane, a friendly grin on a wrinkled face.

"Mr. Fergus—" Jeff breathed life back into his lungs.

"Saw the light on," Fergus commented casually, taking a seat in front of Jeff's desk. "Thought I left it on when I was up here earlier, at first. When I saw it was you, I thought I'd come up and say hello."

Jeff recovered from his fright and slid Everett Greene's Bible back onto the shelf.

"Did I scare you?" Leonard chuckled.

"Yeah," Jeff said. "I guess you did a little. I was just—"

Jeff trailed off, not quite sure what he was doing or why he had thought to look through Greene's Bible after nearly twenty years. He saw it lying on his father's desk only once as a child, and then only the first page, the one that bore the inscription, before his father caught him and removed the book for safekeeping.

Why did I remember that now? What are You trying to tell me, God? Am I surrounded by devils?

"Jeff?"

The young pastor realized he was mumbling to himself, chewing on a fingernail. Suddenly embarrassed, he turned to his old deacon. "Thinking...I was just thinking."

Fergus braced himself on his cane, eyeing the young man with a hint of worry. Jeff sat on the edge of his desk, his mind swimming.

"Mr. Fergus—"

"You know you can call me Leonard," the man replied with a soft laugh.

"Leonard, have you heard the stories people tell about the North Woods?"

The old man slapped his knee and let loose a big belly laugh. "Boy, have I. Those are wild tales folks tell. They've been telling them since I was a boy."

"Yeah," Jeff pondered. "Me too. Isn't that odd?"

"Not really," the man said, shrugging. "I s'pose every town's got its share of ghosts. Comes with being old."

"Yeah," Jeff said. "Maybe."

The mirth left Leonard's face. "Something bothering you?"

Jeff thought a moment, then said, "That was some storm the other night, wasn't it?"

"You bet. Thought I was gonna lose my roof for a while. Hadn't had a nasty wind blow through here like that in a good, long time."

"I saw it, you know? I went outside, and I looked up right as it was coming through town. I looked...I looked right into it. It was—" the pastor sighed, dropping down in his chair, as if exhausted.

"It was what, Jeff?"

"It bothered me." He winced, unsure how his next words would sound. "Spiritually, you know? Like...I don't know, like demonic, maybe?"

Fergus gauged the words carefully, and Jeff was certain the old man was going to request the pastor take a sabbatical to clear his head.

"You think it was something more than a storm," he repeated.

"I don't know what I think." Jeff put his head in his hands. "Ever since the night of the storm there's just been this feeling that I can't shake. Like something's...off around here. Like—OK, this is going to sound crazy—but it's like whatever folks talked about in the North Woods has moved in finally. It's *here*. Greensboro feels...haunted, I guess."

Fergus leaned back in his chair.

Jeff continued talking but spoke to his shoes, too embarrassed to face the old man. "Do you think there was really something out in the woods? The Bible says demons are real."

"That it does," Fergus commented in a measured tone.

"Maybe...I don't know." Jeff finally shook his head, surrendering to the ridiculousness of his babbling. "When you and my dad started this church in the old building out in the North Woods, did you ever see anything? Anything that couldn't be explained?"

"Did we ever see the bogeyman, you mean."

Jeff's face flushed. "Sorry. I'm being an idiot."

"The answer's no on both counts," Leonard said, his expression comforting. "Ha-ha. I think the ol' devil was probably 'fraid of your dad."

But Dad's not going to be around much longer, Jeff thought, his heart grieving.

"You've got a sensitive soul, Jeff. Always have, since you

were a little boy. Could be God is trying to tell you something. Maybe He's got special work for you in the days ahead."

"That's what worries me."

"Don't be worried, son. Be ready. He'll give you direction."

The pastor reclined in his chair, sullenly staring at the spackled ceiling. "I just hope I recognize it in time."

CHAPTER FOURTEEN

DRAS MADE IT halfway through *She-Vampires From Mars* before he fell asleep on the couch.

The worries of the day—the disappearance and possible death of Lindsey McCormick, the inevitable loss of his father—weighed heavily on his mind. But fatigue overruled his concerns, and he rested quite easily.

Then something happened.

From Slumberland, Dras heard a noise emitting from the waking world. It wasn't the movie. That ended hours ago, and now the bright blue fluorescence of the empty screen cast a hollow glow over the room. He stirred as he heard the noise again, louder this time.

Dras woke up, startled. The television's blue glow beat against his head with its abrupt brightness. He fumbled to find the remote, only half awake, just wanting to stop the loud white noise. After tossing aside both his stereo and DVD remotes, he finally found the right one for the stupid TV. *Click*. The television went dark. He yawned, appreciating the quiet. Rising slowly from the couch, stretching away the effects of sleep, he realized he was thirsty. Lucky for him he was the proud owner of a new carton of milk, cold and refreshing and serving as the perfect end to a not-so-perfect day.

With no light to guide him, he still managed to bump his knee only once on the way to the kitchenette. He opened the refrigerator, filling the room with its light, and winced, having just grown accustomed to the darkness. Dras groped around with half-closed eyes, trying to find the carton. After an uncomfortable run-in with his possibly sentient Jell-O, he found the milk and grabbed it, keeping the refrigerator door open for its light.

He peeled open the box top and drank straight from the carton. It had been awhile since he had milk in the house, at least in a drinkable state, and he now realized how much he had missed it. Taking the carton from his lips, he sighed, enjoying the long absent taste.

He started to put the milk back in the refrigerator when he noticed something on the back of the carton.

Lindsey's picture.

He frowned. Big, bold letters above her picture read, "Have you seen me?" But before he had a chance to give it another thought, the picture came to life and spoke to him: "Dras!"

Her voice was quiet and ghostly, her eyes urgent and filled with fear.

"He's in the house!"

Dras jumped a foot and let loose a holler. In his fright, he dropped the open milk carton. The thick white fluid oozed out like blood. Lindsey's lifeless picture looked like the face on a bleeding body.

The room turned ice cold in an instant, and Dras could see his breath leaving him. He left the dying milk carton on the kitchen floor and slammed the refrigerator closed, although somehow he knew the cold had nothing to do with the appliance.

He tried to shake off the encounter, reasoning that he was still dreaming. Sleepwalking was not a foreign concept to Dras. Although most of his nocturnal exploits involved harmless activities like trying to use a pillowcase for a shirt or flipping through channels in the middle of a dead sleep, he decided it wasn't entirely impossible that his sleepwalking adventures had just taken a giant leap into the bizarre.

Backing away, wanting to get as far as possible from the talking milk carton—and fully willing to leave the mess until morning—Dras moved back into the adjoining living room.

As he passed the window, he heard scratching.

He spun toward the window, suddenly wide awake. He remembered hearing that sound once before, when he was little. Scratching. The kids at school—mainly TJ Walker—told him it was the bogeyman coming to steal him away from his home. Those stories used to upset him so much. Jeff, of course, always told him not to worry about it. *It figures. Jeff was probably never scared of the bogeyman once in his entire life.*

Dras watched the window carefully, hoping to see what was causing the noise and feeling like he was nine years old all over again. One time, after the kids at school had ingrained in him the story of the child-stealing bogeyman, Dras heard scratching like this on his window. The sound nearly drove him crazy, until he finally ran to the window and threw back the curtains to meet the laughing faces of TJ Walker and his cohort in elementary school shenanigans, Patch Collins. They'd tricked him, but at least Dras knew the truth. There was no bogeyman.

Right?

In his apartment, he continued to watch the window, trying to piece together the mystery. He was on the second floor, so he knew it wasn't one of the neighbor kids pulling a dumb prank on him. Well, not unless they had a ladder, but he figured the little rug rats weren't that inventive or intent on torturing him— unless it was that weasel Sean Patrick. *Surely not.* He moved toward the window, and the scratching sounded again.

He pulled up the blinds, bathing the apartment in pale blue moonlight and revealing a peaceful neighborhood a story below.

Nothing was even remotely near the window, and no trees grew close enough to scratch it with mischievous branches. He took note of the deserted streets, and when the scratching persisted, he couldn't stop a chill from slithering down his spine.

He told himself that there was nothing to fear. There was nothing outside the window. No bogeyman staring back at him. So what if the image of his dead ex-girlfriend had spoken to him from his milk carton?

I'm dreaming.

Taking a deep, man-sized breath, Dras unlocked the latch on the window and lifted the glass to get a better look at the streets below. Without warning, a cold force exploded in his face, knocking him back. The curtains writhed wildly, whistling as the wind whipped through them. Fighting the gust, Dras slammed the window, quickly latching it. It wasn't until the curtains fell back into place that he realized he was breathing heavily, his breath still unnaturally visible. He stared at the window, trying to determine exactly what happened. He was so intent on watching the window he failed to notice the man in his living room.

The Strange Man.

"Hello, Dras." The monster smiled, his presence turning the air musty and stale.

Dras spun. For a fraction of an instant, he thought it was Rosalyn pulling another, not quite as funny, friendly scare on him. But as his eyes met those of the monster, he knew he was wrong.

The creature was dressed all in black and bound in chains and straps as if contained in a mobile imprisonment, his sickeningly pale features glowing in the dark. At once mesmerizing and terrifying, a crooked nose, the wicked fangs of a beast, and yellow, gleaming eyes captivated Dras.

For what seemed like an eternity Dras stood and gawked at his visitor. All the time the monster remained in the shadows, as if he had control over the light and commanded the moon's rays to avoid him. Never had Dras felt such power emanating from anyone. *Not even Jeff.*

Nor had Dras ever felt such fear. It wasn't the TJ Walker, bully-at-school fear. Dras had faced bullies and authorities alike on more than one occasion over his devil-may-care attitude and wisecracks. What he felt now was different.

It was pure terror. There were no words for it.

He was afraid to blink. The dark and the cold snapped at his feet like snakes, and he could hear the room hissing at him. He must not close his eyes. He feared that if he were to close them and give in to the darkness, even for a blink, he would never open them again. His stomach wanted to expel the left-over pizza he ate while talking to Rosalyn on the phone. His teeth chattered.

Words were no longer an issue. He had no idea what to say to this... *thing* in his house. His mind raced, already beginning to crash, as he tried to think of rational explanations. However, not one emerged.

I'm going to die.

Through stammering lips, he ventured: "Who... who... are you?"

The monster in his living room rose in the air. He perched on the ceiling, where the darkness held him up, his long, encompassing wings constructed of bent light and shadows reaching out across the room. His gaze charmed Dras into a dark trance. The Strange Man smiled as he considered the young man, his yellow eyes glimmering from the dark corner.

"Really, boy"—his slow, raspy voice was the only sound the monster allowed in the room—"can you not tell? I am that which stalks you in your nightmares. Look into your deepest fears, and you will find me staring back at you."

The monster began crawling across the ceiling, suspended in the air by shadows. He hovered closer to Dras and, with extended talons, traced the side of the boy's face.

Never blinking, always smiling, the monster spoke again. "Now do you see me? Now do you know who I am?"

Dras could feel the answer screaming inside him. Yet he was too scared to reply. Now that the Strange Man was so close, he couldn't face the monster and instead stared at the ground, wishing that he would go away. But he didn't.

This is really happening. Reality had found him at last.

His fear was almost too intense to bear. Still, he had to confirm what he suspected. He had to know for sure. Like a frightened child, he confessed, "You're the bogeyman."

The monster in the living room threw back his head with such a cackle Dras shivered uncontrollably. He roared with a hideous, high-pitched laugh, causing the flower left by Rosalyn on Sunday afternoon to wither to its death.

When the Strange Man finished reveling in Dras's despair, he gazed into the boy's eyes. "I am. But what's in a name, really? I've had so many since the day I fell from heaven."

Dras balked, shivering. "You...you're a demon?"

"What's the matter, boy?" the devil chuckled. "Did you think your holy book was all fairy tales? You've been sitting in a pew for years and yet believe very little of your own Christian teaching, yes?" At Dras's silence, the Strange Man shook his head, disgusted by the frail young man before him. "I was right about you. I was right about this place. You're ready for me now."

The devil's come for me. A terrible weight settled on Dras as he remembered his father's sermons and all Jeff's words of warning. *Oh, God, I'm sorry. Please, Jesus, don't let him kill me.*

"What do you want?" Dras forced himself to ask.

The monster pulled back and slithered about and up and down the apartment. He maneuvered around the dirty clothes and magazines piled in various camps on the floor. Taking a good, thoughtful look around him, the monster's yellow eyes spotted something on the wall.

The shadows carried his frail body in the direction of his stare, and the Strange Man regarded a framed picture on the wall. His tapered talons snatched the picture from its place so that he could examine it more closely. It was a picture of Dras and Rosalyn. The monster's eyes fixed on the beautiful young woman. An inscription at the bottom of the picture read:

LOVE YA, GOOFBALL. —ROSALYN

The monster touched the contours of her body. His beady eyes nearly bore a hole into the glass frame. Yes, she was the one he wanted. And only this feeble boy and his love for her stood in the way.

In one exquisite moment the Strange Man thought to eviscerate the boy where he stood, but he knew that was impossible. For whatever purpose, the boy had been marked. Not only by him but—by *Him.* By God.

Repulsive, but true. Yet the Strange Man knew there were other ways to destroy the boy.

"She is a delightful young girl, your friend Rosalyn," he hissed through his fangs. "There's fire in her eyes. I like that."

He recalled seeing her at The Rave Scene. How she danced.

The way her body moved. The way the lights and the music moved for her. How it excited him.

How it made him want to tear her limb from limb.

Dras could only watch the monster holding the picture in his talons. At the mention of Rosalyn, at the very thought of her being involved with the grotesque creature, he wanted to tackle the monster to the ground and fight. He'd never done a brave thing in his life, but there was an uncontrollable and unexpected need to stand up for her. To save her. However, the darkness surrounding his feet pinned him to the floor. Neither had the immobilizing terror left him. He could only wait and watch.

"I have my eye on her, you know," the Strange Man commented.

Dras found himself grinding his teeth, unable to do anything else.

"I had so many plans for this town upon my arrival," the monster continued, "but I must admit I find her distracting. I have roamed the earth and gone back and forth in it and have very rarely seen such a creature as this Rosalyn. Her beauty is unequaled."

Then, almost as an afterthought, the monster sighed, as if sincerely envious of Dras. "You are very lucky to have her in your life."

It was like the kind of remark Dras's grandmother used to make before waxing sentimental and telling stories about the kind of fun she and her friends used to have back in the good old days. It was so conversational. In the space of a heartbeat, the Strange Man seemed harmless.

Then, suddenly, the monster turned his head all the way

around backward and pinned Dras to the wall with an other-worldly stare. With only his glowing eyes visible from the shadows, he said, "Of course, I have been watching you too."

The image of those eyes burned itself into Dras's mind, and he felt that his stomach's persistent desire to rid itself of the pizza was going to overwhelm him.

"Surprised?" the monster cackled. "What did you think, Dras? That no one noticed you? That no one saw how you live your life? Eyes are always watching you, boy. Always watching you."

Then the monster closed his eyes, and the burning glow of the yellow orbs was snuffed out. Now he was completely hidden in the darkness. His raspy voice surrounded Dras.

"You are a bit of a drunkard, aren't you, boy?" The voice seemed to come from nowhere but everywhere at once. Dras shrank back as much as he could, his eyes darting around wildly as he tried to anticipate the monster's next move. He could have sworn that even the shadows were giggling at him, mocking him, as the Strange Man persisted in haunting him. "You must make your father, the honorable Reverend Jack Weldon, so proud. Slipping into church with a hangover and all."

Dras could feel despair swallowing him. The painful shame of his mistakes squeezed him so tightly that tears welled up in his eyes. He hung his head, his stomach twisting into yet more knots as conviction ate into his soul.

The monster was not done yet. Dras could hear pleasure in the Strange Man's voice as he asked, "How does the old adage go? A saint on Sunday, a sinner for the week?"

All of Dras's defenses were peeled away, and he was exposed, raw. When it was only Jeff riding his case about the way he lived, it was no big deal, just a bunch of words from a straight-laced older brother that could easily be tuned out. But to think that some demon was keeping tabs on him, to think that maybe God was actually paying attention too? The burden was so great his knees buckled, and he slumped to the floor, rocking himself, covering his ears, trying to drown out the twitching shadows' constant giggling.

The monster pressed, "Of course, we also have to consider God's side. Imagine how He feels to have a pathetic creature like you claiming to be His child. Oh yes, I know about church camp when you were nine. I was there. Did you know that?"

Dras shut his eyes, trying to wish it all away, but the ghosts of his past refused to disappear. Suddenly the shadows pulled back the veil, ushering in the monster once again. Extending his talons, flicking the air, the monster loomed over him.

"What was it you prayed?" the Strange Man asked as though he needed to conjure the memory from the back of his mind, although Dras somehow knew he did not. *He's been watching me. He's been watching all of us. All this time.*

The demon clapped his hands together and proclaimed to the ceiling, doing a spot-on impersonation of a televangelist, "You prayed, 'Dear, Jesus! Come into my life and save me, Lord! I want to serve You!'"

Slowly, his crooked body twitching, the monster leaned down and whispered into the weeping boy's ear, "Promises, promises."

"Stop it!" Dras screamed, pulling his hair in frustration. "Please...just stop..."

"You are a waste, boy. A hypocrite. And because of the life you have chosen, so very many have rejected God and walked right into my grasp."

"No...no..." Dras sobbed, knowing it was true but trying to wash away his guilt with tears.

Jeff was right. His brother was right.

"Yes! Yes!" the monster urged. "You've helped me for a long time, boy, even though you may not have been aware of it. And now, there is one more thing I require of you."

Dras looked up, his eyes wide with fear. "What?"

The Strange Man leaned closer with a grin. "I want you to stay out of my way. I have grown quite fond of your friend Rosalyn, and I mean to make her mine. You know you cannot stop me, yes?"

Silence. Unending cold. Dras nodded, his fear taking over. "Yes."

"You cannot stop me. And what if you tried? Who would believe you? What good would your testimony be? You are a liar. A fool. Look at you!"

It was too much for Dras. Shock set in. His muscles grew so tense he felt he might pass out. The monster was relentless, tearing away Dras's heart piece by piece, destroying him with his words. And the cold, the punishing cold...

Dras's vision began to blur. He was losing it. *No.* He had to fight. The fear of closing his eyes, of death, was too great.

I don't want to die.

"What do you want me to do?" Dras asked weakly, his body growing colder and colder. Numb. He wondered if he would see Lindsey soon.

"It's very simple. Leave. Get out of Greensboro by night-fall"—the Strange Man's smile had completely vanished—"or I'll come looking for you."

Dras shuddered, his breath leaving his body in intervals that were farther and farther apart. With great effort, he looked up to see the monster's face two inches before him. He was so deeply terrified and shocked by now that the Strange Man's proximity did not even cause him to flinch.

"But what about Rosalyn?"

"She's no longer your concern," the monster hissed. "She belongs to me now."

Dras's mind grew dim as everything blurred together surreally. A spell had been cast on him, and the lines of clarity were fuzzy. He was having trouble remembering his own name as the darkness bathed him in misery.

"N–no..." He fought to protest, but his will was breaking. Feebly, he whimpered, "God—"

The monster jerked. With long, sharpened claws he clutched Dras's chin. The jolt resonated throughout Dras's insides, and he didn't know how much longer he could keep from vomiting. His ears popped, and his knees ached with fatigue.

"God! You call on God?" the Strange Man spat. "What would God want with you? You turned your back on Him long ago. Do you really think He wants you now? If you want to beg a god for mercy, beg *me*." Green drool dripped from the Strange Man's fangs. Then, slowly, his animalistic nature softened, revealing more of the gentlemanly manner he exhibited at the beginning of Dras's horrible nightmare. "I've given you your only hope for salvation. Leave town and save your friend. Or stay here and suffer hell with me. Let's leave God out of this, shall we?"

Crying, Dras begged, "OK. Please, don't hurt me..."

"Pathetic," the Strange Man said. He stood, abruptly loosening his hold on Dras. "Now, let's make sure we understand each other. You tell a soul what we've discussed, and our deal is off. If you let anyone find out about me, you will never be able to run far enough to escape me. Am I clear?"

With his last ounce of strength, Dras nodded, his body fighting to hang on. "Y–yes...."

Too weak to go any further, he collapsed. The monster stood over him, pleased.

Then the Strange Man was gone, taking the shadows with him.

Dras sprang off his couch, failing to suppress a scream. His heart raced, and he was covered in a cold sweat. He looked wildly around the room and realized that morning had arrived. In fact, the television was still on, frozen on the blank blue screen, just as he'd left it the night before. He had never turned it off.

Quickly, he craned his head over the couch and looked into the kitchen. The milk carton was gone, and the floor was clean. Panting, still trying to recover, he struggled to wrap his mind around what had happened.

"It was a dream." Euphoria settling in, Dras jumped to his feet and shouted, "Ha! It was just a dream!"

On top of the television, he noticed the empty case for *She-Vampires From Mars* and reasoned that he just scared himself silly. That was all. A dream brought on by too much leftover pizza and a bad B movie.

His breathing calmed, and he flopped back down on his couch, leaning his head back and grinning with relief. He couldn't help but chuckle at how scared he'd been.

What a crazy dream.

Then he noticed Rosalyn's flower. It was withered. Dead.

"Aw, nuts."

CHAPTER FIFTEEN

DRAS REALIZED HE'D slept late. The moment he awoke, he was out the door. There was only one thing on his mind: Rosalyn.

For a fraction of a second, he'd considered living up to his end of the Strange Man's bargain and hightailing it out of town for parts unknown and less demon-infested. But despite the fact that his nerves frayed at the thought of staying behind and incurring the demon's wrath, Dras knew he couldn't do that to Rosalyn. He couldn't leave her behind to face this thing alone.

Perhaps inspired by a newly purchased and overpriced Snake Eyes action figure, Dras determined to save the day.

His single-mindedness was further proven by the fact that he'd made it a whole block on his bicycle before he noticed that in his haste to save his friend from the clutches of the hell-beast, he had forgotten to put on pants. No matter. He had a job to do.

Pantsless and determined, he continued pedaling toward Rosalyn's apartment.

"OK," he said as he raced on the sidewalk, trying to calm himself back to rational thought, "demons are real. Check. Demons. *Real* demons."

The concept didn't sound any less far-fetched when repeated. Yesterday, demons and monsters were *fun* things—guys in makeup and prosthetics in all of his favorite movies. Now they had crossed the fourth wall and were asserting themselves into his life with deadly intent. His mind fell into the pool of nostalgia, and he waded through memories of too many late nights indulging in Dead Ed Ghoulie's *Midnight Matinee* on TV. He counted all the ways to kill the fictional monsters he had seen on the screen and in stories he'd heard: stakes, holy water, silver bullets, sunlight. But would any of that stuff work on the Strange Man? Dras didn't know, and he wasn't about to gamble with Rosalyn's life. No, he needed to know the truth. *Time to stop living in a comic book, Dras.*

Hopping a curb, his vision blurry with stress and concentration, Dras nearly toppled a bouncy raven-haired beauty on her midmorning jog with her dog.

"Hey! Watch it, creep!" She leapt out of his way. The dog yipped at the rude interruption.

Dras ignored them. "Get a grip, Dras. Real demons. Real, live ones. They're after Rosalyn. Think. *Think.* What to do? What to do?"

Glancing up to round a corner, Dras's heart froze as he faced the word *devil* in bold, black letters. He nearly yelped, fearing that the Strange Man was somehow sending him subliminal messages, and slid the bike to a halt. A moment later, Dras realized he was standing in front of his brother's church and that the message was only part of a marquee. The Good Church of the Faithful's groundskeeper—Dras had no idea what his name was—had a worn box of black plastic letters and had just finished assembling them into a message.

Transfixed, Dras read the message in its entirety:

The reason the Son of God appeared was to destroy the devil's work. —1 John 3:8

Dras stepped off his bike and let it topple to the ground. He stumbled toward the words on the marquee, his heart pounding a steady rhythm in his chest. "Demons are real," he breathed, barely cognizant of the bewildered look he was getting from the groundskeeper. "God's real too." *Exactly.* This insanity had to go both ways. If he was facing a devil, then he had to go to God. *The reason the Son of God appeared…*

"Wait!" he shouted, getting it. "Jesus! Yeah!" Calming, he thought it through, forming a plan. "Yeah," he grinned, nodding. "Yeah, OK."

Containing a laugh, he stepped to his bike, righted it, and was off once more, with the groundskeeper calling behind him, "Boy, you know you ain't got any pants on?"

There was a knock on Rosalyn's door. It was two o'clock in the afternoon.

Rosalyn was immersed in her studies when she heard the rapping. She had gone to a morning class, but by the time Dras arrived, she was off for the rest of the day, left to sit at her kitchen table and ponder the complexities of college algebra. The sudden interruption was a welcome change of events.

The knocking was persistent and hurried. She could hear Dras calling from the other side of the door.

"Rosalyn! *Rosalyn!*"

She had no clue what was so urgent, but she was about to find out. Laying her pencil on her open book and walking to the door in no immediate hurry, she moaned, "I'm coming. I'm coming."

"Yes?" she asked casually as she unlocked the deadbolt and opened the door. Her eyes fell on Dras's bare legs. She cracked a smile. "Nice boxers."

As she faced him, expecting that he was pulling another one of his jokes with no clear punch line, she noticed that he looked horrible. His eyes were wide and panicked. Sweat beaded on his forehead, and he was out of breath.

Dras stormed through the doorway like a hurricane, ignoring Rosalyn. He scanned the room.

"What are you looking for?"

Taking a small but long overdue breath, he turned to his friend, grabbed her upper arms, and stared into her face with worry and compassion. "Are you OK?"

She gave him a quizzical look. "Yeah. Why wouldn't I be?"

"Did anyone come by? Did anything happen? Anything strange?"

"Like you barging in here in your underwear all wigged out and asking me strange questions?"

Dras faced her suspicious eyes. He realized how crazy the situation must seem. He calmly released her arms and tried to relax, now sure of her safety.

Thank You, God, that she's OK.

Once Dras relinquished his hold, Rosalyn moved past him and headed back to her books. "I was just studying. I've got my last final coming up. Ace this one, and I can put this semester behind me."

She seemed confident in her scholarly ability. Dras looked at her as she sat at the table, going back to work. "So, yeah. The pants? Did you forget to do laundry again, or is this some new fashion trend?" She flipped through the pages of her book without looking up.

How can she keep studying for some stupid algebra test when there's an unholy monstrosity out there that wants her soul? Demons are real! With all of the hidden evils in the world stalking lost souls, he didn't see how she could be concerned with something as mundane as math. *How can she not see?* Then he realized that he had not seen either, even though Jeff tried time after time to warn him. *Why didn't I listen? Why was I so stubborn?*

He stared at Rosalyn as she thumbed through the pages of her algebra book, completely oblivious to the horror that was coming for her. For the first time he grasped the enormity of the challenge that lay ahead of him. He searched his mind but could think of no way to convince Rosalyn, of all people, that an honest-to-goodness demon was out to get her. She was level-headed, a realist, and she most certainly did not believe in angels and devils waging war for human souls. Maybe she didn't even believe in God. Things like that just didn't factor into her life. Worst of all, Dras knew that he was partly to blame for her lack of convictions. After all, he was raised on the Bible. His family talked to him about God every day. Dras had been exposed to the truth, yet he chose to ignore it.

Why? Because it was an inconvenience? He sullenly understood. *If I had really thought about it, really admitted that I knew that those things in the Bible were true, I would've had to live life a lot differently. But I didn't do that. Because I was selfish.*

And now Rosalyn is paying for that, moron, he scolded himself. *You should have told her all this already. Maybe it's too late now.*

The monster was already circling her, preparing to make his move. Dras looked at Rosalyn and remembered all the times she'd been there for him. He knew he had to try.

Even if it cost him his life.

It's time to grow up, Dras, and maybe, just maybe, finally make Jack Weldon proud.

As he settled this decision, gathering up what little reserves of courage he had left, Dras failed to notice that he was pacing.

He was so lost in thought that he did not see Rosalyn lift her head from the book and watch him, ready for him to stop at any moment.

At first, Rosalyn figured Dras stopped by to keep her company, and she appreciated the gesture. However, the more he paced, the more nervous he made her. He had barely spoken three sentences to her since he came in. And now he was just pacing. Her heart began to pound as she wondered if his strange behavior had something to do with Sunday. With the kiss. Maybe they were about to have "the talk."

Oh, no...

She could take it no longer. Taking a deep breath and setting her pencil aside, she rolled her eyes at him, trying to appear casual. "You're wearing a hole in my carpet."

Dras continued to pace, but her words broke him from his reverie. "Sorry."

She smiled. "Could you change your pattern or something? You're making me seasick."

Dras stopped but couldn't look at her. *This is it.* The time had come, and he had to warn her. Suddenly all the sermons he sat through in his life came flooding back to him. He didn't know much, but he felt certain that if the Strange Man was, indeed, a demon, then—like the marquee said—the Son of God was the one Rosalyn needed on her side.

If only I knew how to convince her of that. He sighed, not knowing where to begin. *If only Jeff were here. He'd know what to do. But Jeff's not here; you are, goof. So don't screw it up.*

"I need to talk to you."

Rosalyn raised an eyebrow. "About?"

Dras faced her, then looked away. He began to sweat and hoped he could form the words, trying hard to recall what little Scripture he remembered from his youth. Coming up empty, he stammered, "Something you're probably not going to want to hear."

Rosalyn's throat tightened. She feared the worst. Hoping Dras was just kidding around, as usual, she poked back. "That's probably not the best way to begin a conversation. Why not try, 'Good news!' or 'Something great just happened!' I think you'll find you'll get better results that way."

She giggled until Dras turned to face her. His eyes were intense and desperate. She had never seen him like this before. He looked at her dead on with an indescribable fear in his eyes.

"I'm serious," he said gravely.

Rosalyn felt more than a little uncomfortable under the convicting stare of her best friend. Clearly their "fun only" rule was about to be broken. The air in the room changed, and she knew they were about to have a serious talk. Perhaps the most serious talk of their whole relationship.

She nervously joked to hide her worry. "Apparently. Do you need to lie down? I know it's kind of startling the first time."

Dras wasn't laughing.

His eyes were incredibly urgent, and for a moment the two of them relived the awkwardness they shared on Sunday afternoon. That feeling that things were too real. Too intense.

It terrified her, even though a part of her welcomed it. Wanted it so bad.

"Have you ever thought about...the Lord?" Dras began, immediately cringing.

OK. Didn't see that one coming.

"The Lord?"

"Jesus Christ." Dras pointed to the ceiling.

Rosalyn paused for a long moment. It was the strangest feeling, like her heart skipped a beat. And out of nowhere, there was the slightest hint of a warm sensation in her heart. She quickly dismissed it. *This is ridiculous.*

"You're serious?" she said, her tone cynical.

Dras nodded solemnly. With all of the sincerity he had to offer, he said, "More than ever."

Rosalyn studied him, staring into his eyes, trying to see if it was a prank or if something had really happened to Dras, something to change him and cause him to be serious and real when he had avoided reality all his life. *What could have possibly happened to change him overnight?*

She sighed. "Dras," she pleaded, "one of the great things about us is that we stay away from religion and politics. Remember? Let's face it: you were the one who always said that people could believe whatever they want to believe. Right?"

"That's changed," Dras said, sounding sure of himself. "I've changed."

Rosalyn smirked. "Since yesterday?"

Despite her discrediting expression, which Dras knew he fully deserved, he replied, "Yes."

Here it goes, Dras thought. His moment had arrived. He had no idea how to explain his faith to her. He barely understood it himself. All he had at his disposal were some words and catch-phrases he picked up in bits and pieces of his father's and Jeff's sermons. Now he wished he had picked up a Bible before he rushed over here in his underwear, assuming he even owned one.

Dras was ashamed at how unprepared he was, at the years he'd wasted living his life only for himself. Suddenly all the things that seemed so much more important than God—the parties, the girls, the mindless hours watching television—none of it meant anything. It all came down to this: Rosalyn was lost and living apart from God.

Dras had always known it deep down, but he never thought about it or did anything to try to show Rosalyn the truth about her spiritual condition. Now the devil had come to collect, and if Rosalyn didn't change, there wouldn't be anything that anyone on the face of the planet could do to help her.

Me included.

Bracing himself, he began. "Jesus Christ loves you, Rosalyn," he said.

Even as the words left his mouth, Dras knew they sounded hollow and rehearsed. *What reason does Rosalyn have to believe me? It's not like she's ever seen me act like I believe any of this stuff.* Still, he had to press on. The crisis was too serious for him to waste time wallowing in self-pity.

He winced, embarrassed, yet continued. "He loves you. He went to a cross and, um, died for your sins."

Rosalyn interrupted him. "What are you doing?" Her tone was offensive. "Are you Jehovah-Witnessing me?"

Dras's face flushed. The interruption flustered him, and he lost his train of thought, which he was having a hard enough time keeping on the tracks as it was.

He backtracked and tried again. "Listen. This is important."

Rosalyn didn't seem to be listening. She picked up her pencil and went back to studying.

"So is college algebra, Dras." She dismissed him as though this were just a phase Dras was going through and by tomorrow morning it would wear off. But Dras saw the hard set in her face and knew how betrayed she must feel. She retaliated, "And, unlike you, I don't want to flunk out of college and be a townie for the rest of my life."

That hurt. Jeff's words came back to haunt Dras. "Have you ever stopped to think about who your life is affecting?"

Oh, Rosalyn...I'm so sorry...

Dras hung his head, his heart breaking. All of his life he could always count on Rosalyn. Now, when it mattered most, he had failed her.

He could feel his eyes tearing up, because he realized he loved her so much, more than he ever knew, yet he was the one who had hurt her most. With a heavy heart, he said, "None of that will matter if you go to hell."

Rosalyn fumed.

She slammed her pencil down on her book. Scooting the chair back with an abrupt squeak, she stood. Dras took a step back. Rosalyn's face was a mask of hurt and anger.

"What right do *you* have to tell *me* I'm going to hell?" she shouted.

"Wait, I'm sorry. That came out wrong. I'm new at this. I didn't mean it like—"

She cut him off, visibly holding back her pain. "You think because you manage to drag yourself to church every once in a while or just because your dad's a preacher, you're better than me?"

Dras couldn't look at her. He turned away, staring into the distance.

"Of course not," he said lamely.

"News flash! Who's the one who drags you home after you've gotten wasted? You hypocrite!"

All the things she'd kept bottled inside were exploding now. All the years she had taken care of him without so much as a thank-you had created a resentment he never knew was there. "To think you act the way you do, and *I'm* the one people called Trysdale Trash? Now *you* want to get holy on *me*?" Tears welled up in her dark, soulful eyes.

"What right do you have?" Rosalyn said quietly, as if to scream any more would break her.

It killed Dras to see her angry like this. In a way he welcomed the punishment she'd heaped on him because his conscience was so burdened by it all. It felt like a kind of twisted penance. But to see her punished too was something he could not allow. He could not stand to see her suffer because of him.

Desperate to make things right, Dras tried to press on. "I have no right. I know that. I've done horrible things, and I took God for granted. I took you for granted too. You've always been there for me, and I—" His voice trailed off. He was unable to finish the thought. He tried to start over. "But you've got to believe me. I've changed. And I can't take back all the things I did or said, but I want to make things right. I don't want you to—"

Rosalyn sniffled, forcing herself not to cry in front of him. Through gritted teeth, she blurted out, "Maybe you should worry about yourself before you start worrying about me. That's what you're good at."

Unable to bear one more second looking into his eyes, she walked away and sat back down, focusing her gaze on her algebra book. Now that she wasn't facing Dras, she wiped away a tear. Speaking in a voice that was detached and cold, "You should leave. I have a lot of studying to do."

She picked up her pencil and returned to work, putting an end to the conversation by turning her back to him.

He watched her sadly, wondering if there was anything more he could say. Faced with everything he'd done and everything that had happened, there was only one thing *to* say.

"I'm sorry."

He paused, as if waiting for a response, any response. Rosalyn was finished, though. She said nothing. She wouldn't even look at him. Dras turned his back in disgrace and walked out. From the other side of the door, he could hear her softly weeping.

Outside, Dras exited Rosalyn's apartment building, miserable and alone, hating himself for a lifetime wasted.

And still in his boxers.

Passersby poked each other and giggled when they saw him. A week ago Dras himself would have found the situation hysterical.

But Dras Weldon was no longer laughing.

After putting on some much-needed pants, Dras went to sit outside Smokey's, the neighborhood bar and grill, for the rest of the afternoon. There were always chairs outside, usually on opposite ends of a chess set where old men sat and gossiped while testing each other's wits.

Dras sat alone.

He sat there in the heart of town, the place where he grew up, and watched people run back and forth, living their lives. All of them—most of them at the very least—completely unaware that a monster had come to Greensboro.

Dras's eyes were dark and weary, reflecting the anguish in his heart.

Rosalyn hadn't listened to him. He knew that after the way

he had lived for so many years she had no reason to put any stock in what he had to say about God or morality. Still, she remained in danger, and Dras had to help her. He just had no idea what to do next.

But he knew someone who might.

CHAPTER SIXTEEN

ORANGE SKIES SIGNALED the onset of twilight as Dras pulled his bike into his parents' yard. The Widow Cromwell, a frail waif of a thing, stood across the street, tending to her petunias. Dras hopped off his bike and let it fall on his parents' lawn, the lawn that Jeff always kept mowed and manicured. He looked across the street, as he always did, and threw a hand to the air.

"Hey, Ms. Cromwell!"

The elderly woman regarded him with a frown and shook her head disapprovingly. She'd had it out for Dras ever since he pedaled his bike through her garden on his way to school for thirteen years. He thought to go over and apologize for all the times he'd aggravated her, but he had something else to do right now.

Save Rosalyn.

Slipping around back, he opened the screen door to his parents' porch and pushed his way through the wooden door and into the kitchen. His mother was cooking supper, and judging by the portions, it looked like Louise Weldon was eating alone tonight.

"Hey, Mom," he greeted her in a short, strictly business tone.

Dras usually made it a point to sound extra cheery when visiting his parents. That was because he usually wanted money. Now he just wanted help.

Startled, his mother nearly dropped her hot skillet and fried potatoes all over the kitchen floor. Dras held out his hands, prepared to catch her should she tip.

"Sorry. Didn't mean to scare you."

"Dras," she said, catching her breath, finally able to smile. "I wasn't expecting you tonight." Then, as if a revelation had dawned on her, she frowned and set the skillet back on the stove. Wiping her hands on her pants leg, she reached for her purse, which was on the counter. "How much do you need?" she asked matter-of-factly.

Dras guffawed, totally blown away by the insinuation. "Mom, I don't just come over whenever I need money."

His mother chewed her lip, as if pondering how best to break the truth to him. But she didn't have to say anything; her expression told him everything.

With her silence Dras reached his lowest point.

That's all I am to them. A screwup.

"I'm not here for money," he said forcefully, angered by the reputation he'd built for himself.

Surprised, his mother asked, "What's wrong?"

Dras took a courageous breath. "I need to talk to Dad."

Moments later, in the calm coziness of the Weldon family living room, Louise Weldon spoke quietly to her youngest son.

"He had another spell today. He's been asleep most of the afternoon."

Dras turned to her hesitantly. "Is it OK if I—"

His mother's eyes lit up. "Sure. He'll be glad to see you."

She patted her son on the shoulder, leaving him alone with his father.

Dras studied the sleeping man as if he'd never seen him before. He realized then that he'd never actually thought of his dad as a person. For that matter, he usually just thought of him as a go-to guy when he needed someone to fix things. His dad was good at fixing things. Jack Weldon was a strong man once. Able to do anything. Fix any toy. Leap tall buildings in a single bound. Outrun a bullet.

But he couldn't outrun bad health.

Dras remembered the good old days, before his dad got sick.

When Dras was a kid, his father worked in the construction business building houses, as he had since he was sixteen. Of course, he was a pastor too. That was his passion, but the small congregation at the Good Church of the Faithful couldn't afford to pay him a full-time salary, so he kept on doing what he knew how to do, working with his hands. Dras thought back to the many nights his dad stayed up late preparing sermons or visiting sick people, only to rise before dawn the next morning and be at a job site. He never complained.

When Dras was fifteen, his father suddenly started complaining—complaining of aches and pains in his bones. The doctors diagnosed him with osteoarthritis, meaning the cartilage cushioning his bones was degenerating. There was nothing that could be done, so his father carried on as best he could despite the pain. More and more he was bedridden and finally had to give up the pulpit, passing on the pastor legacy to Jeff. At the time, Dras worried more about whether his dad would still be able to drive him to the big comic book store in Russellville to pick up hard-to-find back issues of *The Weird Avenger*. Looking back, he knew that losing the ability to be a pastor had really hurt his dad.

But he didn't lose faith. He didn't give up.

Things worsened even more for his father when, three months ago, the doctors discovered that his problems were more serious than arthritis. He had chondrosarcoma. Bone cancer. They said that if he lived through the year, he should feel lucky.

After that, Dras rarely saw his dad awake. The doctors confessed there was little they could do at this stage. Even chemotherapy or radiation was not considered very effective, so his father spent most of the time on painkillers, confined to a recliner.

Dras gazed down at the old man, sleeping and pale, and found himself afraid to approach him, afraid to disturb him or cause him any more grief. He felt he'd spent a lifetime causing his father grief, bringing shame to the family name. He wasn't responsible like Jeff, and he certainly wasn't fit to walk in his father's footsteps as a leader in the church.

Maybe he doesn't even want me around anymore.

Dras wouldn't blame him if he didn't.

He thought again of all the hardships his dad had faced, all the tight finances and stress-filled days of construction dead-lines and caring for the people of his church, all the sickness and loss of energy. Still, Jack Weldon had faith that even after all he'd been through God was good. And if he hadn't given up on God—*Then maybe he hasn't given up on me.*

Careful not to get too close or bother his father too much, Dras knelt at his father's side and whispered, "Hey, Dad. It's me, Dras."

Tears started rolling, and Dras couldn't stop them. He had come to the end of himself and found that he didn't know anything anymore.

"I don't want to wake you up," Dras said. "I just...I need to talk to you."

As his father continued sleeping, Dras poured out his heart.

"I'm in big trouble, Dad. You know, all my life you tried to tell me about what it means to be a man. You told me that a man ought to love God first, then his family, then himself. I...I haven't been too good at doing that. Jeff turned out a lot better than I did. He's great, you know? Always looking out for me..."

Dras wiped his cheeks.

"I didn't want to be like that. I always wanted to do my own thing no matter who got hurt. But...but now I'm starting to see where that's getting me, and...I'm tired of running, Dad. I'm really sorry for not coming to see you like I should, and I need you to forgive me. I'm ready to grow up now, Dad. I'm ready to be a man."

Overcome with emotion, Dras took hold of his father's brittle hand, holding it close to his face and crying into it, finally repentant, when he heard, "Dras?"

Drying his face, Dras looked up to see his father awake and smiling at him.

Dras smiled back. "Hey, Dad."

"Been awhile, son. Welcome home."

Dras threw himself onto his father, hugging him and crying. Jack Weldon held his son close, patting him on the back, welcoming him with unconditional love.

Dras held open the door, helping his father onto the front porch. His parents' old swing overlooked the well-kept neighborhood, where wrought iron streetlamps flickered in the face of the approaching dark. As gently as he could manage, Dras lowered his sick father into the creaking swing. The old man gave an exhausted sigh. Dras realized how much strength the move had cost his dad, but his father was determined to get out into fresh air for at least a few precious moments—moments he would spend with his youngest son discussing what was bothering the boy.

Breathing heavily, worn from the exertion of nearly carrying a grown man, Dras braced himself against the porch railing, the lush trees in the yard rustling in the breeze behind him.

Once his father managed to catch his breath, he forced himself to sit up despite the pain. Jack Weldon appraised his boy, ready to get to business. "So, what's troubling you, son?"

Dras scratched the back of his head in that way he often did when he was anxious about talking to his father. Usually father and son communicated only when the son wanted something, and Dras knew now was no different.

But it is *different*, he told himself. *This is important. Really, really important.*

Still, Dras struggled with how to begin. Somehow he figured telling his father outright that an ancient demon was gunning for him might be a tough sell, but he desperately wanted his father's advice. He settled for an edited version of his sordid tale.

"I feel like there's something God wants me to do. No—" he corrected himself—"no, I know there's something God wants me to do."

Of that much he was sure. Rosalyn was in trouble, and there was absolutely no doubt in Dras's heart that he was the one to help her. His only doubt concerned how he could help her.

His father nodded thoughtfully, his years of pastoral counseling showing. "How can I help?"

Dras nearly fainted. It was as though Rambo had just offered to ride shotgun with him into war. As much as Dras wanted to hide under his bed and let Daddy fight this battle for him, Dras knew his father was barely able to stand on some days, let alone deal with whatever horrors the Strange Man could unleash. He couldn't ask his dad to do that, not after spending the last twenty-two years making him solve his problems. No, Dras had someone else in mind who could fight by his side, but that was for later. Right now he just needed some wisdom from Jack Weldon: Spiritual Commando.

"What if it's dangerous?" Dras asked, his heart pounding.

Jack replied matter-of-factly, "Serving the Lord usually is."

"Yeah?"

The old man nodded, his sagely blue eyes terrifying and encouraging all at the same time. "Jesus told His disciples to consider the cost of following Him. Salvation is a free gift, but the responsibility that comes with it can cost us everything— our friends, our families, sometimes our lives. Christ gave up everything for us, and He expects no less from His followers."

"But how can I do it, Dad?" Dras pleaded, losing his cool when faced with the enormity of what he had to do. "I'm terrified."

His father smiled, the corners of his mouth crinkling. "If God's called you to do something, son, then He'll be with you. He'll give you everything you need to accomplish what He's put before you. God never gives us more than we can handle."

Dras heard his father's words, but it did little to erase the image in his mind's eye of the Strange Man leering at him. All around him the dying light reminded him that night was falling, and with it, judgment was coming for his rebellion against the demon. In the sunlight he'd been bold, fueled by adrenaline to warn Rosalyn. But now there was only the petrifying certainty that his warning would come at a price. *What am I gonna do?*

Suddenly Dras felt his father's hand on his knee. His father grinned warmly despite the pain the gesture caused him. "Dras," he charged him, his voice strong and bold, "don't be afraid."

Dras's eyes broke from his father's stern gaze, and he looked out over the darkening horizon, listening for hellhounds or zombie moans or anything that might signal the Strange Man's retaliation. "What about...demons?"

His father's brow wrinkled as he half grinned, looking just like Jeff as he did so. "What about 'em?"

Dras folded his arms nervously. "I mean, like, um...metaphorically. Let's just say 'bad things.' Well, I mean, if you're serving God like He wants, then you're safe, right?"

His father leaned back, wincing only slightly, and snorted, "Son, if my life's any indication, it's been the exact opposite."

Dras went white. "Yeah?"

"If you're standing up for God, you'd better believe the devil'll throw everything at you to knock you down."

"Oh." Dras slumped.

"Doing the right thing is rarely easy. But you can't let that stop you if you've got something important to do, Dras. You've got to hold your ground, no matter what." His father chuckled, delicately craning his neck to the door to make sure his wife wasn't eavesdropping. He turned back to his son, a hint of long-dormant mischief in his eye. Wearing an expression that reminded Dras a lot of himself, his father confided, "Don't tell your mother I said this, but...sometimes to serve the Lord, you've got to raise a little Cain."

Dras considered the statement as cold shadows enveloped Greensboro, heralding what he knew could be a night of blood and misery.

Maybe my last night.

He reflected on his father's earlier words about counting the cost of following Christ. Then he thought of Rosalyn and what would happen to her if he didn't take a stand.

Suddenly all fear left him, replaced by a simmering determination.

Let hell come. Dras gritted his teeth, his soul afire. *I'm ready.*

CHAPTER SEVENTEEN

SABELLA WELDON COULD wash dishes in her sleep.

After all, she had been washing dishes and cooking and cleaning since she was five years old, after her mother abandoned her and her father and four brothers. Now the tasks were second nature to her. Sometimes she wondered if she could get through the day without doing something. Jeff was the same way, driven and practical, which was why, she supposed, they were perfect for each other.

As she scrubbed the pan for the night's meat loaf, she recalled that Jeff barely touched his supper. Granted, meat loaf wasn't the man's favorite, but Jeff would never tell her that. He always smiled and ate what she served him. Truthfully, she didn't really care for meat loaf, either. She just wanted to see how long he would persist in his stubbornness before he finally broke down and confessed his distaste of the dish to her. But tonight Jeff avoided not only the meat loaf but also the mashed potatoes, the corn, and the fluffy dinner rolls. Isabella knew there was something on her husband's mind. Since the night of the storm he had been distant and deep in thought, almost as if he were expecting something.

Now he sat outside in the swing on the back porch, slowly rocking back and forth, watching the tranquil waters of Grover's Pond. Sullen and reflective, he sipped a cup of coffee, and Isabella considered the chances that he would tell her what was bothering him if she asked. She decided to give it a shot.

After draining the last of the soapy water and drying her

hands with a towel, Isabella opened the screen door and left the kitchen behind to join her pensive husband on the swing.

"What are you thinking about?" she asked, sliding her shoulder beneath his arm and fixing her eyes on the peaceful pond, the sun safely down and the stars beginning to appear.

"Ah, nothing," he muttered, clearly lying.

"Come on," she playfully coaxed him.

He groaned, the sound he always made when Isabella finally convinced him to reveal his feelings. He said, "Do you ever wonder how we got here?"

"What do you mean?" she asked, turning away from the pond and looking only at him, ready to give him her full attention.

"In high school, I barely even knew you existed."

"Well, I was a band geek, and you were too busy raging against the machine with Kyle Rogers."

Jeff smirked, his eyes twinkling as he countered, "Maybe if you'd taken your attention off Scott Townsend for a second—"

Isabella rolled her eyes, laughing. "Oh, don't get me started."

"Do you ever think about what your life might have been like if you'd left with him to go to the City?"

"No," Isabella replied emphatically. "I don't think I would have lasted long as the wife of a high-society concert oboist, if that's even what he ended up doing. I'm much happier being a humble pastor's wife in Greensboro."

"But just think," Jeff continued. "If my dad hadn't dragged me to your dad's house to help him build his barn seven years ago—"

"Then we never would have gone on that first date, watched that awful movie, and gotten married six months later."

She snuggled closer to him. Jeff set his coffee cup on the porch floor so both hands were free to hug her. He sighed, reliving so many good memories. "None of this would have happened."

She nudged him in the ribs. "You're not starting to have regrets?"

He chuckled. "No, no. It just blows my mind, that's all. I never thought I'd be married to the most wonderful, smart, sexy—"

"Keep going," she grinned.

"Talented, sophisticated...can I stop yet?"

"If you must."

"We've got this great life, and I didn't do anything to deserve it. It just kind of fell in my lap."

"True," Isabella agreed, nuzzling him and enjoying the quiet of the evening. "We're really blessed. God's been good to us."

"It just seems"—Jeff searched for the words, or maybe just the courage to say them—"so fragile. We've had things good for so long and now...I don't know. Now I'm suddenly afraid it's all going to go away."

Isabella sat up a bit straighter, eyeing the side of his face, fixing her gaze on his clenched jaw and the trembling fear in his eye. "Baby, what's wrong?"

Jeff remained quiet—scarily so—but finally broke the moment with a sad grin. "Nothing." Isabella placed her hand over his and gave it a gentle squeeze.

From their cozy spot on the back porch swing, the couple heard a knock on the front door.

"Who could that be?" Isabella asked, looking inside the house.

It was almost eight o'clock. They didn't usually have visitors this late in the evening unless someone from the church needed something.

Jeff got up to greet their guest.

On the other side of the storm door, backed by the starry skies, stood none other than Dras. The two brothers viewed each other for the first time since their argument after church on Sunday. Jeff still had not entirely recovered from the hurtful things Dras had said. Nonetheless, he refrained from giving in to the impulse to slam the door in his brother's face.

"Jeff," Dras sounded serious and purposeful, "I need to talk to you."

By now Isabella had followed Jeff into the living room, curious as to who their visitor could be. When she saw it was Dras, Jeff noticed she grew more curious.

"What do you want, Dras?" Jeff left no room for friendly chitchat. Deep inside he really did want to be kinder to Dras, but the very sight of his brother infuriated him.

"Can I come in?"

Dras stood before the door expectantly. Jeff looked at him for a moment, weighing his options. Finally he set his jaw and stepped aside, allowing his brother passage. Dras walked in and gave a quick nod to Isabella.

Jeff saw something in his brother's eyes that he had never seen before: concern. However, he didn't think about it for long. Instead he saw only his screwup brother who said some hateful things a few days ago and who seemed utterly incapable of any action that was not selfish and self-destructive. Dras never made house calls unless he wanted something. Usually money.

"I need your help," Dras confessed to his brother as Jeff closed the door.

"Surprise, surprise." Jeff's voice dripped with sarcasm. He knew that he should care. Not only that, he wanted to care. But when it came to Dras, a lifetime of disappointment had left him jaded.

Overlooking the remark, Dras looked his brother square in the eye and leveled with him. "Rosalyn is in trouble."

Suddenly concerned, Jeff tried to look past his feelings toward his brother for the moment and be cooperative. He folded his arms. "What happened?"

"Nothing," Dras assured him. "Yet."

Dras sighed. "Look, this is going to sound crazy, OK? But you're the only one who can help me now. You *have* to help."

Pacing, Dras began. "Last night, some…guy came to my apartment. He was this man. This *strange* man. And he…he said that he wanted Rosalyn."

Jeff unfolded his arms. "What?"

Isabella kept her cool. "What do you mean?"

Dras's eyes wandered around the room. Running his hands through his disheveled hair, Dras let out a long, exhausted breath and tried to make himself understood with as little confusion as possible. "You should have seen this guy, Jeff. He—" Dras winced, but he forced himself to voice the ridiculous—"he was like a devil, or he was the devil, I'm not sure which. And really, I don't think I want to know. But he—"

"Wait a minute."

Jeff—ever disbelieving and beginning to think this was a joke—demanded, "What are you talking about?"

"Remember when we were little and we used to hear those stories about the bogeyman? This is the guy! I'm serious, man, he's like everything we were ever afraid of as kids, all rolled into one. You've got to believe me."

The bogeyman.

Jeff froze and felt like he needed to sit down or throw up. Maybe both.

Surely Dras couldn't know the thoughts and fears that had been running through his mind since the storm, the sense that something lurked just out of sight. The shock of hearing his brother speak his worst fear aloud paralyzed him, and he found it difficult to concentrate.

Is this my sign, God? No...no, I'm not ready. I don't want this!

"He's after Rosalyn now," Dras blurted. "I don't know why or what for. I don't understand what's going on here. Maybe he came with the storm. He had to come with the storm. That's when things started getting weird around here. First Lindsey disappears, and now this? All I know is that he's here in Greensboro, and he wants Rosalyn. We have to stop him, Jeff!"

Jeff saw truth in Dras's eyes. Conviction filled him, and although Jeff wasn't quite sure what to say or how to handle it, he knew that—at the very least—Dras believed he was telling the truth. He had seen the bogeyman.

Jeff refused to believe. All his childhood fears grabbed hold of him, and he suddenly felt powerless, frightened, a little boy again unable to sleep during storms. And it made him angry. His only defense was to discredit his brother.

"Have you been drinking?"

The accusation exasperated Dras. "No," he protested, trying to be calm. "I haven't been drinking, and it wasn't a dream. It was real. This is real. It's really happening, and if we don't do something, Rosalyn might get hurt. Or worse."

Jeff kept quiet. He had no idea what course of action to take. *I'm not prepared.*

Of course, he wanted to be there for Rosalyn if she really needed help, but at the same time he couldn't quite believe Dras's bizarre story of devils and the bogeyman. Couldn't believe, or maybe just wouldn't.

"*Please.* You have to help me save her, Jeff. If anyone's strong enough to do it, it's you! I am begging you, man. I can't let anything happen to her. Not to her." Dras's voice broke. He was at the end of his rope. "I tried to tell her about Jesus, but she didn't listen to me!"

His words were the final straw. "What do you think I've been telling you all this time, Dras?" Jeff snapped. "Why would she have any reason to believe you? You think you can just walk in, recite a couple of Bible passages, and talk about 'Jesus dying for your sins' and that's it? Problem solved, bad things go away, and everyone lives happily ever after?"

Dras's face flushed. "Well...yeah. Kinda."

"You still don't see it," Jeff fumed, shaking his head.

"That's why I need your help! I need you to talk to her! You'll know what to say."

Jeff's mind worked the situation over a moment. His skin chilled, and a sweat broke out on his brow. The room was spinning, and he just wanted it all to go away.

This can't be real. This can't be happening. I'm not ready, God!

"I'm sure there's an explanation for all of this." Jeff reasoned. "I'll talk to her tomorrow, OK?"

"No!" Dras shouted, his eyes radiating fear. "There isn't time! He's after her right now! Why won't you believe me? You're supposed to be a man of God! Don't you get it? There is something out there hunting down her soul!"

Jeff's anger boiled over. Hearing Dras tell him about his Christian responsibility sent him into a raging tailspin. "Of course I get it! There was always something out there. I've been trying to tell you that for years! Every day I see people heading down that road because they are too busy with their own lives to see what I see. Do you have any idea the number of people that come into my office who are absolutely miserable, and there is so much pain in their lives they can hardly stand it? Do you? Have you ever stopped for one minute and taken a step out of your self-serving existence to see someone else hurting? Have you even tried to care about anyone but yourself?"

Dras's eyes grew hard, but he did not argue.

Indignant, Jeff said, "That's what I thought. So don't you dare come in here and try and tell me about people hurting. You got that? Don't you dare!"

Dras hung his head, biting his lip to keep from retaliating.

Humbly, Dras confessed, "You're right, Jeff. Is that what you want to hear? Because it's true. You've been right all along. And you've been fighting the good fight, and you've always been the good son, and you are everything you were ever supposed to be, while I was the little screwup brother. But I'm trying here. And it's hard."

"Good," Jeff coldly acknowledged.

Dras's eyes filled with shock.

Isabella too turned in disbelief to her husband. She was as bewildered as Dras. "Jeff!"

Dras shook his head in dismay. "Forget it. I'll deal with this on my own." Sadly and quietly, but with a newfound resolve, he pushed past Jeff and Isabella and headed for the door.

Jeff watched him go and shouted after him, "That'll be a first!"

Dras held back his hurt and walked out.

Jeff slammed the door behind him. Isabella gawked at him, stunned by what had transpired. "You can't let him go off on his own like that."

Jeff didn't even look at her. "Watch me."

Dras climbed onto his bicycle, his mind racing. He couldn't argue with his brother. He knew it was useless to try to explain how his encounter with the Strange Man had changed him. Rosalyn didn't believe it, and now Jeff wasn't listening to him either. Infuriated, his instinct told him to hit his brother or do something to get even. But that was the old Dras. The new Dras knew Jeff was right. Jeff tried to warn him over and over again, and he never listened. Even now, the only reason he took notice of the things Jeff talked about in church was because Rosalyn was in danger. He wondered if, had it been anyone else—if the Strange Man had come to him threatening Lindsey's life—if he would have cared as much. It shamed him.

Yet after all the years of Jeff urging him to come back, now that he was finally here, this was the reception that awaited him? Dras felt utterly betrayed.

He was running out of resources in his fight against the Strange Man, and all he could do was pray that God would give him a little help. When he heard the screen door slap behind him, Dras jerked his head toward the sudden sound and saw Isabella crossing the yard. Her expression was hesitant but determined.

Sincerely taken that Isabella had followed him when her husband shunned him, Dras stammered, "Isabella, what—?"

"It's the Scriptures."

"What?"

"If it's true what you're saying—if you're really up against some kind of evil spirit or whatever—the Scriptures are your only hope. When Jesus was tempted by the devil in the desert, he quoted Scripture. The Word of God has power, and even the demons in hell have to respect it."

Dras considered her words, then smiled. He always did like Isabella.

"Thanks," he said, and meant it.

She nodded firmly, fearful for him and what lay ahead. "Be careful."

Dras picked up his bike and rode off into the night, while Isabella rubbed at the unusual cold in her arms and returned to her house on Grover's Pond.

CHAPTER EIGHTEEN

FIRST ROSALYN HATED his guts, now Jeff. *Zero for two. Not the best track record.*

In a single afternoon he had managed to isolate himself from his entire circle of friends. Now he had no one to turn to. Had it not been for Isabella's tip, he would've been totally alone in his fight.

Nevertheless, Dras was filled with determination. He knew there was no turning back now. After all, he made a bargain with the Strange Man, and though it could be argued that the bargain was not made in his right mind, Dras somehow figured that mattered little to the Dark Lord of Evil. Now that he had clearly violated the pact by trying to intervene and warn Rosalyn, he had no idea what the Strange Man would do next. Frankly, the thought terrified him. But what terrified him most was knowing that the Strange Man might kill him before he had another chance to tell Rosalyn about Christ.

Dras had only one last option. The Good Church of the Faithful.

The hour was late, and the doors had long since been locked, forcing Dras to put to use a skill he learned in the eighth grade from an older kid named Hal Jones, who used to sit next to him on the bus. With a small nail file he worked on the lock to the church, hoping no one would stop him before his task was done. He'd actually only picked a lock once before when breaking into Mrs. Eddleson's desk to repair a disparaging social studies grade. But he was caught, putting a swift end to his criminal career. Until now.

After a couple of tense minutes the lock to the church finally popped, and Dras quietly stole inside. He made his way in the darkness all the way upstairs to Jeff's study. *Even if Jeff isn't going to help, his books still can.*

The books were available to every member of the church, and Dras was technically a member, albeit a mostly absent one, so his action wasn't completely criminal. *OK, OK, so picking the lock is a bit of a slide backward, but this is an emergency. I'll apologize to Jeff later.*

Dras fumbled around Jeff's desk until he found a lamp and pulled the chain, shining a small amount of pale light into the room. The bookshelves were densely populated with research materials of all kinds, and Dras fully realized how much studying Jeff did and how devoted he really was to what he believed. Despite recent events, Dras respected his brother even more.

Dras pulled the first Bible he saw and set the large volume on the desk. Isabella told him that only the Word of God had the power to ward off evil, so he needed to stock up on ammunition and fast if he was going to buy himself more time to help Rosalyn. Not only that, he knew the Scriptures could serve a much greater purpose. His last attempt to convince Rosalyn of the truth had been disastrous. All he had to present were a halfhearted faith and scraps of sermons preached by his father and brother. If he were going to get Rosalyn to understand that she needed a Savior, he was going to need God's Word as proof.

He opened the Bible and began to thumb through the thin pages, realizing he had no idea where to begin. The most he knew about the Bible was that the first book was called Genesis, and he was pretty sure the last book was called Revelation. *Oh, and that nifty Ecclesiastes verse that I used to argue my point last Sunday morning.*

Suddenly, he felt guilty for his little quip. *I really was an idiot.* Of course, though the guilt was unpleasant, his new conviction only proved to him that he really was different, despite what others said. Maybe there was still hope yet that he could become the person he always should have been.

Hey, God... He paused long enough to reflect, catching his breath for the first time today. *It's been a long time since I've prayed, but I have nowhere else to go. I really screwed up, God, and I need You. I can't do this without You. But I'm ready to listen now. Sorry it took me so long getting here. Help me to do this right.*

Dras exhaled, feeling all of a sudden like his bones were made of steel, and set himself to his work. He faced the Bible head-on, wondering where to find the verses he needed to help Rosalyn. Luckily Jeff took great notes. The Bible was adorned with multicolored lines and circles, highlighting passages that Jeff had found useful in his studies. With his brother's road map, Dras traveled down the path of knowledge that his brother had pioneered.

At least one of us was prepared.

As he read, Dras took notes of his own. Scribbling on Post-It notes, he quickly jotted down certain passages that stood out to him. He scanned the pages, praying that the Lord would show him what he needed for the upcoming battle. There was so much in the book that held power and meaning, it was impossible for Dras to retain it all, and he regretted that he hadn't spent more time in God's Word before. It would have certainly made his search easier.

Then something came to mind, something he hadn't thought of in a long, long time. It nearly caused him to laugh.

A dumbfounded smile broke his serious expression, and he realized that God was giving him what he needed. What *she* needed. He carefully and plainly printed something on another piece of paper, folded it, and stuffed it into his back pants pocket. He would save it for later.

Dras closed the old Bible, his heart filled with hope. It wasn't too late. He wasn't powerless. There was still a chance.

Gathering the Scriptures that he had copied, he hurriedly moved for the door. Then he stopped short and took one last thoughtful look at the study. He scanned the bookshelves again before taking his search to the drawers of Jeff's desk. He found what he was looking for—a much smaller, more sensible Bible for the devil-fighter on the run. He grabbed the small book, stuffed it in his jacket pocket, and raced out the door.

I'm not taking any chances.

He didn't bother to turn off the lamp on Jeff's desk or worry about locking the church behind him. He trotted down the steps two at a time, careful not to trip over his own clumsy feet in his haste. Once outside, he moved for his bike.

Then he heard scratching.

Dras spun around, fearful he'd find the Strange Man's grinning skull behind him, but was surprised to see only the shadows cast by the church. Still the scratching persisted. He moved away from his bike, beckoned by the small, peculiar sound. He felt a little bit foolish but was nevertheless compelled to investigate.

Holding his breath, Dras inched closer and closer to the shadows, the scratching low and consistent. His hand rested on his jacket pocket and the Bible he had stashed there, hoping that it would serve as a sort of protection or ward against whatever evil lurked just beyond his line of sight.

Suddenly a small creature jumped out of the darkness and

stood facing Dras, frightening him and causing him to lose hold of the Bible in his pocket. The tiny beast was perhaps two feet tall with a muscular, hairless body, noseless face, round obsidian eyes, and a wide mouth full of needle-like teeth. Dras held his ground, his heart hammering in his chest, unsure of what he was seeing.

Is this *a demon?*

The thing growled at him with all the ferocity of a newborn kitten.

For a demon, Dras thought, *he's awful cute.*

Dras cracked a grin, his heart calming, and leaned over as if to pet the little guy. "Aww, hey there, fella. Was that you making all that noise?"

The gremlin tittered and turned to the shadows behind him, and a thousand slick, black eyes, glittering in the moonlight, blinked back at Dras.

"Aw, nuts."

Dras rose slowly, his throat tightening in anticipation, and stood motionless for six precious seconds before the shadows exploded and a thousand twitching, crawling gremlins spilled out of the darkness like cockroaches. They scurried, their claws scraping across the pavement. He couldn't distinguish one beast from another but only understood that they were legion. Their giggles and whispers filled the night air as the mass, blacker than black and darker than the darkest night, moved ever faster.

And they were coming straight for him.

CHAPTER NINETEEN

PSTAIRS IN HIS home study Jeff Weldon immersed himself in his books, trying hard to forget the events of the evening and move on with his life.

He especially wanted to forget Dras's talk about the bogeyman.

He decided to focus his energies on his studies. He was in the middle of leading his Wednesday night Bible study group in a series on the parables of Jesus from the Gospel of Luke, and he figured now was as good a time as any to outline next week's lesson. Surely it would get his mind off the gnawing, persistent burning in the pit of his stomach, that feeling that evil walked in Greensboro.

And that he was ignoring it.

Isabella had avoided him since his fight with his brother. He knew he'd upset her, and he felt guilt setting in. Yet his pride was resolved. Dras was just going to have to deal with his problems on his own. It was time for him to live with the consequences of the life he led. After all, Jeff wouldn't always be there to bail him out.

The justification sounded good, but deep down Jeff knew he was only kidding himself. So he assembled his study materials, trying to escape the reality of the situation. But God, it seemed, had other plans.

Isabella quietly entered. "What are you doing?" she asked, as if nothing was wrong, as if harsh words had never been said.

Jeff didn't look up. He couldn't. Not yet. "Preparing my Bible lesson for Wednesday night."

"What's it on?" she sounded interested but restrained, carefully trying to bridge the gap of communication.

"Um—" he thumbed through his Bible until he found the passage—"I don't know, whatever's next. Luke...chapter... fifteen. There it is. Oh—" He paused and put the book down, backing away from it a bit.

"What is it?"

Jeff stared at the Bible, reminded of the night of the storm. Just like on that strange night, the Bible seemed alive, as if it were trying to impart something to him. He replied, "The prodigal son."

Isabella nodded knowingly. "Right, right. I remember that story. About the two brothers. One left home and wasted all his father's money on wild living, and the other stayed home and dutifully did the work. Then the foolish brother realized his mistake and came back home to get forgiveness. The father welcomed him with open arms and threw a big party, but the other brother was jealous and bitter because he had been a good and faithful son, and no one ever made a big fuss over him. But his father told him, 'My son, you are always with me, and everything I have is yours. But we had to celebrate because this brother of yours was dead and is alive again; he was lost and is found.'" She smirked, finding the irony poetic and a perfect example of God's timing and sense of humor. "*That* prodigal son?"

Jeff was quiet for a long moment, staring at the Bible.

He had been an idiot. Dras needed him now. Maybe more than ever. This was no time for rivalry or disputes. Souls were at stake.

Rosalyn was at stake.

Turning to Isabella, Jeff said, "I think God's trying to tell me something, Iz."

She smiled and folded her arms. "Could be. What are you going to do about it?" She waited on his response.

A moment later Jeff stood, like a warrior preparing for battle. "Let's go."

CHAPTER TWENTY

"Maybe Baby" by Buddy Holly played on the old jukebox in the darkened corner of Smokey's Bar and Grill. The clock over the bar read 8:45. Earl Canton glared at the moving hands on the clock face and gulped down his beer.

Clancy, the large woman who ran Smokey's, sauntered up to the bar with a wet rag, wiping down the evening's stains. Seeing Earl staring at the clock as if they were in a western standoff, Clancy warmed and leaned on the counter with a dimpled elbow.

"Better finish off that beer, Earl," she smiled. "Fifteen minutes before the sheriff's new curfew takes effect. I gotta close down so I can get home."

Earl set his beer down with a *clunk* and grimaced, finally voicing what was already evident in his eyes. "Where does Hank get off trying to tell me what time I gotta be in? Ain't that my right?"

Clancy shrugged, her meaty hands on her round waist. "I just do as the law tells me, Earl."

"If you ask me, that's half Greensboro's problems. We all just do what we're told, like nice little cattle."

With a disgusted look, Earl turned around to view the other pre-curfew stragglers. There weren't many. Greensboro was pretty much abandoned after 8:30 these days, just because most folks didn't want to be out getting involved in something only to have to wrap it up at nine. The few that were sharing in his childish defiance of the curfew were mostly hardworking guys determined to enjoy their downtime, despite Hank Berkley's orders. Exhausted-eyed men lounged around tables enjoying beers and onion blossoms, sharing the stress of the day.

And what's wrong with that, Sheriff Berkley? Ain't we earned that?

"That goes for the rest a'ya too," Clancy called out, flicking her towel as if to say, "Git." "Closin' time, boys. You all can come back tomorrow."

Her admonishment was met by good-natured groans, but her customers obliged, gathering their things and making preparations to leave.

Not Earl. He remained fixed to the stool at the counter, still clutching his beer and paying little attention to the half-eaten ham sandwich on the counter, prepared to take his good, sweet time in finishing it. If Hank wanted to come around and give Clancy flak for that, he'd stand up for the good woman.

"You all scared a' Hank?" Earl loudly asked the shuffling patrons. He spun around on his bar stool to face them. "We're grown men, and we're letting him tell us when we gotta be home for the night? Is he the sheriff or our mama? Last I checked, I pay my bills. I pay my taxes, his salary. Way I see it, that gives me the right to stay out as late as I want."

Some of the men paused, listening to Earl's talk, their eyes faltering with doubt for a moment. Clancy shooed Earl. "Oh, don't you listen to him. Now, Earl, you hush. Hank's just trying to keep our folks safe."

Earl leaned back on the counter, laughing. "Well, if Hank's keeping us safe, we'd all better be worried. The only thing that ol' boy could save us from is a buffet line."

Laughter rippled through the men as they approached the counter and paid Clancy for their meals and drinks.

Seeing he was gaining some followers, Earl went on. "Yeah,

he'd throw himself on a pile of doughnuts to save one of us, wouldn't he, boys?"

Clancy sighed, shaking her head in disapproval as she tallied up totals.

"I don't know who took Lindsey McCormick," Earl told the cluster of men, "but I'm guessing he's only good at overpowerin' young girls. I'd like to see him try and take one of us. What do we have to be afraid of?"

Clancy giggled nervously. "You *hush*, Earl. I gotta get home. I don't want to be breakin' no laws."

Earl waved off the protest, rolling his eyes. "Let Hank come down here and start a squall. He don't scare me."

By this point the other men had begun nodding and muttering, "Yeah!" Clancy worried that she was going to have some late-night guests.

A voice came from across the diner.

"That's about enough, Earl."

All eyes turned to the back, where Deputy Miller stood, his tie loosened and the top button on his uniform undone. He looked worn from another long day of searching for Lindsey or her captor/killer. Miller had pull with the men in Greensboro, and those who had only seconds ago agreed with Earl now hung their heads and hurried to pay for their food, their thoughts of publicly protesting the curfew dissolving.

Earl watched their shift in attitude and shook his head with disdain at the lot of them. *Stupid cows, all a' ya.*

Setting his drink down, Earl puffed out his chest and rose from his stool as Miller left a tip on the table and made his way to the cash register.

"Hey, Roy," Earl said, obviously not threatened. "Didn't see you back there."

"Figured you might not've. You seemed awfully busy runnin'

your big mouth and all," Miller replied, joining the line. Clancy shot anxious glances between the two men, fearing a confrontation she'd be ill-equipped to referee.

"Still a free country—" Earl tugged on his belt loops, pulling his pants up a little higher—"unless Hank and you boys are trying to put a stop to that too."

"Seems to me you do a lot of talking, Earl." Miller appraised the other man with a bold eye. "You ever back that up with more than tough words?"

Earl snickered, catching the expectant looks on the other men's faces. Calmly he put out his hands and waved the off-duty deputy forward. "Why don't you step on over here and find out, Roy?"

Clancy stepped in now, leaning over the counter. "Quit it, both of you. It's late, and we're all irritable. Just cut it out, and let's all go home before we do something we'll regret in the morning."

A defiantly savage grin remained fixed on Earl's face as he challenged Deputy Miller. "Come on, Roy. What d'you got?"

Before the deputy could respond, every man froze at the sound of roaring wind outside. Earl, so caught up in proving his manhood, was the last to hear the howling sound. Everyone in Smokey's slowly looked to the window, but it was Earl who started for the glass, hesitant but curious.

"What is that?" Clancy asked. "That the train?"

"Sounds too close to be the train," Miller responded, pulled to the window by interest as well.

Earl reached the front window and peered out the glass into the ebony sky. Miller soon joined him, both men forgetting their past grievances in their effort to understand the situation.

"You two better get away from there," Clancy warned.

"Sounds like a tornado. We'd better get in the kitchen in the back, just to be safe."

Earl held up a hand. "Hold up. Listen. You hear that?"

Miller mused, "Sounds like—"

At that moment, Dras Weldon went screaming past, pedaling furiously on his bicycle.

"Help!" he shouted, his face twisted by blind terror.

Earl scratched his head as the boy carried on down the street. "What d'you suppose that's all about?"

He did not have to wait long for an answer.

Without warning, a tiny black shape slammed into the glass, ripping a scream out of Clancy and all the men with her. Earl fell backward, landing on his rump on the hard floor, yelping in surprise. Miller stepped back in retreat, his eyes struggling to comprehend what he was seeing.

The thing looked like a small child but with charred reptilian skin, large, lightless black eyes, and a wide mouth full of teeth. The little critter banged on the glass and squealed like an angry hog, as if hungry for the flesh of all those who hid inside Smokey's.

"What is that?" Clancy shrieked at the top of her lungs as the deafening roar outside picked up like an oncoming phantom train. An instant later the creature was joined by a billion others just like it flying past the window like a murder of crows, their dark bodies blotting out the lights on Main Street. More things latched onto the window, banging and screeching, cracking the glass and threatening to spill in.

Miller reacted, pulling Earl away from the window. But the rest of the patrons froze in terror, forgetting to run or hide. With bated breath they all waited for their bloody fate to come. Thankfully, just as the glass was about to shatter, the things pulled off and joined the dark mass of their kin, disappearing after Dras and his bicycle.

Blissful silence settled among those inside Smokey's until Clancy slapped Earl on the back of the head, then faced him with her hands solidly fixed to her wide hips.

"That's what you get for staying out after curfew!"

Whether the Strange Man was, in fact, the devil himself or not, one thing was certain: whoever he was, he had a lot of friends.

Dras pedaled faster on his bicycle, trying to keep ahead of the crawling darkness that seemed intent on devouring him whole. He only dared throw a few quick glances behind him, for he knew that he had to keep his mind on going forward. Had to stay ahead of them. But when he looked back, he saw many shiny eyes blinking back at him like the twinkling of stars in the vastness of space. Their chattering teeth and the clicking of their claws seemed closer.

Always closer.

A nervous and panicked sweat formed on his brow. Dras stood on his bicycle to increase his speed, but the things were so incredibly fast, coming at him like a driving whirlwind, consuming everything that fell in their path.

Dras slipped through an intersection to the sound of honking cars as angry drivers—trying to duck in before the nine o'clock curfew—hung their heads out of windows, shaking fists and hurling insults. All protests silenced, however, when Dras's demonic entourage fluttered past. Suddenly red lights were ignored, and a Bronco, its driver captivated by the horrifying sight of hell's legions, drifted right into the path of little Miss Jenkins's cream-colored 1970s' Buick, which was barreling down the road away from the monsters. The speeding Buick clipped the rear side of the Bronco, peeling off its bumper and sending it into a tire-burning tailspin.

Smoke and the smell of burnt rubber lingered in the air as the gremlins abandoned the chaos, continuing their determined pursuit of the young man on the bicycle. Dras heard their dark-stained claws scraping against the metal as they hurdled the stalled and wrecked vehicles, leaving them in ruins. Like a plague of locusts they moved, unstoppable, a raging army of many dark and nameless things ravaging the land and leaving nothing behind.

Their laughter was the worst. A never-ending cacophony of high-pitched squeals of devilish delight hummed behind Dras, reminding him much of the Strange Man's own laughter. The twitching creatures in the shadows cackled in glee, savoring the hunt with Dras as their prey.

He pedaled faster still, knowing that time was running out. With their multitudes so uncountable, their bodies vibrated against each other as they forged on, creating a deafening buzzing sound, like a swarm of angry bees.

As Dras continued his frenzied tour of Greensboro, he neared the video store where sun-bleached VHS cases once beckoned him to monster-filled childhood adventures. Dave sat behind the counter, his back to the glass, once again captivated by his guitar magazine.

"Dave! Dave!" Dras shouted as he pedaled by. "Call the cops, man! Help me!"

Dave only held up his slush—a blue one, tonight—and lazily called out from behind the glass, oblivious to danger. "Later, dude."

Streetlamps overhead exploded in sizzling sparks as the monsters tore through them. Dras groaned in frustration as he rounded a corner, leaving Dave and Main Street behind.

Leonard Fergus reclined in an old wooden rocker on his front porch, a sweating glass of sweet, iced lemonade on the small glass table beside him serving as his faithful late-evening companion. The neighborhood was quiet, save for the nighttime insects gossiping about secret things and the sound of "Stormy Weather" lazily drifting through the screen door from the record player in his front room.

With half-closed eyes, Leonard rocked in the old chair his daddy made, savoring Lena Horne's silky voice and thinking of better times. Life was souring in Greensboro these days; everyone said it began when the highway moved, but Leonard wondered if maybe it started before that, if maybe his town was just one more to fall to the impersonal, self-centered way of the world. His church was filled with gossips and backbiters, and the few faithful members were driven away by the elders' church politics. Neighbors didn't talk to each other anymore but were content to lose themselves in cell phones, computers, DVDs, and loud music. People wanted to be immersed in pointless noise, it seemed, but nothing was ever really said.

The problems of a world and a town moving on without him seemed too large to contend with, so Leonard retired to his porch, looking out over the same neighborhood he used to pedal down on his bicycle when he was a boy. The Bible warned in Ecclesiastes against losing oneself in the days of youth. Leonard assumed the good Lord meant for time to be better spent savoring the present than longing for nostalgic memories. Still, Leonard couldn't resist a peak into the sparkling years of childhood when things were simpler. Back then there was such a thing as community, and family was important. Society these days prided the individual, the man who could make his own way without the help of anyone. Children were reared to be fully self-reliant.

But at what cost? Leonard mused. *In the animal kingdom the pack means survival and security. Wander too far, try to take on too much on your own, and what predators await you in the dark?*

Greensboro had become a town of strangers. Leonard worried what predator awaited them in the dark. Lindsey McCormick was already missing and feared dead. He knew in the pit of his stomach that the terror would not end with her.

What have we brought down on ourselves?

Down the street, Leonard heard the sound of a pedaling bicycle and leaned forward in his chair, almost expecting to see a specter of his childhood self emerging from the innocent past.

But Leonard only saw Dras Weldon, huffing and struggling, riding his bike down the deserted road. Leonard smiled, revealing his pearly white dentures, and propped himself up to a standing position, leaning on his cane.

"Where ya off to tonight, son?" he called out casually. "It's past curfew."

Dras did not answer; he only stared at him with pale-faced hysteria as he breathed in furious gasps, pedaling faster still. Leonard's grin faded, replaced by a worry he couldn't quite explain.

Then he heard the buzzing. A split second later a loud explosion ruined a transformer, casting the block into blackness. Leonard gasped, standing on wobbly legs, leaning against his cane. The wind whipped about him, chilling his blood, and his senses immediately heightened with anticipation. A surge of adrenaline shot through his veins, making him feel like a younger man again, but his newfound strength sent only one primal impulse into his mind: *run.*

Fixed to his porch by some morbid desire to stare into the abyss that was spiraling toward his house, Leonard gazed into the inky sky as Dras split past and saw it.

Fluttering shapes flickered in silver moonlight, things with gleaming, metallic eyes. Leonard felt a mad giggle rise in his belly and forced it down, his eyes bonded to the unclear sight, his mind trying to determine what lived within the tumbling ball of movement. Greensboro had weathered its share of tornados in its history, but this—

This was unnatural.

"What—" his voice trailed off, trying to understand; his brain raving at him to flee, to save his life.

The buzzing sound intensified, followed by clicking and crunching, cackling and crowing. Telephone poles splintered and toppled over, crushing cars. Roofs were torn off houses as the dark whirlwind hurtled itself toward the petrified senior. Finally, he was able to tear himself away from the devastation and nearly jumped into his house, slamming the door shut. Outside, what sounded like a freight train passed, rattling the foundation of his home. China fell out of a glass cabinet, shattering on the floor below. Pictures bobbled and jumped off walls. And through it all giggles chorused outside like the sound of a classroom full of mischievous schoolchildren.

Tears welled in Leonard's eyes as insanity flooded the streets beyond his door, and he slumped to the floor, praying for deliverance.

"Oh, Lord," he said. "What have we done?"

Dras sped through the run-down neighborhoods of the East Side, racing for Rosalyn's apartment. One by one the lights along the street blinked to black as power lines snapped and whipped about violently, succumbing to the indescribable mass weighing down on his back.

In response to the commotion and sudden blackout, curious eyes peeped out windows, while other residents opened doors, stumbling onto their lawns, disgruntled that their quiet evening was interrupted.

"Help!" Dras shouted at them, getting his voice back. "Help me!"

Neighbors exchanged bewildered looks but were caught in utter shock at the sight of the unexplainable monstrosity tearing down their streets. Blinds snapped shut, and doors slammed closed.

"No!" Dras yelled, calling out into the night. "Wait!"

But no one answered his call. Everyone was either too afraid to intervene in the supernatural phenomenon or thought it was best not to know, not to get involved. It angered Dras to watch them turn their heads, but at the same time he understood.

Every time I looked at Rosalyn, I looked the other way too. Not anymore, though.

He determined not to be imprisoned by his fears any longer. He was ready to stand for his rediscovered faith, even if it meant death. As the twitching, clicking things in the darkness edged closer, almost touching the rear tire of his bike, he knew that death might very well be his fate, but he did not let that knowledge deter him.

I have to get to Rosalyn.

She was all that mattered now. In a moment of clarity he realized she was all that had ever mattered to him.

I can't let her down.

He thought to follow Isabella's advice and wield the Word of God against his pursuers, but as he tried to remember the verses he had just read in Jeff's big Bible, he came up empty. If his memory was his only defense, he was in big trouble. Still, there was the smaller Bible in his jacket pocket, but he couldn't spare a moment to reach for it and thumb through his notes.

All he could do was pray.

Stay with me, God. Help me do this.

Despite his fear, Dras felt a momentary warmth in the pit of his stomach reminding him that God was near.

If I could just convince Rosalyn of that...If I could just convince her of the truth...

Something whizzed past his ear, and he jerked instinctively to dodge it. He turned his head and saw the shadows bearing down on top of him. One of the things within the shape sprang close enough to strike with its talons. The thing's chattering laughter rang closer to Dras's ears than he cared to endure.

He cried out at the sight of their dull, gray flesh. Their enormous eyes, luminescent with dark energy, glared back at him with murderous hunger. Their gleaming teeth, long and mismatched, reminded him of a wood chipper, and he hoped he'd never find out if that analogy proved accurate.

Turning his back on them, forcing himself to face the road ahead and not the dangers behind, he pedaled faster.

But they moved closer. Closer.

He roared in frustration, his face twisted in a grimace of terror, feeling their warm, rotted breath on the back of his neck.

Faster, Dras! Go faster!

His legs threatened to collapse, but he kept pedaling. Leaning forward, he put all of his weight into the effort, breathing heavily but thankful to be breathing at all. He felt drops of sweat rolling down his forehead and back from the exertion, but the things moved closer still. One of them grabbed on to the scruff of his jacket. He screamed in desperation.

"Agh!"

Faster!

Suddenly the chain on his bike fell loose, unraveled, and spiraled away from him. In abject horror he looked down, wide-eyed, as his feet spun around without gaining any ground.

"*No!*" Dras cried, almost in tears.

With his attention distracted by the disassembling of his bicycle, he was caught unprepared for the parked car.

Bam!

He hit the stationary automobile full force. His bike stopped instantaneously, the momentum propelling him forward, sending him flying over the car. Dras landed hard on the pavement, skidding a few inches before he scraped to a stop in front of Don's Barber Shop.

Inside, Don, having just awakened from an impromptu nap in his tiny apartment in the back, swept the store after hours, preparing for tomorrow's business. Dras jumped to his feet, his mind wheeling and his lungs burning, to face the gremlin horde. The barber looked up and saw, as Dras did, the swarm of creatures form a single arm and swat at the parked car on the curb.

Dras let out an astonished half shout and hurled himself sideways to the concrete as the car *whooshed* past him, exploding through Don's storefront window. Don dove behind a sink.

Dras swayed to a standing position, the small Bible tumbling out of his coat pocket to the ground as he prepared to dodge another attack.

But the monsters stayed their many hands.

They buzzed about but did not cross over the Bible. Dras noticed the book on the ground, and Isabella's description of the Word of God as a weapon came back to him. As quickly as he could, for he couldn't afford a single wasted moment, Dras dropped to the sidewalk and picked up the Bible, ready to brandish it as a sword. But by the time he rose again, the monsters were gone. The night sky was clear once more, and their laughing had vanished.

"Ha!" Dras shouted, his face brightening in the quieting breeze of the evening. "How about that?"

His victory subsided as he realized how much pain the catapult over the car had inflicted. The impact left him short-winded. He wheezed, trying to regain his breath. He could feel that one of the knees was torn out of his pants, and the sting in his flesh told him he was beginning to bleed.

Yet he was safe, for now.

He turned to see the car parked inside the barber shop. From behind it Don slowly rose, his face white, still clutching his broom.

"What—" Don said in a hoarse whisper.

Dras cracked what began as an uncertain grin—met by stings and throbs moving through his body—and ended as more of a wince.

"Uh...Sorry?"

But his concern for Don's establishment paled as he realized the threat that still loomed over his best friend.

"Rosalyn!"

Her fate flashed before his eyes, reminding him that he had work to do.

Dras abandoned his bike and ran down the street toward Rosalyn's apartment as Don the barber surveyed the devastation of his shop and threw down his broom in surrender.

CHAPTER TWENTY-ONE

THE STRANGE MAN hovered ominously above the streets of Greensboro, moving with an uncanny speed despite the frail appearance of his body. As he wandered the roads, a cold green mist that reeked of burnt flesh followed him, leaving withered grass in its wake. His body fixed in the air like a hanging man as he crept through the night, and a wicked shadow fell on the neighborhoods as he came upon each house, stopping only for a moment to peek in the windows with his orb-like yellow eyes.

Woe to the little boys and girls who choose to disobey their parents and stay up late tonight!

Elsewhere his legions were already dealing with the idiot boy who broke his promise to remain silent, but the Strange Man feared that the Lord was protecting the boy now, and if that was true, then there was nothing that all the armies of hell could do to change it.

There must be another way, he reasoned, *another way to remove the boy. Anything to get to the girl.*

Inside the dark recesses of his soulless heart the monster prepared to set a plan into motion. He held his crooked nose to the starless night sky, trying to recognize the scent of the child he sought. Yet he could not find his prey.

It was on nights like this, when the monster was engaged in hunting, that legends and the darkest of fairy tales were born. "The bogeyman," the storytellers called him. A droll name, true, but it served a purpose, carrying with it fear and a reputation he could use to his advantage.

The feared bogeyman drifted along the lonely roads of Greensboro, searching for the last cog in his plan for the evening. The Strange Man peered in yet another window and saw only a sleeping baby. He grew impatient, but then at last the darkness spoke to him and led him to the spot where the little one lay. The monster smiled.

Aha!

He interlaced his long fingers, pleased that his journey had proven fruitful. He strolled to the white picket fence in front of the slumbering house, and the bogeyman of Greensboro slithered toward the bedroom window.

Rebecca Walker prepared, once more, to put her daughter, Millie, to bed. Ever since the night of the storm, Millie had been especially goosey, her big, searching eyes frozen to the picture window beside her bed. Rebecca had done her best to assuage the child's fears, even going so far as to make a grand production of locking the latch on the window, pulling the curtains, and even keeping a lit candle at her bedside. It was ridiculous now—even dangerous, Rebecca feared—to keep a burning candle beside her daughter's bed when a lamp or nightlight would have sufficed. But Millie insisted. She had only herself to blame. She herself had told Millie it was candlelight that kept the bogeyman at bay, and so now Millie would settle for nothing less.

"It's really not necessary, honey," Rebecca said, pulling the covers to Millie's cherubic face. "The storm's long gone. There's nothing to be afraid of anymore."

"Just one more night, Mommy," Millie pleaded, just as she had every night since the storm.

Rebecca sighed patiently, but before she could make her argument, the phone rang.

TJ will answer it.

"Millie," she said—the phone rang a second time—"nothing's going to happen to you, OK? The bogeyman's not real."

"But—" Millie pouted, the phone ringing a third time.

Rebecca threw a look to the door, waiting any moment for her son to answer the phone. When it rang a fourth time, she quickly kissed her daughter on the head.

"Go to sleep, sweetie." She rushed out of the room.

Hurrying down the stairs, taking two steps at a time, Rebecca found her son sprawled out in the recliner, blitzing through channels. The phone rang again.

"TJ?"

"What?" he mumbled.

"The phone?"

"What about it?"

Rebecca growled and raced into the kitchen, snatching the receiver off the cradle, nearly ripping the whole thing out of the wall.

"Hello?" she said, stressed.

The ER at Greensboro Community Hospital was in chaos.

Men, women, and children, all wrapped in bandages or blankets, crowded about, shouting over each other regarding the strange, unexplained events they had seen that night.

Nurse Consuela Margolis glanced over her shoulder at the sight of the EMT workers wheeling Miss Jenkins through the ER's double doors on a stretcher, the old woman suffering nothing but some bruises and a cut on her left temple. The paramedics fought to restrain the town gossip as she cried out hysterically, "Dogs! It was wild dogs! They were trying to kill me! They were following that Weldon boy!"

"Try to remain calm, Miss Jenkins," an approaching nurse offered, checking the woman over for serious injuries and coming up empty.

Miss Jenkins fanned herself, sobbing dramatically, "Oh, why did he sic those dogs on me? I'm just a poor old woman. What could I have done?"

It was when Miss Jenkins resorted to telling the paramedics how "that boy" had never been any good and how her current woes were just the most recent of pains she had sustained due to Dras Weldon's delinquent antics that Consuela turned back to the phone.

Rebecca had answered at last. Consuela attempted to speak to her, though her ears rung with the commotion of the emergency room admissions.

"Rebecca, we've got an emergency at the hospital. Doctor Brown wants all the staff to report in immediately."

"What's going on?"

"Haven't you seen the news? There've been reports of a huge flock of birds, a pack of wild dogs, a tornado—"

"*What?*" Rebecca nearly laughed.

"No one knows what's going on out there, but there've been wrecks, and power lines are down all over town, and people are hurt and confused. It's a madhouse here, and we need you to come in ASAP."

"O...OK," Rebecca said, overwhelmed. "I'll be right down."

Rebecca hung up, her mind whirling. Adding to her mystification, a parade of police cars blurred by her front window, their lights and sirens drowning out TJ's television.

TJ just turned up the volume. He got up to fetch another drink from the fridge.

Rebecca took a tentative step to the window, peeled back the sheer curtains, and watched the speeding law officials responding to—

What? Dogs? Birds? A tornado? What's going on out there?

An uneasy sense of anxiety blossomed in her stomach, numbing her hands, as she realized she was going to have to go out in that—whatever *that* was—and deal with its victims. She thought of Millie and worried that whatever was happening might hit her home next, but just as quickly she assured herself that her paranoid motherly instincts were just in overdrive. She had a job to do.

Whether she liked it or not.

Rebecca moved toward the closet to retrieve her jacket. "I need you to watch your sister tonight," she yelled into the kitchen.

TJ pulled another beer out of the refrigerator and popped the top before meandering back into the living room. "I got plans," he said, and took a drink.

"There's an emergency at the hospital. I have to go in."

Dropping into the old comfy recliner he'd inherited when his father left the family, TJ took a good, long swig of his beer. "Whatever."

"And put that away," Rebecca whispered harshly, hoping to keep the sounds of the argument from reaching Millie upstairs. "I don't want your sister seeing you with that."

TJ's reply was to gulp another mouthful of beer and let loose with a rippling belch.

"TJ, I need you to work with me," his mother begged him. "I can't do everything by myself."

"Fine," he said loudly. "Go. I told you I'd stay already."

It relieved Rebecca to win the latest power struggle with her son, but she didn't want to leave estranged. Softly, she said, "TJ—"

He turned up the volume, drowning her out.

"I love you," she told him, but he didn't care.

Sadly, Rebecca gathered her things and walked out of the house.

Good night, Millie. Be safe.

Little Millie Walker had trouble sleeping again. Luckily no storms were on the horizon, and it was not the sound of thunder that was keeping her awake. The candle burned on the night-stand as it had burned every night for the last week, assuring Millie that the bogeyman was no longer anything to fear.

But sounds from downstairs told her that Mommy had to leave to go to work again, and Millie could never sleep when her mother was gone. TJ was here, true. But he was the guy who told her about the bogeyman in the first place. Suffice it to say, he wasn't the most understanding when it came to her fears. Not like Mommy. Still, Millie had her candle, and she knew that everything would be OK. She just needed to go to sleep, and Mommy would be back when she woke up in the morning.

Lying there, trying to think of something that would cause her to fall asleep, she heard a noise and grew instantly worried. Although Mommy told her that the strange man she saw outside her bedroom window on the night of the storm wasn't real, Millie could not bring herself to believe her. After all, she hadn't seen him. Millie had.

Again, a sound came from her window as it had on that night, only this time it wasn't scratching. It was shaking. The panes on her window vibrated as if…as if…

Someone was trying to get in! The thought terrified her. She wanted to cry out for TJ but froze in anticipation, clutching her covers tighter.

The panes on the window shook. They rattled more and more violently, causing a horrible racket. Surely TJ heard the noise. It was too loud to go unheard.

Please come and get me, TJ.

The shaking stopped.

Silence.

It was over.

Millie's eyes grew wide as she watched the tiny hook latch, the only thing protecting her from an intruder, slowly raise and come undone, as if lifted by a ghost.

The window unlocked.

Suddenly a cold force slammed the panes open, pinning them to the walls on either side. Her curtains, printed with playful puppy dogs, took flight and writhed in the powerful wind. Millie sank almost completely beneath her covers, biting her lip to keep from whimpering, and watched helplessly as the flame of the candle was extinguished.

Darkness drowned the room, save for the eerie glow of a green mist that began to roll along her floor. Her stomach twisted in knots. She saw him.

The bogeyman.

He had the same long fingers, like claws, just like on the night of the storm, and as he stretched them forward, the shadow they cast seemed to reach all the way across the room. His shadow touched her. She felt cold. Only her frightened, tear-filled eyes were visible above the covers. She remained perfectly still, praying he could not see her. That he *would* not see her.

The monster lurched across the foot of her bed, his breathing raspy. Millie heard the bogeyman's pointed boots grating across the floor as he passed her by. He crept so slowly, yet she knew that if she dared move he would snatch her in the blink of an eye.

With elongated talons, he seized the doorknob. Slowly he turned it. The door opened without a sound, and in an instant he left Millie's bedroom. To go downstairs.

TJ.

What a way to spend Friday night.

TJ flipped through the channels, grumbling under his breath about his mother leaving him to watch the kid. TJ was eighteen when Millie was born, and the news of a baby sister came as a shock to the high school senior. He was resentful of the little brat, who came along at just the time when he needed his parents' attention the most. They knew that his knee injury cost him his shot at a bright future. He needed their help, their guidance. And most of all, he needed their pity. But they were more concerned with the baby. As it turned out, they shouldn't have been so happy, because it was only a year later that TJ's dad decided he didn't want to be a new father all over again. Instead he wanted to recapture the freedom he'd sacrificed when Rebecca gave birth to TJ, back when *they* were fresh out of high school. So he took up with a girl who was barely older than TJ and ran off with her for greener pastures.

TJ didn't blame him. He blamed Millie for breaking up his family. He blamed his mother for not trying harder to make his old man happy. Most of all he blamed God for sitting by and letting it all happen.

An image of Lindsey flashed on the television. A reporter commented on the local manhunt for the missing girl.

Lindsey—

The only thing TJ had going for him these days was her. Lindsey McCormick was a babe. Granted, that was about all he knew about her, but she was a great kisser and believed in proving it often. Now she was gone.

He didn't know her well enough to really miss her as a person, he guessed, but he was sure going to miss the good times they had shared.

TJ pressed the remote control, abruptly ending the announcer's report, flipping the channel to *COPS*. Stretching and scratching, he got up from the recliner. Wearing shorts and his old high school jersey, he was settled for the night.

TJ Walker, the football star cut down before his prime, moped into the kitchen for another beer. His mother didn't approve of him drinking, but she wasn't the greatest at enforcing her authority. TJ was the man of the house these days, and if he chose to drink a beer, his mother would just have to like it.

As he passed the staircase—the house illuminated only by the soft flicker of the television screen—he failed to see the lurking monster slowly descending the stairs with outstretched fingers.

Millie choked back tears and kept a considerable distance between herself and the bogeyman. She watched as TJ disappeared into the kitchen and noticed with trepidation that the bogeyman was almost at the bottom of the staircase.

Dropping to her knees, pressing her little worried face to the back of the bars on the banister, she stared as the monster joined TJ in the kitchen. Silence hung in the air a moment before—

"Wha—? Agh!"

Pots and pans, the new ones that Mommy hung over the center island, banged together. Millie flinched when she heard her brother scream again. It was so awful she couldn't hold back a cry.

"TJ," she whispered.

He screamed again, only this time it was accompanied by a sickening ripping that sounded as if his jersey had been torn in two. The struggle was so loud and his screaming so scary that Millie put her hands to her ears as she cried.

"TJ." Her bottom lip quivered.

Then, as suddenly as it began, the screaming ended. The banging stopped. It was over.

Millie gazed into the quiet living room below her, feeling sick to her stomach. All was still.

Then she saw him.

Slowly creeping around the corner just until he was in her line of sight, the bogeyman poked his head out and looked straight at her. A twisted smile stretched grotesquely across his face.

"Hello, Millie."

She gasped for breath and jumped to her feet. Instinctively she ran to the only place she knew to go. Her bedroom.

The bogeyman followed. He reached out his fingers, pointed toward his prey, and began to float up the stairs. The shadows carried his twisted body to her room. He flung the door open. As Millie's screams filled the house, he closed the door behind him.

The phones at the Maribel County Sheriff's Department rang off the hook. All over town people reported bizarre sightings of tiny creatures wreaking havoc. Power lines were down and stoplights were awry, causing car wrecks at nearly every intersection. Greensboro was in a state of total anarchy, all of it apparently caused by "gremlins," as one old-timer called them. The more calls that came in, the stranger the accounts became—the teeth got longer, the claws got sharper. Sheriff Hank Berkley didn't know what in the Sam Hill was going on in his quiet little town.

Concerned and frightened citizens crammed themselves into the station trying to make their voices heard. Most of them had dressed in a hurry due to the late hour. They were a mismatched bunch with messy hair, all clamoring to get the sheriff's attention as he and his men strained to hear phone conversations.

At last the sheriff, always slow to anger, raised a hand. "All right! I need you folks to calm down for a minute. Someone will be with you as soon as they can."

That only quieted the crowd for a brief, heavenly moment before their hysteria resumed. Hank rolled his eyes and sighed as Deputy Adams approached him.

"We just got another call," Adams informed him. "Folks at Smokey's. Said they saw those things chasing Dras Weldon on a bicycle."

The sheriff sighed and rubbed his head. "You'd better go check it out."

The deputy nodded, already rushing into the fray.

"Be careful!" the sheriff yelled after him, knowing his deputy wouldn't be able to hear him.

The phone rang again.

"Merciful heaven," he moaned before picking it up. Placing the receiver in position, he stuck his finger in his free ear to block out the noise. "Maribel County. Sheriff Hank Berkley speaking."

"Sheriff?"

The voice was soft and distant. Hank strained to hear.

"Hello?" he repeated.

The voice had sounded like—well, it almost sounded like a little girl.

"Sheriff—"

"Hello? Are you all right?" Hank grew concerned.

On the other end of the phone, halfway across town, little Millie Walker, wide-eyed and in a catatonic state, whispered into the phone.

"Something happened, Sheriff." Her tiny voice was hollow and terrifying.

"What's that, honey?" the sheriff asked, his compassion showing through.

With little Millie on his lap, the Strange Man sat in the rocking chair in her room, creaking back and forth. He smiled at her and stroked her hair as she talked to the sheriff on the phone.

In the same creepy, unwavering voice, Millie reported, "TJ—he's hurt...He's..."

The sheriff strove to make out her words. "What? Honey, are you OK?"

Millie thought to begin again, all life having left her eyes. "He—"

Millie looked up to the Strange Man. He met her empty

expression with a nod and an encouraging smile. Millie turned back to the phone.

"He wants me to tell you Dras Weldon killed him."

"Now hang up," the Strange Man quietly urged her.

She did as she was told. She remained seated, her eyes frozen in a fixed position on some distant place in front of her, never blinking. The Strange Man smiled and patted her head.

"Good girl. Now, remember, it's our little secret, OK?"

Millie stared blankly.

At the station, Hank leaned into the phone, trying to hear over the din of the townspeople.

"Hello? He–hello? Are you there?"

The line went dead.

He rested the receiver on its cradle. Immediately the phone rang again. The caller was sure to deliver another tale of a gremlin-related disturbance. The blood drained from the sheriff's face as he stood in the middle of the nightmare.

"God help us all."

CHAPTER TWENTY-TWO

"ROSALYN!"

Dras banged on the door of her apartment, frantic and out of breath. He called out again as he pounded with his balled-up fist.

"Rosalyn! Let me in! I have to talk to you!"

Nothing.

Finally, in a burst of adrenaline, Dras threw himself against the door. The lock broke, splintering the wooden frame. Dras managed to catch himself before his momentum tossed him to the floor.

The place was dark. Abandoned.

He ran his fingers through his sweaty hair.

Where could she be?

As he pondered his friend's mysterious disappearance, he leaned against her couch, taking a much-needed breather. He had never worked so hard in his life, and he knew he would feel it in the morning.

If I ever see morning.

No, he couldn't think like that. He would make it through this. Rosalyn would too. He just had to think. His head hurt. The only sound in the room was his own breathing, and even that was too loud.

Trying to think but only confusing himself more, Dras moved through the dark apartment, his mind scattered and disoriented. The moonlight shining through the window pulled him into its path. He edged closer and looked through the glass at his quiet, wholesome town of Greensboro. The place where he grew up. His home.

But tonight it looked different, like a sham. Most of the people out there didn't know the truth any more than he had twenty-four hours ago. They were blind. Deceived. He could see a number of red and blue lights in the distance. The town came alive below him, panicking as reality visited each man, woman, and child. It was pure pandemonium, and Rosalyn was lost somewhere in it.

With that thing looking for her.

However, Dras was mistaken. The monster wasn't looking for Rosalyn, but for him.

And the search was over.

As Dras stared out the window, wondering what had become of the predictable town he once knew, the Strange Man quietly slinked through Rosalyn's open door. The monster was wearing his mask of beauty. Lazy, unconcerned eyes and unblemished skin replaced his crooked nose and pale face. He looked as if he hadn't a care in the world. Instead of black and chains, he was adorned in a rich blue suit that perfectly fit a well-built frame. He reflected power and wealth. No longer was he a picture of death and evil but of civility and charm.

"She's not here." The Strange Man greeted him with the singsong voice he used when in human form.

Dras spun around. Caught off guard, he stared openmouthed at the stranger.

"Who are—?"

"I already looked."

Dras recognized him.

It's the guy who danced with Rosalyn at the club. The one who made me feel so jealous. But what's he doing here?

Then, looking into the man's eyes—dark, soulless eyes—he knew.

"*You.*" Dras seethed, terror beginning to grip his heart.

The Strange Man parted pouting lips in a trademark half grin.

"Me."

Without warning, the Strange Man flew across the room and threw a punch that smashed into Dras's jawbone.

Dras stumbled backward, surprised. No one had ever actually hit him before. Threatened, sure. But Dras had never fought a day in his life. Rosalyn always settled his disputes with bullies with her own fists. Even when TJ Walker picked on him at school, it was Rosalyn who sent the bully home to his mother with a bloodied nose.

Now, for her, Dras was prepared to step up to bat.

Setting fear and precaution aside, Dras lunged for the Strange Man with a right hook, putting all of his weight behind it. Of course, the Strange Man picked Dras's first punch ever to dodge out of the way. Dras's own force sent him tripping over himself and tumbling over the couch, causing Dras to question God's judgment regarding the "clumsy gene" He'd encoded in him.

But the trip over the couch turned out to be a hidden blessing, as Dras came face-to-face with a small footstool. He picked himself up and hurled the footstool, breaking it over the Strange Man's shoulders. Then Dras leapt off the couch and jumped squarely onto the man's back. But the Strange Man, with an effortless and graceful hand, removed Dras, redepositing him on the floor.

Dras stubbornly rose, refusing to admit defeat. He threw another punch.

The two of them danced in the moonlight, trading blows. It was a valiant effort on Dras's part, and the battle was fierce.

The Strange Man connected another uppercut, and Dras bit the inside of his mouth. Wincing in pain, he tasted the metallic tang of his own blood. Enraged, he retaliated, tackling the Strange Man and pinning the masquerading devil to the ground. Again and again Dras beat at the Strange Man with clenched fists yet never drew blood. In fact, Dras managed little more than to muss the Strange Man's hair. Furious with his fruitless efforts, Dras continued to scuffle with the creature until the Strange Man made a most unexpected move.

He laughed.

Dras stopped short as the Strange Man laughed arrogantly, amused by the attack. "She's mine, you know," he said. "You can't save her. It's too late."

It could have been a bluff. A diversionary tactic. But the confidence in the Strange Man's voice caused Dras's surety to waver for a moment. The enemy needed only a moment.

Placing his strong feet on Dras's center of gravity, the Strange Man catapulted the boy through the air. Dras landed across the room in a crumpled heap before his mind even caught up with what had just occurred. Seeing stars, he gathered himself to his knees, trying to recollect his thoughts and prepare for another attack.

The Strange Man approached.

The beautiful image flickered, revealing the terrible, chalky white head and the chains and straps that covered his sickly form. The creature extended his claws, nearing his fallen foe, and Dras's heart hammered violently in his chest.

I'm going to die.

The Strange Man hissed with delight, drawing ever closer, his pointed shoes scraping the carpet. "You could've avoided all of this, boy, if you'd only left town when I asked."

"Why are you doing this?" Dras asked, desperate to know.

"For eons I sat before the throne of God watching over you—His precious creation. And do you know what I saw?" The Strange Man's upper lip curled in repulsion. "I saw a race of creatures that delighted in wallowing in their own filth. The things you do to each other, not to mention what you do to God. If only you could hear the halls of heaven weeping over the mess you've made of this once perfect world. You disgust me. I look on you, and I feel hate in my heart. I hate you all."

Dras edged back. The Strange Man slithered closer, his rage building.

"And I hate God for loving you so much," he concluded.

"You really are the bogeyman," Dras said, not afraid but amazed. "All those stories... They were true."

"I've been confined to those contemptible North Woods for over a century," the Strange Man seethed. "Longer than I expected. I was bound there by the faith of the forebears of Old Greenesboro, able only to watch the generations pass from afar. Every so often a few unlucky ones would wander into my web, and I relished the chance to visit upon them a small portion of the horrors I planned for your pitiful town."

Dras inched back as the Strange Man closed in.

"But now the faith of that bygone era has finally faded. This new, modern world has forgotten the things of the night. People have stopped believing in demons, and they've stopped believing in their God too. The walls have fallen. I'm free. And soon I will remind them that there are things left in the shadows to fear."

"But why Rosalyn?" Dras nearly broke into tears. "She's nothing to you."

The Strange Man's eyes lit up. "Ah, but she's everything"—a crooked finger tapped Dras's chest—"to *you*, isn't she?"

At last Dras understood. The creature standing before him

was pure hatred. He stammered, "That's all this is to you? Some sick game?"

"No, no, no," the devil countered. "Don't trivialize it. Suffering is its own reward. Seeing you, like this…I'd kill a thousand Rosalyns just to watch you weep."

Dras tried to rise, but with the wave of a hand the Strange Man fixed the trembling youth to the ground, forcing him into subservience.

"What did you hope to accomplish by telling her about God's love, boy? Did you think that knowing would protect her from me? But it's about more than knowing, isn't it? What have you ever shown her of it? It's just words coming from you—hollow, empty words—and words will not save her." The Strange Man loomed larger than life, his cold shadow settling over Dras. "You have failed."

"No," Dras shook his head, fighting off the cold spell of the Strange Man's influence.

Unexpectedly he felt a flare of assurance inside, something wholly supernatural, and he knew what to do. Without hesitation, Dras rummaged around in his coat pockets until his fingers found one of the Post-It notes he took from the church. He brought it into the moonlight and found one of the verses he scribbled: Psalm 16:1.

Bracing himself, forcing his wobbly legs to stand, Dras read the scripture aloud and with authority.

"Keep me safe, O God, for in You I take refuge!"

The Strange Man recoiled violently, his eyes afire. Dras grinned in surprise and satisfaction.

The twisted monster unleashed a terrible glower. As before at The Rave Scene—only exponentially magnified—a force slammed into Dras like two invisible hands, pushing him off his feet and sending him flying backward, smashing him through the window and plummeting him two stories straight down.

Shards of glass decorated the street as Dras crashed, landing on an unsuspecting parked car below. The impact dented the hood and cracked the windshield. Glass rained down around him.

After the storm of sorts subsided, he slowly rolled over, feeling a cracked rib swimming around inside him.

He moaned. "Ouch."

Trying not to lose consciousness, he stared with blurry vision up to the heights from which he had fallen. Rosalyn's window, now completely devoid of glass, stared back at him. No sign of the Strange Man following to make sure of the kill.

Again, Dras had been spared.

He quietly thanked God he was still alive. Painfully he rolled off the car, falling to the pavement. He was weak, and his broken body ached, but he managed to pick himself up. Sucking up air hard and fast, trying to refill his lungs, he remained bent over, just in case the need to vomit decided to overwhelm him. He heard sirens.

Wincing from pain and fatigue, he looked into the bright headlights of a squad car. Shielding his eyes, he watched as the car rolled up to him and stopped. The lights remained on, but the siren was—much to his appreciation—switched off.

Out of the car stepped someone whom Dras immediately recognized as Deputy Dane Adams, who went to high school with Jeff. He and Jeff had played baseball together, back in Dane's slimmer days.

"Dras?" Deputy Adams seemed surprised. "Is that you?"

"It's me."

Dane assessed the situation—the damaged car, the bits of broken glass strewn across the pavement, and the window above.

"What happened here?"

"I fell."

"I should say so." The deputy whistled as he surveyed the damage.

Suddenly the police band crackled to life.

"Attention all units—"

Instinctively Dane tuned his ears to listen.

"Be on the lookout for Dras Weldon. I repeat, be on the lookout for Dras Timothy Weldon. He is suspected in the murder of TJ Walker and wanted for questioning concerning Lindsey McCormick's disappearance."

TJ? Dras thought. *What does he have to do with this?*

Dras began backing away, his mind racing with the realization that he'd been set up. *For murder?* Something told him that the police would also pin on him whatever other atrocious acts the Strange Man had committed.

Dane, reaching for his firearm, turned toward Dras, unsure as to his next move.

"OK, boy," he said.

"Whoa, Deputy." Dras held out his hands, the sight of the gun making him extremely nervous. "It's not true. I've been set up. I didn't do it. I didn't do anything."

Dane wasn't looking to take any more chances than he had to. "Let's just go down to the station, Dras. We'll sort all this out."

"You've gotta believe me," Dras pleaded.

"I believe you," Dane said, although the gun in his hand didn't imply a world of confidence to Dras. "Let's go."

Dras raised his hands, knowing he had to give himself up, even though it meant that he couldn't keep looking for Rosalyn. He didn't know what else to do. Maybe the sheriff would listen to him.

As the deputy edged closer, he reached for his handcuffs, taking every necessary precaution.

Dras heard scratching. Squeaking, scraping across the pavement. Chattering teeth, clicking claws, and hungry growls.

The Strange Man's friends were back for more.

Dras and the deputy both looked into the distance. Dras, having seen the horror before, was initially less shocked by their appearance, although after recalling what they could do, he was filled with horror.

"What is that?" Dane asked.

Before Dras had a chance to explain, the buzzing horde of locust-like creatures closed in on them. They broke rank, splitting from a central swarm, each drone carrying out its own impulses.

Dras inched back, but not too far, for fear that in the heat of the moment he would get a bullet in the back from one very terrified deputy.

"We have to get out of here!" Dras shouted, trying to break through the deputy's trance.

The creatures came closer, and Dane stood paralyzed by confusion. His mind couldn't handle what he was seeing. He was beginning to lose his sanity. But not his gun.

He aimed and fired madly into the swarm of descending gremlins, digging bullets deep into their charred bodies. The bullets didn't stop them. Dras continued to back away, trying to stay on the outskirts of the droves.

"Let's go!" he cried, giving the deputy the opportunity to save his life. He had seen how fast the gremlins could move, and he knew that time was running out.

But Deputy Adams wouldn't budge. He continued firing into the plague of creatures, shouting like a madman, until they overwhelmed him. As they began to cut at him and bite him, shredding his clothes and moving on to his flesh, Dras couldn't watch anymore.

With the deputy's helpless screams behind him, Dras ran to the squad car, slid across the hood, and jumped in. Instantly a gremlin pounced on the hood of the car and roared, its terrible teeth chattering. With its vacant eyes staring back at him, Dras yelled in fright as he threw the car into all sorts of gears before he found the right one.

Finally slamming the car into drive, he pinned the pedal to the floor. Revving up and peeling away, the car barreled full steam ahead into the raging droves of unholy creatures. They bounced off the car, unfazed in their pursuit. Leaving the bloody remains of Deputy Adams behind, they came together and united to make one shape, as before. This time Dras was better prepared.

He tore through town, the image of the hungry shadows staring back at him in the rearview mirror. At such a high speed he had to fight to keep the squad car on all four tires, but he managed. He wasn't a great driver to begin with since he was never able to afford a car of his own, but necessity overcame his lack of skill. Zipping and zooming through traffic, running lights, Dras drove, the red and blues of the squad car illuminating the darkness.

"Dane?" A worried voice came through the police radio.

Startled, Dras jumped, banging his head on the top of the cabin. The radio squawked once more. "Dane! Come back, over."

Hands shaking, the sounds of the gremlins scraping the trunk of the police car, Dras fumbled for the radio, bringing it to bear.

"He–hello? Hello, is anyone there? I need help."

"Who is this?" The voice sounded annoyed, even through the static.

"Uh, Dras. My name's Dras Weldon."

"*Dras?*" The voice paused. "This is Sheriff Hank Berkley. What's your situation? Is Deputy Dane Adams with you?"

Dras felt faint, the gremlins laughing and screaming behind him.

"Dane's dead, Sheriff. They got him."

Silence. "Who got him, son?"

"They're going to tell you I did it, Sheriff, but you gotta believe me. It's him. It's…it's the bogeyman."

A roar that reminded Dras of a Hollywood-style T-Rex accompanied an earth-jarring crunch as the police car bounced up on its front two tires before crashing down on the pavement in an impressive fireworks display.

"Whoa!" Dras shouted, losing hold of the radio. The car did a doughnut in the street.

A barrage of tiny monsters assailed the vehicle, cracking the windshield, obscuring the light of the streetlamps, and cutting into metal. Dras shielded his face, terrified that the gremlins would break through at any moment. He jerked the car into reverse. Pedal to the metal, he zoomed backward, dividing his frantic attention between the monsters bearing down on him and the street behind.

People gathered outside to investigate the commotion.

Dras shouted, "Get out of the way! Move!"

Screams ensued as the curious dispersed and took shelter, the police car wailing in the night.

"Dras!" Sheriff Berkley barked from the radio.

Dras flinched, having forgotten there was a radio in the car. Somehow he dove for the handset and returned to the wheel without crashing his rear end into a pole.

"Sheriff!" he screamed, real fear taking hold. "They're everywhere! I can't shake them!"

An especially agile gremlin catapulted itself on the head of its demonic kin, caught the side of the police car, and pumped its legs. With one ferocious kick it busted the driver's side window. There was an explosion of glass, and Dras shouted once before discovering he had a hell-born gremlin in his lap.

"Ah!"

The gremlin wrapped its clawed hands around his throat and throttled him, laughing all the while. Dras banged at the thing's head with the radio handset, steering blind now. When the handset failed to harm the creature, he threw it to the side and reached into his jacket to procure his Bible. The battle-thirsty monster sniggered and squealed, strangling him. Dras's fingers brushed the holy book, but in the midst of the struggle he could not pull it out, and he knew that he would have to conjure a verse from memory to defend himself.

Distracted by the flailing beast, Dras struggled to recall a single verse out of the dozens he'd read not so long ago. *Please, God, give me something. Help!*

"Oh!" he croaked as 1 John 3:8—the Scripture from the marquee—popped into his mind, surprising him. He quoted: "The reason the Son of God appeared was to destroy the devil's work!" Laughing, he added, "Jesus has already beaten you!"

The thing shrieked in pain, its blackened flesh sizzling as if burnt by the words. It retreated, fleeing the car, rejoining the blitzing mass of shapes.

Dras shouted in dumbfounded triumph, watching the army of demons fading into the night.

"Ha! Word of God, baby!"

The squad car hit a fire hydrant.

It wheezed and died. Dras sat there watching a geyser of water rain down on the car.

He'd done it. He'd survived.

Thanks, God.

The radio crackled. Dras wasted no time raising the handset to his lips.

"Sheriff Berkley, they're leaving! They're gone!"

"Dras, we need you to come in to the station, all right? We need to sort this out."

"I can't. He's still out here. He's after Rosalyn, and I have to warn her."

"Son, that's not a good idea. We need to figure this out together. Turn yourself in and—"

"What do you mean?" Dras snapped back, his heart pumping. "Turn myself in? I didn't do anything! You don't understand."

"I understand. I believe you. We want to help."

Dras felt faint. The sheriff was lying to him, trying to negotiate him into a surrender for murders he had no part in committing. Suddenly he worried that even if by some divine miracle he survived the night, the only future that awaited him was a cold prison cell.

The world slowed in that moment. Just days ago he'd barely been able to convince himself to go to church and listen to a sermon for an hour. Now, now he had given up everything for his faith.

What have I done?

Then he remembered Rosalyn, and nothing else mattered.

Sheriff Berkley continued reasoning with him. Dras reached over and switched off the radio. He didn't need any more distractions. He started the car and returned to the road, his mind focused. He had to get to Rosalyn. If only he knew where she was.

He spotted the line outside The Rave Scene. Ignoring the curfew, the place stayed open, offering drinks and dancing to those brave enough to rebel against the sheriff's edict.

"Of course!" Dras exclaimed, overjoyed with relief.

He slammed on the brakes, and the car fishtailed to a rubber-burning halt in front of the factory, drawing stares from the would-be clubbers lined up outside.

At the sight of a squad car—which looked as though it had just survived a demolition derby—some of the partygoers walked away, fearful of being punished for breaking the curfew. But when Dras kicked open the dented and scratched door, to their relief they realized they were in no danger of police involvement.

Dras tumbled out of the car, expecting to be overwhelmed by gremlins any second, but a quick glance around told him the devils had vanished. Either they were afraid, which seemed unlikely—*Or they're saving me for their boss.*

Trying not to think about the grim alternative, Dras pushed toward the entrance, shoving his way through the crowd.

"Out of the way!" he hollered, allowing nothing to stand in his path to Rosalyn.

When some of the offended partygoers made their protests known, Dras rudely knocked them down. Even when he reached Pete, the burly dark-skinned bouncer he'd always kind of liked, he spared no time. He pushed past him, and when Pete grabbed his arm with a, "Hey, hold up a sec! You know you gotta pay the cover, Dras," Dras elbowed him in the stomach, doubling him over.

"Sorry, Pete," Dras said as he disappeared inside the club.

Pete recovered from the hit with a cough as one of the other bouncers rushed to his side. Grimacing, Pete said, "Better call the cops. We might have a situation."

CHAPTER TWENTY-THREE

EFF LEANED OVER the steering wheel, willing his old pickup to go faster. He scanned the streets and sidewalks as his mind worked to anticipate where Dras would go. His only guess was that Dras would return to Rosalyn's apartment, so that's where Jeff headed first. Despite his new desire to help his brother, Jeff still had doubts about what exactly they were trying to save Rosalyn from. Isabella rode quietly in the passenger seat, doing her part to keep a lookout for her brother-in-law. Jeff wondered if she fully believed what Dras said.

That the bogeyman was after Rosalyn.

It was about the craziest thing he'd ever heard, and a small part of him felt utterly foolish for being so worried and speeding through the all-but-abandoned streets of Greensboro after curfew.

I'm a grown man, he told himself. *What do I really expect to find out here?*

But the moment he thought to turn the truck around and head back home, ready to chalk up the whole strange escapade to Dras being a dork, he remembered the desperation in his brother's eyes. There had been hopeless terror there—not for himself, for Rosalyn.

Jeff wouldn't be able to live with himself if something happened to her and he'd done nothing to stop it, even if Dras's perception of the situation was ridiculous. Whether there was a literal bogeyman haunting Greensboro or not, Jeff couldn't let anything hurt Rosalyn.

"What are you thinking?" Isabella asked.

Jeff started at the sound of her voice. She had turned off the radio when they began their goose chase to quiet her mind and keep her focus.

"I don't know," Jeff said truthfully. "I don't really know what we're doing out here."

Isabella didn't remind him, knowing full well he knew what they were doing—it was just the *why* he couldn't grasp. "You don't believe him," she said.

"You *do*?"

Isabella flushed. She gazed out the window, suddenly quiet. A second later, "Jeff—"

Jeff laughed. "Do you really think a demon—a real, flesh-and-blood *demon*—is after Roz? I mean, seriously, what do you think's going to happen tonight?"

"Jeff!" she screamed, pointing, blood draining from her face.

Jeff slammed on the brakes.

Ahead of them was Rosalyn's apartment building, cordoned off by a police barricade that held back gawking neighbors shuffling about in their evening attire. An ambulance screamed past Jeff's old truck.

"Rosalyn."

Amidst other stalled motorists caught out past curfew, Jeff shut off his engine. He hopped out of the truck and pushed through the mob of people. Isabella matched his movement. A quick examination of the scene revealed Rosalyn's busted out window, a blanket of shattered glass below, and blood.

Lots of dark crimson blood.

"No..." Jeff paled.

Deputies milled about the crime scene, kneeling with ashen faces, taking pictures, making notes, and interviewing wildly gesturing neighbors. Jeff spotted young Deputy Hollis nearest the barricade, nervously trying to keep the crowd at bay with feeble explanations.

"Everybody, just stand back," he said shakily. "Everything's under control."

"Deputy," Jeff shouted, shoving his way forward, nearly toppling over the standing barricade. "What happened?"

"Uh... There's been a murder, Reverend," Hollis explained, eyes darting back and forth.

"Where's Rosalyn Myers?" Jeff asked, struggling with his emotions. "That's her apartment! Is she OK? Is she here?"

Hollis shifted, blushing. "Um—"

Deputy Carter Ross, seeing Hollis crumple under the raving pastor's pressure, pulled off his latex gloves with a plastic snap and approached. "Hey there, preacher."

Jeff cooled, realizing he was causing a scene. "Carter, what's going on?"

"One of our deputies was killed."

"Is Rosalyn Myers OK?"

"We haven't seen her."

Isabella gripped Jeff's arm with both hands, breathing deep. "Thank God."

"What about my brother?" Jeff asked.

Carter looked away, as if expecting that question to come sooner or later.

"Is he here?"

"We're looking for him," Carter said evenly.

"Why do you say it like that?"

"Surely he's not a suspect," Isabella argued. "Is he?"

"We're looking into that, Isabella," Carter said in a way that made Jeff step forward, drawing the deputy's attention to him rather than his wife.

"It was bats, I tell ya!" a middle-aged woman shouted. She

wore a fuzzy blue nightgown, her bottle-blonde hair up in curlers. "It was like a whole flock of bats! They were following that boy!"

Jeff's mind raced, trying to process the information. Isabella tugged on his sleeve.

"We'll find them," she said, her voice sure as stone.

Jeff put a hand to his head, feeling sweat breaking out, his heart picking up in nervous anticipation.

Everything is spinning out of control. What's happening?

Garbled static crackled simultaneously on Hollis's and Carter's radios. Deputy Ryan Stevenson's growling voice followed, clear as a bell.

"Calling all units. We just got a call from The Rave Scene. The Weldon kid is there. Repeat: all units converge on The Rave Scene. Suspect is considered armed and extremely dangerous."

Carter and Hollis shared an awkward look before looking to Jeff. Eyes locked on the preacher, Carter radioed, "Negative, Unit 4. We're stuck at the scene."

"Copy that, Unit 6." Stevenson chuckled, darkly. "We'll manage without you."

"N–no," Jeff stuttered, staring between Hollis and Carter. "No, you don't know what you're talking about. This... There's got to be a misunderstanding."

"This is police business, Jeff," Carter said, his voice full of pity. "You'd do best to go back home."

Jeff glared at the deputy, his hands balling into fists. Without a word, he turned tail and marched for his truck like a man possessed.

Isabella was caught between her husband and the apologetic deputies, but determined to find Dras and Rosalyn, she threw Hollis and Carter a final pleading stare before running to catch up with Jeff.

The lights inside The Rave Scene swirled. The music was deafening, and the bass shook the house. As every night, the youth danced, laughed, and drank to escape their worries and concerns.

Dras tried to break free of their numbers. He never before realized how many people came here, how many unhappy, lost souls there were in Greensboro. These people, who used to be his friends—or at least his compatriots—now stood between him and Rosalyn, holding him back. They overwhelmed him with their masses, and he fought harder and harder to push through. The more he struggled, the thicker the crowd became.

Yet through the crowd, he caught a glimpse of her.

Rosalyn.

His heart warmed; newfound energy coursed through his veins. She was here. She was all right.

It's not too late.

Rosalyn, completely unaware of any danger, danced on. Three strapping young men surrounded her, and she flirted with them all, gyrating and running her hands through her hair as she made promises with her body she never intended to keep. But the fellows didn't seem to mind. Playfully she danced in their midst, dividing her attention and energy between them.

And as she danced, the Strange Man watched.

He studied Rosalyn as she moved, judging her truly magnificent. Casually he prowled, circling her, biding his time. She would not be able to resist him now. She would give in and receive him willingly.

She will be mine.

He thought of all the terrible things he would do to her.

As he watched her sway, as he considered the way she teased her partners with her eyes and smile, he knew she was perfect. It was his time to own her, to consume her.

"Rosalyn!"

The Strange Man's ears picked up a voice that the others in the factory could not hear over the pounding music. He turned and saw Dras, much to his surprise. The boy had not spotted him yet, and the Strange Man hung back in the shadows to ensure that his presence remained unknown. He had not expected the boy to last this long. No matter. It was too late.

Breaking free of the crowd, Dras rushed to Rosalyn. He pushed one of her dancing partners aside and faced her. "Rosalyn! I have to talk to you!"

Rosalyn's beau moved to retaliate, but she held him off. She turned to her boy toys.

"Take five, guys."

Disgusted with Dras for ruining their chances, they found other girls to dance with. When they were gone, Rosalyn spun around.

"What are you doing here?" she demanded, angry that he had interrupted her when she was so clearly trying to ignore her problems with innocent flirtations.

"You weren't home!" Dras tried to explain, shouting to be heard over the thundering bass. "I have to talk to you!"

Rosalyn shook him off. "I need some space, Dras. I'll talk to you later."

"No!" Dras cried.

Rosalyn took a step back. Dras realized how forceful he sounded and tried to recover.

"There's no time! You're in trouble!"

"What are you talking about?" She gave him her discrediting expression.

Dras growled, looking at the nearby speakers in frustration. "I have to tell you about Jesus!" he shouted.

Rosalyn, unable to hear over the racket, shook her head. "What?"

"I have to tell you about Jesus!" Dras stressed the words.

Deeming it all unimportant, Rosalyn rolled her eyes and shooed him away. She turned and walked toward the bar. Finding an empty stool, she waved Larry over.

The bartender nodded, but before he went to get her a drink, he noticed Dras.

"Hey, Dras. You wanna get started tonight?"

"Not tonight, Larry."

Larry stopped in a moment of pure shock. Dras Weldon had never turned down a drink. Even Rosalyn was surprised, but then, Dras was full of surprises lately. Everything was changing between them. She didn't know what to feel or what to think or who they were anymore. First she was planning to go to Vermont; then she met the beautiful man who filled her thoughts. Then there was the weird kiss between her and Dras, and to top it all off, Dras had experienced some kind of religious conversion. Life was moving too fast, and she needed a break.

"Can we go outside and talk?" Dras pleaded.

Rosalyn sighed. Growing annoyed, she said, "Go home, Dras."

"Listen to me." His tone was quieter. Less forceful but still urgent. "Please, Rosalyn. There isn't a lot of time. Please just listen."

She turned to him. In a hateful, biting tone, she said, "No, you listen, OK? Don't do this. If you want to get religious or whatever, that's your business. But leave me out of it."

"It's not *religion*. I'm talking about the truth!"

"What do you know about truth?" she demanded, then relaxed. "If this is going to be a repeat performance on how Rosalyn is going to hell, then I'd like to sit this one out."

"I know, I know, that was not my finest moment." Dras sighed. "I was scared and..." He trailed off, then took a deep breath, bracing himself. This was the moment he had fought all night for. Praying for God to help him get through it, Dras began. "Look, I've seen hell." Dras thought of the Strange Man, the sheer pleasure that the demon exhibited at the torture and destruction he had wrought. He shivered at the thought of a place like hell existing, a place where untold legions of Strange Men lurked, visiting nightmares upon the damned. "It's like this hungry *thing*, and it's always looking for more souls to swallow."

Rosalyn groaned and hid her face with her hands. "Dras, let's please not do this again."

"But God doesn't want that for you," Dras interjected. "I get that. That's what Jesus came to do—to destroy the devil's work. To save you from hell, if you'd just reach out to Him."

Rosalyn blew out a sigh and rolled her eyes. Dras was losing her. He forced himself to calm down, determined not to blow this as he'd done earlier. Softly, he began, "Rosalyn, God loves you. God said that He has plans for you, to give you hope and to give you a future."

Rosalyn eyed him strangely and chuckled. "He told you that, did He?"

"Well, *yeah*," Dras shrugged. "Sorta." Excitedly Dras reached into his pocket and pulled out the small Bible and the handful of scraps of paper with verses written on them. He dumped them on the counter and shuffled through the mess. Flipping through the pages of the Bible, he tried to find the scriptures he'd previously marked.

"It's all in here," he told her. "It always has been. I just never thought to look before. I didn't realize how *important* it was before now."

Rosalyn sat in silence, taking it all in. "So, why now? Let's just say, for one insane moment, I believe that you're serious about this. Why do you care all of a sudden? Not once have you ever talked to me about this stuff. Why now?"

Dras turned away for a moment. "I was wrong. The world turned out to be a lot bigger than I thought it was."

Rosalyn watched him, curious as to what had gotten into him. Never had she seen him like this. He was absolutely passionate. Sure, he was always giddy when telling her about the latest X-Men comic, but he never showed so much interest in anything serious. *Had he become a man, and I missed it?*

Dras took a moment to shuffle through his pile once more. He found what he was looking for: "Romans 8:38 and 39 says, 'For I am convinced that neither death nor life, neither angels nor demons, neither the present nor the future, nor any powers, neither height nor depth, nor anything else in all creation, will be able to separate us from the love of God that is in Christ Jesus our Lord.'"

Dras finished and began refolding the scraps of paper. When he looked up, Rosalyn was staring at him, quiet and thoughtful.

"That's... That sounds really nice," she said.

Dras touched her hand. "It's like God gives us these moments where we have to choose. He wants us to choose Him so He can protect us and provide for us... but... there are these... *other* things out there that are trying to pull us away." He leaned back, his heart full of regret. "I get that now. I listened to that other voice for too long, and I don't want to anymore. I... I don't want you to listen to that other voice if—*when*—it starts calling out to you. I want you to make the right choice."

Rosalyn smirked after a quiet moment. "OK, I appreciate the concern, I do. But Dras, come on. This is all a little hard to believe."

He stared at her.

She chuckled. "You're telling me that all my life has been leading to this one moment with you in a bar telling me about God?"

"Why not?" Dras laughed, marveling at how simple it really was. "Maybe this is your moment. Rosalyn, God loves you. He wants good things for you. You gotta believe that."

"He doesn't even know me."

"Sure He does. How can you even say that?"

Dras couldn't believe what she was saying. After all that God had done to get Dras here to talk to her. Of course He loved her. This was all about her. Everything that Dras had gone through tonight, the battles and the crashing through windows. Deputy Adams lost his life, buying Dras time to get to The Rave Scene so he could tell Rosalyn these things. God moved heaven and earth and changed the heart of an immature child and molded him into a man. All for Rosalyn.

How can she not see that?

"What about my dad, then?" Rosalyn asked him pointedly, her jaw tense, eyes cold and confrontational. "Was that all part of the awesome Plan-to-Give-Rosalyn-a-Great-Life too?"

Dras sank into his chair. *Her dad. Of course...*

"Rosalyn—" he began, though he had no good answers to give her.

"Hello, Dras."

The voice was familiar, and the crawling feeling he got in his stomach was even more so. Now Dras realized Rosalyn couldn't see God right in front of her because the Strange Man was standing in the way.

Rosalyn spun around to see the mysterious man she danced with almost a week ago grinning before her. "Hey." She smiled warmly, wiping away tears.

The Strange Man winked at her, but his attention remained on Dras. "I hope I'm not interrupting anything." He cocked his head to one side, as if daring the boy to speak about God in his presence.

Dras glared at him. "You can't have her."

Rosalyn stood, confused. She looked at the man to see if he shared her bewilderment, but the Strange Man bore recognition on his face. "You can't stop me."

"What's going on?" Rosalyn said, not appreciating being left out of the know.

Dras became all the more resolved as he took a stand between the Strange Man and Rosalyn.

"Try me."

The Strange Man appeared amused.

"Dras? What's he talking about?" Rosalyn demanded.

Suddenly the doors to the factory burst open, and the combined efforts of the Maribel County Sheriff's Department stormed in like an efficient task force. News of Deputy

Adams's grisly death had reached the reinforcements. Deputy Ryan Stevenson stood at the forefront of the task force, violence burning in his blue eyes.

"Everybody *freeze!*"

CHAPTER TWENTY-FOUR

OUTSIDE, JEFF PULLED to a screeching halt in front of The Rave Scene as droves of screaming youth broke rank, flooding into the street in all directions. Fearing the worst, he and Isabella burst into a mad run, fighting upstream through the people, pressing toward their friends.

Please, God. Don't let me be too late.

Inside, the factory was an uproar. Despite Deputy Stevenson's command for everyone to remain still, panic broke out. As if feeling busted for their dirty little sins, everyone in The Rave Scene stampeded. Everyone but Dras, Rosalyn, and the Strange Man. The three of them stood facing each other, frozen in time, oblivious to the chaos that raged all around them. Rosalyn was still lost in Dras's eyes, though his were focused on the interloper in their midst.

"You'd better run, boy." The Strange Man smiled. "They're onto you."

Dras knew the police were here for him. He knew the Strange Man was to blame. At his fingertips on the bar was his pile of scriptures. Any one of them would be enough to repel the Strange Man, but only for a time. Hell had its sights on Rosalyn, and Dras realized that he wouldn't be able to ward off evil forever. No, Rosalyn needed God's presence in her life to give her that kind of protection. But she would only have that if she invited it in—if she chose—and he couldn't seem to find a way to convince her that God loved her.

Unless—

Dras turned to Rosalyn, his eyes filled with compassion and a depth she had never seen in their twenty-two years together. They had shared a lifetime. Soul mates. She was sure she knew everything about him. Every thought he'd ever had. Every goofy thing he'd ever done. And yet, when he looked at her now, she wondered if maybe she didn't truly know him at all.

"I'm sorry," Dras apologized. "I tried to save you, but he's too strong for me. You've got to make the choice yourself to stand up to him."

"There he is!" Stevenson shouted. He pointed at Dras so his brothers in forest green could spot the suspect.

Immediately the officers shoved their way forward, pushing back the onrush of people. Dras turned slowly and saw them coming.

"This is it," he breathed, the hint of tears in his eyes.

"You have to get out of here," Rosalyn pleaded with him as the police neared.

She didn't know what was happening, but she knew Dras was in trouble, and she wanted to protect him. She was always good at protecting him.

"*Please,*" she begged.

He shook his head.

Stevenson and his men turned over tables in their reckless pursuit to get their man. They were almost on top of him now.

The Strange Man, wanting to avoid any attention this early in the game, quietly disappeared into the shadows and was lost in the unseen realm, leaving Dras and Rosalyn alone.

Taking his time, seeing no need to hurry anymore, Dras reached into his back pocket and pulled out the very special note that he was saving for Rosalyn. He handed it to her and clasped his hands around hers, making sure she took it.

"You don't believe God loves you. But you're wrong. God loved you enough to send Jesus to die for you, to give you another choice. Choose *Him*. I should've been showing you that love all this time, but—" he paused, then took a deep, resolved breath—"this is the only way I know how to now."

He started to pull his hand away. Rosalyn shook her head, unable to understand what was happening. "No. Dras, wait. What are you doing?"

"I gotta face them. I can't run forever. God's got a plan; I *have* to believe that. I hope one day you know why I had to do this. Just remember what I said, OK? No matter what happens. It's up to you now."

Rosalyn reached for him, but he had already stepped back, the deputies about to crash over him like the tide against the shore. The Strange Man had wanted him to leave town. Dras knew that it was more important to stay with Rosalyn, to tell her the truth, no matter the cost. Now he was ready to face the consequences for that decision, realizing he would have to pay for his stand against the Strange Man with his freedom. Maybe even his life.

But I get it, God, Dras silently prayed. *She's worth the sacrifice.*

Jesus knew that, and I finally get it too. I'm not going to run away and let the devil win. So whatever You've got planned, I'm ready.

Rosalyn clutched the folded paper tightly as the police overtook Dras. Stevenson was the first. He used his nightstick to beat Dras over the back. With a shout of pain, Dras doubled over and went to the floor.

"*No!*" Rosalyn screamed hoarsely.

She moved to help him but was stopped by a deputy trying to protect her from the suspect. She tried to contest, fully capable of handling herself in a fight, but the deputy was twice her size, and he held her back. She could only watch as they beat her friend.

The deputies tore at Dras's hair and spit on him, crying out for blood.

Rosalyn screamed for them to stop, but her tearful cries were lost in their cheers of victory.

Just then Jeff and Isabella finally made it into The Rave Scene, but it was too late. Isabella stopped, shocked by the horrible violence being committed by the men sworn to protect the people of Greensboro.

Unable to stand helplessly by, Jeff ran, full force, and tackled one of the deputies. Desperately trying to defend Dras, he fought with tears in his eyes. They were pounding the life out of his little brother, the brother he held wrapped in a blanket just hours after he was born, the brother who was his biggest fan in Little League. They fought together and rode bikes together. They stole Mom's cookies together and loved each other.

And now these men were beating him. It wasn't right. It wasn't fair. Dras was his little brother. His little screwup brother.

The police came to the aid of their own and pinned Jeff to the ground. Broken by the sight of his little brother being stolen from him by these upholders of justice, he cried, "No! Please, stop!" His voice shook with tears, but they would not listen.

Helpless, Jeff, Isabella, and Rosalyn watched as Dras was kicked in the face, his teeth knocked loose. His clothes were ripped from him, and the small Bible that had seen him through the night's battles fell to the floor. Dras moaned, unable to come to his senses enough to defend himself or even protest. He clawed for air, his blood-soaked hands scraping across the tiled floor while he desperately fought to breathe. In the end, it was not the twitching darkness that he had so feared that overcame him but rather the evil of men.

Isabella turned around, unable to watch anymore. Jeff shut his eyes, weeping. Dras's agonizing cries filled his ears. That and the men's laughter.

They're enjoying this.

As Rosalyn watched, everything seemed to dim and play before her eyes in ghastly slow motion. In the middle of it all, with cuts and bruises covering his face, Dras looked up at her. Right at her.

Why? she wanted to scream at him. *Why did you do it?*

As she sobbed, he almost managed a weak smile, and she knew. It was for her. All for her. She didn't understand why, but she knew that Dras gave himself up to the deputies for her sake. He was trying to show her something.

But what? What did you have to show me that could possibly make you do this?

A gunshot split the air. Rosalyn jumped.

"*That's enough!*" roared Sheriff Hank Berkley.

The deputies, Stevenson last of all, subsided in their blood-lust and succumbed to their better senses. They regained their composure, leaving Dras's bloody remains sprawled on the floor of The Rave Scene.

The sheriff holstered his gun and marched toward them, shocked and disgusted by what they had done.

"What is this?" he demanded. "I never ordered this! Who's in charge?"

Stevenson was pushed to the front. Although he looked sorry to be caught, he seemed fulfilled by the blood on his hands.

As soon as the mob released Dras, Rosalyn, Jeff, and Isabella broke free and ran to him. Crying, they fell to their knees and cradled his broken body. Even the sheriff, ashamed of the actions of his own deputies, stooped down to the boy. Reaching over, he checked for a pulse and pulled back slowly.

Jeff cried harder still as he held his brother.

"I'm so sorry I didn't listen. I'm so sorry."

He wept bitterly, and Isabella held her husband close, squeezing him tightly as if to keep them both from falling to pieces.

With a whimper, the tragedy was finished.

Rosalyn stood, unable to comprehend the horror before her eyes, unable to believe it had all happened. She watched as Jeff and Isabella held her best friend in their arms, weeping. She felt colder and more alone than ever. She didn't know how to exist without him. Her future seemed so uncertain now. Everything seemed so uncertain.

She felt small. Insignificant. Lost.

"Rosalyn." The Strange Man called to her with his sing-song voice, laying his hand on her shoulder like claws of ice. After shedding his corporeal form, he had slipped back into the spiritual realm, where he was stronger. Here, unseen by mortal eyes, without having to concentrate on maintaining a physical manifestation of his evil, he could concentrate all his power—all his influence—on calling out to her spirit. "Come with me." He leaned closer to her ear, his voice filled with compassion, "Let me take you away from all of this," he breathed, tempting her away from her place at the boy's side. "*Stay with me,*" he hissed, dreamlike, his pleas seeping deep into her soul, beckoning her.

Rosalyn's shoulders drooped, her physical body reacting to his spiritual pleas.

She's mine, the Strange Man hissed inwardly, eyes afire. He could feel her now, her resolve waning. "Stay with me," he repeated again, hypnotically. *Come with me into the darkness, and I will show you such wicked wonders.* He felt her despair and breathed it in like a drug. She was so wonderfully miserable, her spirit broken and torn apart.

Just like me, he suddenly realized.

He'd only thought to glory in her death before, but now—now he understood how much sweeter it would be were she to join him. *I can remake her in my own image.*

"Look at me." he entreated, hungry for her degradation. "Rosalyn, look at me."

All she must do is look at me. Accept me, and we will be together in perfect hell.

Instead she looked at the boy.

"Look at me." he growled, his face darkening and his eyes beginning to glow.

With barely an effort, she took one step forward, one step away from him and closer to that insufferable boy. Her back remained to him, shutting him out.

She had made her decision this night.

The Strange Man's spell snapped as Rosalyn tore free. Raging, he trembled, impotent. "Come back to me!" he projected to her, exerting all his effort. "Look at me!"

But she would not.

Her heart remained fixed on the boy as she shed tears for him. The Strange Man reared back with outstretched talons and charged, determined to gut her here and now—to sate his uncontrollable lust. He roared like an animal, tears of desperation and rejection welling in his glowing eyes, and lunged forward to strike. However, the girl's love for the boy—or perhaps the boy's love for her, which he had demonstrated in his one selfless act—shone from Rosalyn like a bomb blast, and the Strange Man staggered back, halted.

He retracted, his face aghast with this outcome.

In removing the boy he had given him more power.

Glowering now, his teeth stretched in a tight grimace, the Strange Man stood away from her, denied his prize. His hate blossomed, and he thought to destroy everyone tonight, to turn hell loose on this town and not stop until he waded in streets of spilt blood. Then they would know his retribution!

But he calmed himself, forced himself to remember his true purpose. He did not come to Greensboro to seduce schoolgirls. He had bigger schemes to set in motion. The boy was gone now. Soon the girl's love would fade—her defenses would fall—and she *would* be his, one way or another. He had waited over a century already to come to this town and visit his vengeance upon its inhabitants. He must only be patient awhile longer. *It's only a matter of time*, he repeated in his dark mind.

In the meantime, the Hour still waited.

The Strange Man loosed a grim chuckle that rumbled the heavenlies and vanished.

Shaking off a sudden chill, Rosalyn looked at her hand, where she saw the small folded note that Dras gave her only moments before. His legacy.

She thought to open it, to read it and find out what his last words were to her, what he was trying to tell her by allowing himself to be trampled and abused. Maybe the letter would hold the explanation she needed. However, she couldn't muster the courage to read it. She just wasn't ready.

Not yet. Maybe not for a long time.

She slid it into her back pocket, its contents still a mystery. For now, she could only grieve.

From his place on the floor, Dras saw his friends surround him, felt their tears splashing his face when he felt nothing else. His arms and legs wouldn't move when he commanded them to. His jaw hung loosely on a hinge, broken. No words came out.

In those moments—his last moments on Earth, he assumed— he thought back to his conversation with his father earlier in the night. Their words came back.

"I'm scared, Dad," he had said back then before he knew what fate awaited him.

But you did know, he told himself. *You knew it would end badly, but you did it anyway.*

"What if it doesn't work out? What if I fail?"

"Son, when it comes to doing the right thing, it's not about

winning or losing. It's about making your stand." Brave Jack Weldon, who had faced every obstacle meant to test him and survived.

Dras felt Jeff cradle his head and wanted to tell him it was going to be OK. He worried how Jeff would take this, if he'd blame himself for not believing Dras and coming to his aid. But Dras understood now that this was something he had to face alone.

He shifted his eyes, trying to get a glimpse of Rosalyn. He barely saw her standing away from the carnage, her face a mask of disbelief and shock. Had he failed her? *No.* No, he told her that he believed God had a plan, and he had to keep believing that now, even at the end. God would make some good come out of this. He *had* to. Dras had only to play his part.

Now it was Rosalyn's turn.

She had the truth now, and Dras had to believe that the truth would set her free.

Again, Jack Weldon's words came back to him as his vision dimmed to blackness.

"When it comes to doing the right thing, it's not about winning or losing. It's about making your stand." His father had smiled at him, stood on the front porch, and put an arm around his son. *"In the end, that's all that really matters."*

Yeah, Dras thought, a sudden peace washing over him. His eyelids were heavy now, his breathing shallow and sparse. *I made my stand.*

I can live with that.

"I want to make you proud, Dad."

"You don't have to do anything to make me proud, son. I love you, and I always will. No matter what."

"I love you, Dad."

I love you, Rosalyn.

EPILOGUE

FAR FROM THE tragic drama unfolding in The Rave Scene, the Strange Man slithered through rolling green mist, moving deep into the North Woods toward Greensboro Park Lake. The lake remained taped off—quarantined—while the police continued their investigation. Stories were spreading in town regarding little Timmy Whitaker's bizarre discovery, and everyone had a theory.

But by the time they learn the truth, it will be too late, the Strange Man delightfully mused.

He hovered above the dark water and stooped down to twirl his hooked claw in the muck. As he had expected, the consistency was shifting. The lake was getting thicker. Darker. It was changing.

First the lake. Then the town, the Strange Man thought.

It began with his sacrifice of Lindsey McCormick. The shedding of her blood began the corruption, cursing the lake and its surroundings. *Haunted* was the term folks would use to describe this patch of country, but humans rarely appreciated the full meaning of the word. There was so much to the world they did not understand, so many old things that had existed since before time began, before simple human intellect sought to conquer the mysteries of the universe, old things that were forgotten or reasoned away by the diminutive mind of man, old things that would soon rise again and reclaim their hold on the earth.

Greensboro—a simple, average, insignificant town—would

be the first to witness the resurgence of those unspeakable horrors.

The surface of the lake bubbled like thick tar, and the Strange Man withdrew his finger, wringing his hands over his swirling cauldron of dark power. In the air around him the birds of the trees took flight, cawing and flapping, desperate to get away from the supernatural pull of the transformed waters. The insects chirped and buzzed fearfully and scurried off into the distance as quickly as they could. The North Woods emptied their creatures, and the Strange Man closed his eyes in silent ecstasy, hearing their turmoil, sensing their terror.

Flee. He smiled to himself. *But you will never escape.*

Soon the dark water of the cursed lake would start calling lost souls to its depths, changing them as it had been changed, making them the first of its children.

Then the real fun will begin.

Until then the Strange Man would be content to wait and watch from the shadows. He had achieved some small personal victory in removing the boy, it was true. His secret work was safe for now, and only time would tell if others would rise up and challenge his machinations. But if that happened, he would see to them just as ruthlessly.

Yes, the battle is just beginning.

To Be Continued...

O Jerusalem, Jerusalem, who kills the prophets and stones those who are sent to her! How often I wanted to gather your children together, the way a hen gathers her chicks under her wings *and you were unwilling.*
—Matthew 23:37, nas, emphasis added

THE COMING EVIL: AMONG THE DEAD

by Greg Mitchell

*Historian's Note: This story takes place ten years before
The Coming Evil, Book One: The Strange Man*

PEGGY McDOWELL OWNED a lot of cats.

Her trailer in Trysdale always smelled of mildew and feline urine, and the weeds from her overgrown yard had latched onto the home, fixing the rotted mess to the ground. Wallace, Peggy's husband of thirty years, had suffered a stroke and died last summer, leaving the widow a ghost of a woman. Nowadays she could be seen wandering the nearby North Woods at night, dressed in her silk flower-patterned nightgown and carrying an oil lantern, calling out, "Wall–ace. Wall–ace… "

Trysdale children feared her yet made a game of sneaking up to her leaning, weed-covered trailer to steal a peak through the grimy windows and catch a glimpse of the spooky old crone. But today Rosalyn Myers's best friend decided to take the game a step further.

Dras Weldon, the same age as Rosalyn to the day, ventured a knock on Peggy's front door.

Rosalyn pulled on his arm with a hiss. "Are you nuts?"

Dras cracked a goofy grin, scratching at his already disheveled blond hair. "I'm just going to knock."

"What if she answers?"

"The idea is that I'll already be out of there by then."

"This is stupid." Rosalyn placed her hands on her hips.

"Well, if your mom had cable out here—"

"I'm walking back home. If you want to be an idiot and do this, you're on your own."

Rosalyn threw back her long, bouncy auburn hair with a huff and stormed in the opposite direction. Dras watched, not at all bothered by her threat. He called after her. "Scared?"

The girl halted instantly and waited only a moment before marching back toward Dras, waving her index finger. "Dras Timothy Weldon, if you ever—"

"Ha ha. Gotcha."

Rosalyn fumed. "Just shut up and knock already so we can get out of here."

Dras took a bow. "Certainly." He made his way to the front steps of the rickety trailer.

Rosalyn rubbed her arms nervously, shooting suspicious glances to each side, fearful that something in hiding might pounce on them. She was afraid. She was mature enough to admit that but not mature enough to admit it to Dras.

Dras turned back, his eyes alight with mischief and his face smeared with a silly euphoria. He stuck out his tongue, then rapped hard on the aluminum door.

The door flung open, and Old Woman McDowell's plump face appeared before them, her thin lips drooping, her eyes tiny beads of fire.

"What do you want?"

Dras jumped back in terror, then took off running for the country fields beyond. Rosalyn's breath caught in her throat as she turned tail, Dras's heels little more than specks on the distant horizon.

"Dras, you goofball!"

Suddenly she heard crying behind her and skidded to a dead halt. Hesitantly, Rosalyn turned back to the shabby trailer and saw Old Woman McDowell leaning against the doorframe, her fat face in her meaty hands, weeping.

Rosalyn's expression softened. She approached the woman.

"I'm sorry," the girl said meekly. "That was mean. We were mean."

The old woman jerked to attention, startled. She wiped away her tears with the sleeve of her flower-patterned nightgown.

"You're not the first." Her voice was little more than a warble.

Rosalyn stepped closer.

Her double chin trembling, Old Woman McDowell said, "I hear the stories they tell about me in town. They think I'm crazy." Then softer, to herself, she muttered, "A crazy old fool."

Rosalyn frowned, her heart torn between pity for the poor woman and guilt for her part in the ridicule. "I don't think you're crazy."

As if spotting an oasis in the desert, the old woman's thin, falling lips lifted ever so slightly in a wrinkled smile. "My name is Peggy."

Rosalyn extended a hand. "I'm Rosalyn."

"Can you hear them? Can you hear the hounds of hell baying in the full moon's light? They're looking for you!"

Just a week ago Dras ran like a sissy from a completely human and in no way supernatural elderly woman. But his fears of the widow McDowell were long since forgotten, and now he and Rosalyn were making time for the kind of horror

Dras was perfectly comfortable facing—the kind that stayed safely behind the glass of the Weldon family television.

He grinned as the show's familiar opening monologue began. Canned sound effects of howling wolves played over organ music as the camera zoomed through a mist-enshrouded forest. The words *Midnight Matinee* dripped in bright, animated blood, and Dras stuffed his face with another handful of popcorn.

"Want some?"

Rosalyn sat beside him on the floor, leaning against the couch. She was clearly lost in thought, and Dras tried to break the spell by bouncing a piece of popcorn off her nose.

"Hey!"

He crunched on another mouthful, gently shaking the bowl before her as one might coax a kitten out of hiding with a ball of string.

"Ooh 'ahnt ahny'hing?" he managed between chews.

"I'm fine," she answered, mindlessly staring at the screen as the image dissolved to a black-and-white mad scientist's laboratory, complete with beakers of bubbling fluid, dry ice, and cobweb-decorated stone walls. In the center of the stage a coffin rested. The lid slowly creaked open, and a portly bald man sporting a bushy mustache, dusty suit, gloves, and a magician's cape sat up with a moan.

"I'm your frightful host, Edmond Ghoulie, back from the dead to guide you through these monster-infested territories in order to bring you another terror-filled film of yesteryear."

Dras ignored Rosalyn, his attention devoted to "Dead Ed" Ghoulie. The late-night horror show host was somewhere between a rotting corpse and a stage magician. His pancake makeup crinkling around his mascara gave him a decomposing look. The scene cut to Dead Ed already in a standing position— to spare the poor overweight actor from awkwardly climbing out of the coffin on camera—and with every syllable, the ghoul gave a flourish of his cape, reaching out toward the camera with black-gloved fingers.

"You're in for a truly petrifying treat, kiddies. Tonight you will bear witness to 1963's blood-soaked *Crypt of Dracula*, starring the late great vampire killer himself, Donald Cushing. Beware, dear viewer, lest your heart grow faint at the horrors that await you. And try to remind yourself... it's only a movie."

Dras's grin grew wider. Eerie music swelled as *Crypt of Dracula* began.

"This is going to be so good." Dras dug around in his bowl of popcorn.

But when he took notice of his best friend's downcast expression, Dras's giddiness faded. Rosalyn was quiet tonight. True, she didn't share his enthusiasm for the local Saturday night horror host or his cheesy B movies, but she at least enjoyed spending the night at Dras's house goofing around and talking about the trivial things of youth while his parents slept soundly upstairs.

That was before her father committed suicide around a month ago.

"Wanna watch something else?" Dras asked quietly.

The subject was fresh and painful, and he was careful to be supportive of Rosalyn without actually mentioning the tragedy in conversation. Suddenly he felt like a heel for sitting next to her, scarfing down popcorn as innocent victims on the screen were eviscerated for his adolescent entertainment. Death had touched the Myers family—for real—and Rosalyn would never be the same. Here he was gleefully anticipating the grisly demise of the Count's victims.

Rosalyn snapped to. "What? No, no. You looked forward to this all week."

"We can change it. Vampires are kind of boring, anyway."

Dras's parents made it a standing offer for Rosalyn to spend the night with their family, but following her father's death, Dras's mom nearly insisted the girl stay with them on the weekends at their home in Greensboro, nine miles away from Trysdale. Dras's dad was the pastor at the Good Church of the Faithful, and his mom believed that now, perhaps more than ever, Rosalyn needed a good Christian influence in her life. Dras agreed Rosalyn needed something, especially something that would get her away from home for a while.

Rosalyn's mom was not taking the loss of her husband very well and had decided to cope by screwing the caps off liquor bottles and searching for solace inside. Rosalyn had a four-year-old sister, Annie, and the burden was upon her to take care of the little one while her mother descended into alcoholism. The Weldons always offered to babysit the preschooler too during Rosalyn's overnighters, hoping to decrease the risk of something happening to Annie during her mother's drinking binges, but Rosalyn's mother refused, as if sensing her parenting skills were being called into question. Nevertheless, the Weldons recognized that a twelve-year-old was far too young to keep a family together and believed Rosalyn needed a break from time to time.

A break she didn't seem to be enjoying at the moment.

Rosalyn said, "I talked to Peggy again yesterday."

Dras's hand froze inches from his face, buttered popcorn suspended before his gaping mouth. "You what? That crazy old lady in Trysdale?"

"She's not crazy. You haven't even talked to her."

"I don't want to, either." Dras shuddered and completed his popcorn's pilgrimage to his awaiting mouth. "Gives me the creeps."

"Do you know why she goes out to the North Woods night after night?"

Dras shrugged. "Looking for her marbles?"

"Looking for her husband, goof. He died, you know. Peggy said that when she was a little girl, people around here used to say that you could hear the voice of your dead loved ones in the North Woods."

Despite Dras's unbridled love for scary movies, he found the idea that something spooky like ghosts or the things Donald Cushing faced every Saturday night really existed simply hysterical. He demonstrated his amusement by laughing out loud, totally forgetting that his parents were asleep upstairs and would scold him dearly for staying up so late when they had church first thing in the morning.

Rosalyn raised an aggravated eyebrow while Dras guffawed, popcorn bits dribbling down his chin.

"You're dumb."

"Aw, come on, Roz. Do you really believe that?"

He turned to see if she was going to join him in his laughter, but when he saw the hurt and confused look on her face, her reason for wanting to believe the scary old lady became terrifyingly clear.

"Oh," he said, his giggles silenced. "You want to go out there, don't you? You think you might hear your dad?"

Rosalyn's eyes welled. She bit her lip, forcing back her emotion. "Do...do you think it'd work? Do you think the stories are true?"

Dras didn't answer. He found he'd lost his appetite and all hopes of enjoying *Crypt of Dracula*. Silence settled in the room, and neither dared move. Even the TV's droning in the background seemed to fade as the darkness around them pressed in.

Dras's voice was barely above a whisper. "Roz—"

"Hey, skeeve!" A deeper echo startled Dras, and he tossed his popcorn straight up in the air, bringing down a rain of fluffy kernels on his head.

Rosalyn and Dras swiveled to see Dras's seventeen-year-old brother Jeff enter through the kitchen, quietly closing the screen door behind him, lest it should slap shut and betray his crime.

The hour was after midnight—way past the teenager's curfew—and Jeff was decked out in his usual black attire, including a long, dark coat and fingerless gloves and with his hair gelled to retain a messy, devil-may-care quality.

At the sight of the older boy Rosalyn instantly blushed and looked to her lap. Dras's brow cinched up.

"Jeff, you jerk!"

Jeff chuckled savagely, enjoying the scare he got out of his little brother. Then he spotted rotund Dead Ed Ghoulie on the screen, relaying some fun behind-the-scenes facts from *Midnight Matinee's* latest creature feature. The teen rolled his eyes, "You know Mom hates you watching this crap."

Dras's grin curled in innocent devilry. "That's why I wait until she's asleep."

"I'm telling."

"Go ahead. I'll just tell Dad where you hide your cigarettes."

Jeff huffed. "I hate you."

"Right back at you, Rebel Without a Clue."

Jeff headed for the stairs, prepared to sneak up to his room. He noticed Rosalyn.

"Hey, Roz."

Rosalyn glanced up, her face tight. "Hi, Jeff."

Dras was dimly aware that his best friend had a small crush on his older brother, but he was too grossed out to acknowledge it. Looking up at Jeff, he whined, "Where you been, anyway?"

Jeff paused, tapping his finger on his chin and staring at the ceiling, as if recalling a long mental list. "Um...Let me think. Well, first I went to Noneofyourbusiness, and then we stopped off at Buttout for a soda."

Dras harrumphed and resumed his *Crypt* watching. He was seriously tempted to holler for his father and get Jeff in trouble for sneaking in after curfew, but he knew that he too would incur the wrath of Jack Weldon for staying up past his bedtime to watch a movie.

As much as he hated to, Dras kept quiet and let Jeff have his little triumph.

Jeff, seeing the defeat in his brother's eyes, snickered and moved up a couple of steps.

"Jeff?" Roz called.

Jeff and Dras froze in their brotherly bickering to regard her. Dark curiosity shadowed her bright brown eyes.

"What?" Jeff's tone softened.

"Have you ever heard the stories about the North Woods?"

Jeff came back down the stairs and asked lightheartedly, "Which ones?"

"The ones about being able to hear your lost loved ones."

Jeff gave Dras a reproachful glare as if blaming him for not shutting down this line of thinking before now. "Rosalyn, they're just stories."

"Maybe not," she added hopefully. "It's worth a shot, right?"

Jeff moved into the living room and even went so far as to sit on the edge of the couch, engaging the conversation. In an understanding tone, he asked, "What would you want your dad to say?"

Dras's eyes flashed angry for a second, upset that his brother so acutely zeroed in on Rosalyn's plan when it took him a fit of foolhardy laughter before he pieced it together.

"You know your dad loved you. What more could we want to know from our parents?"

"I want to know why he died. I want to know why he did it."

Jeff nodded, thinking about her response. The whole night was becoming uncomfortable for Dras.

"Maybe..." Jeff started. He paused, then continued, "Maybe there're some things we're better off not knowing. Maybe it should just be enough to know that he was proud of you and loved you."

"Maybe," Rosalyn repeated. She turned away from Jeff coldly, shutting him out, and stared at Dead Ed Ghoulie—the grown man dressed up like a clown—making a fool of himself on public access.

Jeff stood, his long coat billowing, rudely flapping against Dras's face. The older boy didn't offer an apology to Rosalyn for saying what she didn't want to hear, and he certainly didn't offer an apology to his brother for nearly knocking him out with his coat. Instead he disappeared upstairs, leaving Dras and Rosalyn alone in the living room, the glow of the television flickering against their quiet and awkward faces.

Needless to say, Saturday night was a bust. Dras and Rosalyn's usual routine was interrupted by stark reality, and the situation ruined any chance of Dras enjoying the exploits of Donald Cushing: Vampire Killer. The following Sunday wasn't much better.

Dras and Rosalyn sat with Dras's mother on the front pew at the Good Church of the Faithful while Jack Weldon preached in his bold and magical way. The congregation was captivated by his sincere and impassioned presence. Even Dras, despite being so sleepy from his *Midnight Matinee* viewing, couldn't help but listen. Out of the corner of his eye, though, he caught Jeff and a few of his buddies about halfway back, their heads low, whispering and elbowing each other as they passed notes and snickered, drawing disapproving stares from the likes of Miss Jenkins behind them.

Dras shook his head at his disrespectful jerk of a brother, then turned to Rosalyn. She did not come from a religious family and only attended church when Dras's mother insisted. Usually she was courteously quiet and attentive while listening—she genuinely loved Dras's father—but today it seemed the stories of the North Woods still lingered in her mind. Her eyes were distracted, her face blank.

Making sure his mother wasn't paying attention, Dras discreetly scribbled a note on his church bulletin and placed it in Rosalyn's lap.

She glanced at it:

YOU OK?

Rosalyn nodded affirmatively, though she didn't look at Dras.

He frowned and prepared to write another note to press her further when he felt his mother slap him sharply on the thigh. He flinched and looked up to see her shaking her finger at him, her eyes nearly crossed with indignation. He slumped and turned his attention back to his father.

He'd just have to check on Rosalyn later.

After church the Weldon family was on display, as usual. The congregation circled Rev. Weldon, commenting on his wonderful sermon. Dras's mom stayed close to her husband, always his biggest fan. Jeff sneaked around back with some of the rowdier teenage boys to steal a smoke, hoping Leonard Fergus or one of the other deacons didn't catch them.

Dras searched for Rosalyn in the dispersing crowd. She'd managed to avoid the traditional Weldon family handshaking, as she was from Trysdale, the tiny country community on the outskirts of town. No one from Trysdale seemed able to earn the respect of Greensboro proper—small town prejudices— so very few people went out of their way to say anything to Rosalyn Myers outside of, "Good morning, young lady." Her white trash origins were compounded by the fact that her dad had committed suicide, leaving her a twelve-year-old pariah in the eyes of the upper crust. She just wasn't "from a good family."

Dras managed to shuffle through the old ladies wanting to pinch his cheeks and broke free. He found Rosalyn wandering alone in the yard, staring at her toes.

"Hey, I lost you for a sec."

"Sorry. Just needed to think."

Dras shoved his hands in his pockets, trying to play it cool, like Jeff had done the night before. "Wanna talk about it?"

"I really miss my dad."

Dras couldn't begin to imagine what she was going through. His own dad seemed like the strongest man alive. He worked in construction building houses for people in the community and still had time to lead the bustling congregation and do all kinds of charity work. Sure, the man was very busy and had little time for goofing off with his youngest son, but Dras knew that if he ever really needed his dad, Jack Weldon would move heaven and earth to be there for him. The thought of losing his dad was as alien to him as a third eye.

Before he could think of anything to offer in reply, Rosalyn's mom pulled up to the church in her station wagon and sounded a quick toot of the horn. Recognizing the familiar sound, Rosalyn looked up, her dark eyes gloomy, to see her mom leaning across the front seat, calling through the rolled-down passenger side window.

"Rosalyn!" the woman shouted, bleary-eyed and puffy-faced. "I've been looking everywhere for you, young lady. You weren't at Dras's house."

"It's Sunday, Mom. The Weldons are always at church on Sunday."

Her mother blinked. "Oh. Well, come on. I don't want to have to get your sister out of her seat."

At the mention of Annie, Dras glanced toward the backseat, where the tot was nestled in her car seat wearing an oversized T-shirt stained with chocolate and Kool-Aid, dried day-old food stuck to her fat cheeks, and sucking on a sippy cup of amber liquid that the boy hoped was tea. She ignored him and amused herself by playing with a naked Barbie doll.

Rosalyn noticed the state of her sister too, and Dras watched as his friend's eyes grew heavy with heartache.

Mrs. Weldon exited the church just then. She stood behind the sullen Rosalyn like a patient but fierce lioness. The woman placed protective hands on the girl's shoulders, as if defending her from an attack.

"Hello, Meredith," Dras's mother said in a friendly but firm voice.

Rosalyn's mother glanced up and showed a toothy smile. "Hey, Louise."

"We were hoping Rosalyn could stay with us for lunch. We're making spaghetti, her favorite."

Meredith chewed on her lip, then fixed her gaze on Rosalyn. "You want spaghetti? I'll make you spaghetti. Come on. Get in."

"We'd love to have you too," Louise added.

Dras was too young to remember, but his mother had told

him stories about how once upon a time she and Meredith were best friends. They took some college classes together and had a lot of fun with each other. That association was why Dras and Rosalyn began to play together. But somewhere along the way, Meredith grew into her Trysdale Trash reputation, and now the friend Dras's mother once had was lost.

Meredith quickly declined. "We need to get back. Rosalyn, I need you at home taking care of your sister. She's too much of a handful for me alone. You know that."

Rosalyn hung her head. "I know." She opened the door and climbed in with her mother, leaving Louise's guarding hands behind. Dras's mother wrapped a loving arm around her son, and he admitted to himself that his mom was all right. She was always on his case about what comics he read and movies he watched, but he knew that she loved him and would die fighting for him.

When faced head-on with Rosalyn's mother, he was thankful to God to be the son of Jack and Louise Weldon.

"I'll call you later," Dras told his friend in an upbeat tone.

Rosalyn smiled in return, but the gesture was faint. "OK. See ya."

Meredith drove the car out of sight, leaving Dras to watch and worry that one day he would lose Rosalyn just as his mother lost her best friend.

At home, Rosalyn gave her sister a bath, nearly crying as she scrubbed off the dirt and food that her mother had let build up on the child.

"I'm so sorry, Annie," Rosalyn mumbled, gently washing her as Annie hummed and examined a plastic boat. What she was sorry for, Rosalyn couldn't say for sure. A part of her was sorry that she left Annie overnight with her mother. A year ago—two months ago—it wouldn't have been a concern. Rosalyn's father was great with Annie, with both of his daughters. While Rosalyn's mother was out in the evenings attending school board meetings and trying to elevate her social status in their small town, he stayed home, laughing and joking with his kids. He and Rosalyn would tickle Annie's toes together, or he'd get his guitar and play a new song that he'd been working on. It was all folksy Americana stuff, not anything remotely like what the kids were listening to on KDZY back in Greensboro, but it spoke of country living, of family, of hard work, and Rosalyn loved every bit of it.

All she wanted now was to be with him again. Maybe that was why she told Annie she was sorry. If the talks were true about the North Woods, if the dead waited out there ready to be contacted, then that's where Rosalyn needed to be.

Among the dead.

Night fell, and Rosalyn put Annie to bed, then went downstairs, where her mother snoozed soundly on the couch, the television still on and a bottle of hooch sideways on the floor. Rosalyn put the bottle away, took the throw blanket off her father's chair—the one he covered himself with on nights when he fell asleep in his recliner listening to old records—and pulled it to her mother's neck.

Her two charges tucked in for the night, Rosalyn checked the clock on the microwave. It was just shy of nine o'clock, far too early to be done with the day. She knew Dras would call soon, and while the thought of chatting it up with him for a couple of hours usually lifted her spirits, tonight it seemed hollow. Rosalyn felt like she had outgrown her small-town life. Her dad was gone, and he took all the magic of her childhood with him.

In his place was a cold vacancy as the walls of routine grated across the sands of time, closing in on her.

Suddenly she flash-forwarded ten years and saw her mother a complete lush, Annie a wayward child, and as for her—well, she had no idea where she'd be in ten years. Probably in the same place, cleaning up after her mother, taking care of her sister.

What about me? What about what I want?

There was only one thing she wanted now. She wanted her father back, and she was going to find him tonight. On a mission, she rushed to her sleeping sister's room and leaned over to give her a kiss.

"Good-bye, Annie. I love you. I'm sorry."

Then Rosalyn left her home. She did not look back.

Peggy McDowell heard a knock on her door. She answered it. Rosalyn Myers's face was as bright as the stars that twinkled overhead in the navy blue sky.

"Hi, Peggy."

"Rosalyn." The old woman held a calico cat in her flabby arms. "I didn't expect to see you. Come in, come in."

Rosalyn entered, the color in her cheeks restored now that she had a plan. The old woman returned to her messy kitchen, shooed away two of the seven cats that shared the trailer with her, and poured oil into her signature lamp. Rosalyn noticed the elderly woman had sandals on her feet, and her heart skipped with excitement.

"You're going, aren't you?" Rosalyn asked, trying hard to contain her enthusiasm. "You're going out to the North Woods tonight."

Peggy wrapped a shawl around her neck to ward off the chill of the woods, her eyes distracted. "I hope you won't try to stop me, Rosalyn. I've...I've grown to really enjoy our talks. You've been so kind to me, and kindness has been hard to find these days. But—" her thoughts drifted until she shook them straight—"I don't belong here, I'm afraid. My Wallace is out there. I hear him. At night."

The woman looked out the small window above her sink, staring into the dark of the trees that bordered her backyard, a mix of horror and bliss swirling in her haunted eyes.

"He says I can join him. It's where I belong." The rambling woman hurriedly snatched her lamp and turned to the young girl. "One day I hope you fall in love with someone special. Then you'll understand."

"But I do," Rosalyn interjected. "That's why I came."

The old woman paused, a quizzical look on her sagging face. Rosalyn grinned. "I want to go with you."

The movie theater was crowded, but very few people were there to watch the movie. Greensboro kids were no different from the kids in any other small town, and they sought amusement and trouble anywhere they could turn them up. Most were content to "drag the strip," and the theater's parking lot was one of two turnaround points, much to the dislike of Mr. Miller, the owner. At least two police cars—one parked, the other cruising—kept tabs on the goings-on at the parking lot. Cars lined the pavement, crowding out the patrons, as teenagers hung around their vehicles playing music, crowing, roughhousing, and just generally making a scene.

Jeff Weldon leaned against his black 1992 Grand Prix SE, showing off the new ground-effect light kit he'd gotten slapped on the car as the rock band Korn screamed from his sound system. A couple of blonde bombshells were "ooh-ing" and "aah-ing" over the new additions to his ride, but he continued to puff nonchalantly on his cigarette as if their words of praise meant nothing to him. By his side, scruffy and shabbily dressed, Jeff's best buddy, Kyle Rogers, watched the girls with growing interest as they bent over to check out the effects.

Kyle nudged Jeff and pointed at the girls' revealed effects, wiggling his eyebrows. Jeff rolled his eyes and shook his head without a word.

One of the girls, Jennifer, bounced to Jeff. "This is a nice car."

Jeff nodded, taking a hit on his cigarette as Kyle nearly panted at his side.

"We're meeting over at my friend's place in an hour," she informed him, her eyes lustful and enticing. "Wanna come?"

Jeff shrugged. "We'll see. Me and Kyle got to go see a guy tonight."

Kyle spun to Jeff, silently outraged. Jennifer looked the right blend of disappointment and intrigue. "Well, if you change your mind, we're going to Julie Beckins's house. You know where that's at? It's right past McKinley."

"Yeah," Jeff replied casually. "I think I could find it."

"Cool. Hope to see you later."

Then Jennifer and her equally blonde friend scampered across the parking lot to another group. Kyle immediately whirled and slapped Jeff full force across the arm.

"Dude!"

Jeff reacted in pain, his smoke clenched in his teeth. "What?"

"What 'guy'? There's no guy. We're the guy. They want to be with us because we're the guy!"

"Of course there's no guy," Jeff drawled. "It's just the way the game's played."

"So we're going, right?" Kyle asked.

"Shyeah, we're going," Jeff laughed. "Did you see Jennifer tonight? I'd be nuts not to go."

"That's what I'm trying to say. Man, don't scare me like that. What's wrong with you?"

Jeff chuckled as his friend breathed a sigh of relief. Then, without warning, Kyle nearly jumped over the top of the car, banging his hands on the top and whistling.

"Woo-hee, Isabella Evans!" Kyle called across the parking lot as the early show moviegoers exited the theater. Isabella Evans was a beauty, her simmering Latin features an instant appeal to the white-bread farm boys of Greensboro. But unlike Jennifer, she carried herself with regal dignity, her shapely body hidden beneath respectable clothes.

Much to the disapproval of boys like Kyle Rogers.

"Looking hot tonight!" he howled like a hungry wolf, despite the fact that Isabella's polo-shirt-wearing boyfriend, Scott Townsend, had his arm around her. The girl turned to Kyle, at first shocked that someone was calling her name, then grimaced in anger when she realized who had taken notice.

"Kyle Rogers! Don't make me come over there and black your eye!" she hollered. Her carefully manicured boyfriend looked completely at a loss for words.

Kyle whistled some more, hooted and hollered, and banged on the top of the car again before Jeff grabbed him by the scruff of his tattered Army jacket and spun him around. "Knock it off," he said.

Kyle chuckled wildly while Isabella's boyfriend, red-faced and impotent, helped the young lady into his car several yards away.

"Hey, doesn't she go to church with you?" Kyle asked Jeff.

"Yeah, so?"

"Think you could hook me up?"

"Forget it. She's *way* out of your league."

Kyle moped.

"Besides," Jeff added, "she's in band. Those chicks are boring."

Kyle sighed wistfully, defeated again by the opposite sex. "I guess I'll have to set my sights lower." He grinned, rubbing his hands together. "Like Julie Beckins."

"There you go. Now you're playing in the right field."

But Kyle's smile faded as he glanced across the parking lot. "Oh, great."

Jeff looked over the mass of traffic and crowds of loitering teenagers. "What?"

"It's your brother."

Jeff sighed, frustrated. "That skeeve."

Sure enough, Dras rode in furiously on his bicycle, bringing it to a skidding fishtail halt inches in front of his brother.

"Jeff!"

"What do you want?"

"I can't get a hold of Rosalyn," Dras said, his face flushed from exertion.

"Try her tomorrow," Jeff replied, tapping Kyle on the arm and pointing at the car. The two boys made ready to get inside and head off to their romantic rendezvous. "Good-bye."

Dras dismounted his bike, let it crash to the pavement, and hurried to his brother, pulling on his long coat. "Jeff! I've got a bad feeling."

Jeff huffed and flashed his best teenage put-upon look.

"She really misses her dad." Dras spoke fast before his big brother's patience completely ran out.

Jeff nodded. "It's natural."

"But I can tell something's wrong. She's been talking about what Old Woman McDowell told her about the North Woods."

Kyle snickered from the other side of the car. "The North Woods? You looking for the bogeyman, little man?"

Dras glared through his brow at Kyle. Jeff knew his brother hated Kyle enough without him butting into family business. Despite Kyle's good humor, Jeff grew serious.

"You think she went out there?"

Dras replied, "I'm sure of it. Jeff, she's really messed up, man."

Jeff remained stone-faced, his eyes flickering with thought. At last he said, "The North Woods aren't safe."

"Aw, man," Kyle sneered. "Don't tell me you believe in monsters too."

Jeff fixed Kyle with the same through-the-brow look his brother had used. "Of course not. But it's nighttime. She won't be able to see anything. She could fall. Get hurt."

"We need to hurry." Dras rushed to his bike.

Jeff reached into his car and pushed a button to pop the trunk. "Put your bike in the back. You're riding with me."

Kyle watched the brothers work. "Jeff, dude? What about Julie Beckins? Jennifer? Being the guy?"

"Find another ride, Kyle." Jeff took one last drag off his cigarette, then flicked it into the wind.

"But nobody else tolerates me," he whined. "You know that."

Jeff grinned. "Then try not being a jerk for a night."

Kyle scratched his head. "You think that'd work?"

"Later, Kyle."

Dras pushed past the greasy boy, taking his place at his brother's side, and closed the car door. Jeff started the engine, revved it a few times for effect, and sped off.

Kyle continued to mull over his new life direction but stopped short when he saw Jennifer and her friend cruise by, preparing to head to the party. He licked his hand, slicked back his unruly hair, and put on his best smile.

"Hey, Jennifer! Looks like my schedule just cleared up and I can go to Julie's house, after all! Wanna give me a lift?"

Jennifer snarled before pulling away. "Drop dead, creep."

Kyle slumped and muttered. "Thanks a lot, Jeff, ol' buddy. Thank yew, very much."

⁂

"Wallace?" Peggy called into the dark woods, shining her lantern across the trees and foliage. "Wall–ace!"

Rosalyn stayed close, almost pressed to the back of the old woman, her fearful eyes darting expectantly all around. The stars were in hiding overhead, and the air was surprisingly cold this deep into the North Woods. Older kids were notorious for stealing off to the North Woods and on to the Old Greenesboro ruins, mysterious charred brick foundations that served as evidence of the town's first settlers. The place was a perfect spot for teenagers looking for a secluded hideaway where they could indulge in their baser instincts far from the prying eyes of their parents. Rosalyn was always curious to see what the older kids did and wondered what was so fun about drinking and necking. She and Dras had ventured into the woods a couple of times in the past for much more innocent pursuits, but always during the day. Always when they could find their way back.

Now in the all-encompassing darkness, Rosalyn had no clue where she was going or which path led home. She could only rely on the guiding light of Old Woman McDowell's lantern and the bereaved lady's memory to lead the way.

Rosalyn knew why she was following the woman into the woods: to find her father. The idea had seemed the only rational thing to do in a life that was ripped apart. But now that she was here, clinging to the flowered nightgown of Peggy McDowell, who was calling out her dead husband's name in tear-streaked hysteria, she didn't quite feel the same. Once Rosalyn halfheartedly called out, "Dad?" but the act felt stupid and vain, and she kept quiet afterward while Peggy wailed again and again, "Wallace! Wall–ace!"

Soon thoughts of little Annie filled Rosalyn's mind. She worried who would be there to take care of her sister if she woke. Their mother was helpless to care for herself or her youngest child these days. Horrible images filled Rosalyn's mind: Mom falling asleep or passing out with the stove on. A fire catching. Annie crying, trapped in the house.

Rosalyn shuddered and stopped in her tracks. "I think we should go back."

"Wallace!" Old Woman McDowell hollered, then turned back to the young girl. "What, dear?"

"We should go back. I want to go home."

The old lady slowly metamorphosed before her eyes, changing from the sweet, misunderstood old woman she befriended a week earlier into the demented hag from the stories told about her.

"Oh, I'm terribly sorry, dear. We can't go back. I know my Wallace is out here. I've heard him. I won't be going back."

"But...what about me?"

"Your father is out here too." The woman crunched through dry leaves as she overshadowed Rosalyn, her lamp casting twisted shadows across her craggy face. Her eyes were mad with grief and desperation. "I'm just sure of it. You have to trust the voices, Rosalyn. The dead are out here. This is where we belong."

Rosalyn shook her head. "I–I don't belong here. I want to go back."

The crone stepped forward and snatched Rosalyn's arm,

as if prepared to make the girl follow. Her face was wild and monstrous, and Rosalyn felt real fear. Then, just as suddenly, the old woman stopped short. Her face turned cold, and she loosened her grip. "Fine. Turn back. I'll go on without you."

"But how will I see? I need a lantern."

As if the girl had threatened to take it, Peggy McDowell clutched the lamp close to her abundant bosom. "No! I need it! Wallace will be guided by its light. It's how he'll find me!" No longer paying Rosalyn any attention, the crone turned back to the woods, holding out her lantern and shouting, "Wall–ace. Wall–ace."

Rosalyn watched the woman leave to chase a ghost, and something inside her died. She came to the North Woods with hope—with faith—but reason bested her instead. Her father was dead. He was never coming back. He wasn't out here, waiting for her in some beautiful afterlife. The world was exposed as the cold, empty place it truly was, and Rosalyn felt utterly betrayed by the glamour of youth. She thought of Dras, of his goofy optimism, his ability to find joy in the simplest of pleasures, like watching *Midnight Matinee*, and worried he'd never see the world the way she could now.

What worried her most was the thought of losing him because he didn't understand.

Sobbing and alone in the darkness, Rosalyn stumbled through the brush, working her way backward. She was certain that Old Woman McDowell had led her through twists and turns, but she hoped that if she just kept moving back, she'd find some familiar location to lead her home.

She just wanted out of these blasted woods.

"Staaayyy with meee…"

She froze, her hackles rising.

"Who—?"

"...commmeee baaaacckkk..."

Hissing in the trees. A voice in the darkness. Far away. It was a man's voice, loving and kind.

Her heart stopped. She whimpered, "Daddy?"

A tremendous snapping, like a huge tree, startled the quiet. Birds flapped away in fright, and a large black shape rustled overhead. Rosalyn cringed, hating Old Woman McDowell for leaving her alone with no light.

When the terrible noise subsided, the distant whispering resumed.

"...staaaayyyy..."

Now the voice sounded closer. Nearly on top of her. Still quiet, hardly recognizable but decidedly male.

"Daddy?" she braved the question louder.

Drip.

She heard a snapping branch behind her, on the shadowed horizon. Rosalyn spun, tearing up. "Who's there? Where are you?"

Drip. Drip.

She peered into the darkness beyond and nearly shrieked when she saw two glowing orbs floating toward her.

"Rosalyn?"

A voice called her name, but it wasn't the same voice as before. This one she knew and trusted.

"Dras! I'm over here!"

Dras and Jeff hurried into view, holding flashlights and waving them in Rosalyn's direction. Rosalyn relaxed for a moment before glancing back up into the black leaves above her. She saw nothing in the shadows but heard a weak dripping, like water droplets in a puddle.

Dras rushed in her direction until he almost fell on top of her. "You're OK!"

Rosalyn huffed, forcing her voice not to quake. "Well, yeah, I'm OK, goof. What did you think?"

"We've been calling you—" Jeff said, his breathing heavy— "trying to get you to come back."

"That was you?" She felt childish for thinking anything else.

"Yeah," Jeff bent over, supporting his hands on his knees, catching his breath. "Come on. Our folks are going to be mad enough as it is."

Without waiting for protest or agreement, Jeff the fearless leader headed back the way they came. Dras stood still for a moment, his flashlight illuminating Rosalyn.

"You all right?" he asked.

Rosalyn warmed. The world was indeed a scary place, and that knowledge felt like a burden that only she carried. But with Dras around, maybe things weren't so bad.

"Yeah," she said finally, meaning it for the first time since her father died. "Let's go home. There's nothing out here for me."

Dras beamed and led the way home, Rosalyn at his side.

Behind them, high in the lush branches of the trees, catlike eyes glowed in the darkness. Caught in spider-like clutches, the body of Peggy McDowell twitched in death throes, her throat ripped open and her blood dribbling to the soft earth below.

Drip. Drip. Drip.

Meanwhile her killer looked on, watching the girl escaping his grasp.

"Staaayyy with meeee..."